The audacity of the guy!

Having the responsibility of the camp passed to Rick, a virtual stranger, had made Summer's heart sink then...and every time she'd thought about it since—including now.

She had tried to show her assertion at the meeting. But when she'd brought up the subject of downtime, Rick had poo-pooed her ideas.

No doubt about it: Rick Warren put her on edge, made her feel as if he were hiding something. Snooping around her cabin that morning, hiding the file he held. She didn't know what he was up to, but she didn't like it. Or him.

Right at that moment, Rick's face broke into a dazzling smile, directed at the mother who was standing too close, and a flare of anger shot through Summer. *Tsk, tsk. Flirting with the parents. How inappropriate.*

Inappropriate images of Rick Warren had come to her in her sleep the past couple of weeks. Remembering them now caused her cheeks to warm, along with a few other parts of her traitorous body.

Dear Reader,

If you've read my Harlequin Superromance debut *Out of the Depths* (August 2012), you've already met Rick Warren, the former marine whose heroic nature begged for his own story. But what fresh, new challenge could I come up with for a man who stared death in the eye and never blinked? Inspiration for Rick's story hit during a day of fishing with my husband on Kentucky Lake. Well, actually, he fished, and I read.

As we trolled along the banks of a secluded cove, an unexpected sound floated through the tree line… the loud, excited laughter of children. We'd happened into a cove that bordered a summer camp. The sound warmed my retired-schoolteacher's heart, but it also reminded me how children's unpredictable actions day after day would make some people uncomfortable. People such as Rick Warren. A month with eight- and nine-year-olds would challenge even a hardened marine.

When I concentrated on the sound, an image of diminutive Summer Delaney solidified in my brain. Although Rick towered over her, she was holding her ground against him, hands on hips, chin jutted forward defiantly. She stared him down with not so much as a blink. Here was the woman who could bring Rick to his knees—or at least, cause him to kneel on one of them!

I hope you enjoy your stay at Camp Sunny Daze…it's *The Summer Place* to be!

BFF,

Pamela Hearon

The Summer Place

PAMELA HEARON

ISBN-13: 978-0-373-71847-4

THE SUMMER PLACE

This edition published by arrangement with Harlequin Books S.A.

For questions and comments about the quality of this book, please contact us at CustomerService@Harlequin.com.

Printed in U.S.A.

ABOUT THE AUTHOR

Pamela Hearon lived thirty-one years in western Kentucky before love with a handsome Yankee lured her away. She and her husband raised their family of three children and several cats while she taught English to quirky eighth-graders. Life has taught her that, no matter the location, small-town America has a charm all its own—a place where down-to-earth people and heartwarming stories abound. And although the Midwest is now home, Kentucky still holds a generous piece of Pamela's heart. When it's time to tell her stories, the voice in her head has a decidedly Southern drawl.

Books by Pamela Hearon

HARLEQUIN SUPERROMANCE

1799—OUT OF THE DEPTHS

To Dick,

the True North of my life's compass. All the routes led me to you.

Acknowledgments

It's been a long time since any of my children were in summer camp, so writing a book about one required a great deal of research, which, in this case, translates as picking the brains of my friends. As a result, I have many people I want to thank.

Thank you to my neighbor, Chad Mowery, a former marine. The information you shared made Rick come alive for me in a way that my imagination never would have.

Thanks to Mhairi Kerr, my expert on current summer campery.

Many thanks to my dear friend Gary Bielefeld, aka Mr. Fossil, for consulting with me on mammoth molars and for having the uncanny ability to always make me smile.

Thank you to my editors, Megan Long and Karen Reid, for being so great to work with and for making suggestions that make my stories stronger.

Thanks to my agent, Jennifer Weltz, for continuing to believe in me.

Thank you to my critique partners, Kimberly Lang, Sandra Jones, Angela Campbell and Maggie Van Well, for your willingness to read my stuff no matter how many times I run it by you and whose kind words of encouragement keep me going.

Thank you to my children (all adults now), Heather, Nathan and Michelle, for being so easy to blend into a real family.

Thanks to my friends for putting up with my preoccupation and my odd choices of conversation topics.

Most of all, thank you to my husband, Dick. You've taught me not to take myself so seriously and just how much fun true love can be.

CHAPTER ONE

"BET YOU'RE LAUGHING YOUR ASS off, aren't you, Dunk?" Rick Warren directed his comment skyward. He unlatched his seat belt but made no move to exit the car, rethinking the favor Gus Hargrove was calling in.

One summer, that was the commitment. Compared to his former tours of duty, two months was nothing, and anything was better than unemployment—sitting at home, putting on a beer belly. Besides, he'd already said yes. *Honor. Courage. Commitment. Time to face this like a marine.*

He opened the car door and strode across the street and up the walk of the gray stone house. Neither his confident manner nor the doorbell's seraphic chime could lift the dread from the pit of his stomach.

The wisp of a woman who was Agnes Delaney opened the door and welcomed him into the house with her genial "Come in, come in." Her husband, Herschel, showed up close on her heels, his beefy, red face broken by a toothy grin.

"Rick." Herschel's large hand clapped hard on his back. "Glad to have you on board."

Rick forced a smile. "Thank you, sir."

"I slept better last night than I have in months." Agnes's eyes shimmered with gratitude as she looped her arm through Rick's and led him down a wide hallway. "Let's go in here and sit while we talk. I need to keep an eye on Peewee."

Agnes steered him into a great room, which opened onto a large lawn and pool area. A Yorkie was doing laps around the pool, chasing birds, squirrels, butterflies—anything that moved.

"Very nice." Rick indicated the room with its rich leather furnishings and fabulous view.

"Well, hopefully, now you're here we'll be able to keep it," Agnes said, and gave his arm a motherly pat, and he began to feel a little better about his decision.

"You see, Rick..." Herschel indicated a chair, then sank heavily into his own well-worn one. "I didn't say anything before, but Agnes and I invested our complete retirement fund into this venture. With the downturn in the economy, we've had several years of barely breaking even. If things don't go well this year, we'll have no choice but to sell."

Wow, no pressure here. Dread took another swat at Rick's insides. He waited to sit until Agnes perched lightly on the end of the couch. "Well, sir, I'll do my best. How many campers are we expecting?"

"Since we can only afford a skeleton crew of six adults, we've cut it off at twenty. Ten boys and ten girls for each month-long session. The first month is eight- and nine-year-olds. The second is ten-, eleven- and twelve-year-olds. There'll be a week between."

Rick nodded. "That sounds manageable."

"Would you like some iced tea?" Agnes jumped up and moved toward the bar.

"Yes, ma'am, please." What he really wanted was a cold beer.

"We have four barracks that sleep ten each, but we'll only use two of them this summer to cut down on utility expenses," Herschel continued. "Each one has a counselor's room at the back. Both assistants indicated they'd like the night duty since it ups the pay a little for them, but if you want..."

Rick shook his head. "No, that's fine." After a long day

with the kids, a few hours off would be imperative to his sanity.

Herschel seemed to read his mind. "Long days. Six in the morning to ten at night."

"I've never had a job that didn't have long hours." Rick took a drink as he processed all the information being thrown at him. "Will I be bunking with the other boys' counselor, then?"

"No, we don't expect you to do that, and like I said before, I'd rather not open up the other dorms. We own a couple of cabins just across the path from the camp property that we rent out during deer season. If you'd like one of them for the summer, you can stay rent free. Gus and Nadine always moved into one of them. Saves the drive back and forth from Paducah to the lake every day."

No pets. No girlfriend. Rick couldn't foresee any reason to drive back home to an empty house every night. "I like that idea. Thanks."

Agnes handed him a glass of tea and a piece of paper. A quick glance showed him it was a contract, and his throat threatened to cut off the sweet tea making its way down the passage. He breathed slowly to loosen the muscles and focused back to what Herschel was saying.

"…assistant director and head counselor for the boys. Charlie Prichard's been camp director for several years, so he knows what he's doing. He'll make sure the place runs smoothly and just wants you to take care of the activities like Gus did. Hell, you've headed up a government office, so twenty kids should be a piece of cake."

Rick cringed inwardly at the mention of his recently defunct position, but he kept his face impassive.

"We hired a couple of new graduates for the assistant counselor positions." Herschel took a long draw from his tea and smacked his lips appreciatively.

"And what about the girls' head counselor?" He'd have to work closely with whoever was in that position.

Agnes cocked her head and shrugged, reminding him of a bird listening for a worm. "We thought we had someone hired, but she backed out yesterday. That's why I sounded so anxious when you called." She gave him a warm smile that made him feel quite heroic and terribly uncomfortable. "We're still looking."

"Nadine says she'll stay on, but only as our last resort." Herschel gave a lopsided grin. "She and Gus are gonna miss having summers off together. Neither of them wants to make the drive from the lake every day even though they've always said the little cabin in the woods is like a second honeymoon."

Having twenty kids within spitting distance hardly sounded like a romantic haven to Rick.

"What about the assistant counselor?" he suggested. "Is she a possibility?"

"Tara doesn't want the responsibility." Agnes dabbed at her mouth with a napkin. "We still have a few weeks. We'll find someone."

Rick wasn't so sure. "And if you don't?"

"Couple of possibilities," Herschel said. "We could make the first session an all-boys camp this year. Plenty of applicants. That would buy us some more time."

Rick considered the option. "Sort of a boot camp? Give the young men a little taste of a soldier's life?"

Herschel shrugged. "As long as it's fun. Gotta make sure they enjoy it."

Rick nodded. "And the other possibility?"

"Send the deposits back, call it quits and put it on the market." Herschel grimaced as if in pain. "Gus said you're getting your real-estate license?"

"I've just started the online class," Rick explained. "My mom's a Realtor in Little Rock, so it was a knee-jerk reaction when I found out the Department of Wildlife office was closing."

"Maybe you can make some notes? You know, just some suggestions of things that need to be done, in case it ever comes down to having to sell the camp?"

Agnes interrupted before Rick could answer. "Let's not talk about that until…until we have to." Her voice faltered, and she looked at Rick again as if he were a godsend. "Selling's a last resort, and we'd rather not do it unless we're forced to. Our hope is to pass the property on to our girls someday."

His own selfishness poked a finger in Rick's chest. *Man up, Warren. These people need you to save their camp.* He clapped his hands together in a show of enthusiasm. "Well, let's get started. You mentioned you had copies of the applications for me? I'd like to start getting to know my soon-to-be charges."

"Sure." Herschel eased out of the chair. "I'll get those for you." His heavy tread up the stairs echoed across the spacious room.

Agnes smiled sweetly. "You'll be good at this, I can tell. Children say and do the cutest things."

"Yes, ma'am, but they have to be watched constantly." Rick's brain flashed an image of the little Afghani girl who sprang up in his nightmares sometimes. He blinked the image back into the recesses.

"Are you married? Any children?" Agnes asked.

"No, ma'am, to both questions. But I led my share of nature hikes when I was a park ranger. Inevitably, there was some kid who wanted a closer look at a copperhead."

"I've known one or two like that." An amused glint lit her eyes.

Peewee's yelp pulled their attention to the backyard. An irate blue jay swooped down at the dog as he made his laps.

Agnes rolled her eyes. "Such a baby. We got him after our youngest moved out, and I'm afraid we've spoiled him rotten. Just like we did the girls."

"How many children do you have?" Rick killed some time with polite conversation.

"Three girls. The oldest two are married now. The youngest is, well..." Agnes's eyebrows drew in as if she were searching for the correct word.

"Agnes!" Herschel's loud bellow echoed from somewhere upstairs. "What'd you do with those forms?"

"They're on your desk." Agnes's voice rose to a screech. "I saw them this morning."

"Well, you must've stuck them somewhere."

"I know where I'd like to stick them," she muttered under her breath. She sat her glass down. "Herschel had triple bypass surgery a year ago, and he still has some brain fog. I'll be right back."

In the couple's absence, Rick looked over the contract. It seemed to be standard, so he went ahead and signed on the line, then tried to get his mind off what he'd just committed to by sipping his tea and watching the bird taunt the dog some more. The dog's yelp was irritating. He found himself rooting for the bird.

Suddenly, Peewee made a beeline toward the corner of the yard, giving happy little yips.

Rick's gaze followed the dog. He blinked. *Hell-pee-roo!* A fairy had appeared through the wooden gate. He blinked again. Not a fairy, but a girl—maybe a tiny woman?—dressed in a fairy costume, complete with a long, full pink dress, a sparkling crown and wings.

"Stop it, Peewee." The high female voice admonished the dog, who was springing up and down like he was attached to a pogo stick. "You're going to get me dirty. *Stop it!*"

The dog paid no heed to the command.

The fairy stooped down and set her bag on the ground. It fell over, startling the dog, who yelped and jumped back a few feet. Then, with lightning speed, he darted to the bag, grabbed something and took off around the pool.

"Damn it, Peewee," the fairy shrieked. "Give me back my wand."

Rick walked over to the door and stepped outside, waiting until the dog came around the shallow end and headed his direction, then he moved directly into the dog's path. "Pee-wee! Halt!" he bellowed.

The stunned dog dropped the stick and let out a yelp like he'd been kicked. He darted past Rick and launched him-self into the arms of the fairy, who Rick could tell was most definitely a young woman now that he had a closer look. He picked up the stick lying at his feet.

"Oh, poor baby," the fairy cooed, moving in Rick's di-rection. "It's okay. Calm down now." As she neared, the dog shrank deeper under her arm, whimpering and trembling vio-lently, and pushing her cleavage into a splendid presentation within the round neck of her gown. "Thanks." She smiled with gratitude as she took the stick and held it for the dog to sniff. "But you nearly scared him to death."

"Dogs, kids and marines—you have to let them know who's in charge."

The fairy's chin rose a fraction. "And who's in charge is determined by who yells the loudest?" Her smile wavered and then vanished completely. "I've never felt his heart beat this fast. You don't think he could have a heart attack, do you?" Her eyes—the bluest Rick had ever encountered—grew wide with concern. She puckered her lips and pulled the pooch against her cheek. "Shhh. Shhhh. You're my good little boy, aren't you? Yes, you are. You're my good little Peewee boy."

The top of the woman's head only came to Rick's chest. He gazed down at an ocean of golden waves cascading down her back. Glistening in the sunlight, they created quite an intoxicating vision.

"I'm Rick Warren, by the way."

"Hi, Rick." She shifted Peewee to her other arm. "I'm—"

"Nubbin!"

Herschel's voice boomed from behind them, followed by Agnes's high-pitched "Summer! What are you doing here?" Agnes's and the fairy's voices were almost identical.

The fairy's concerned expression softened into an angelic countenance when the couple appeared. "Hey." She gave them hugs. "I had a little time between parties, so I thought I'd drop by."

Herschel looked pleased, but Agnes's brows pinched into a worried frown.

"Rick, this is our youngest daughter, Summer." Herschel made the quick introduction. Rick wished now that Agnes had finished her earlier description of their youngest daughter.

"Summer, this is Rick Warren, the new assistant director for Camp Sunny Daze."

The smile, which had returned, vanished again from the young woman's eyes, instantly replaced by a hint of something that made Rick uneasy.

"Glad to meet you, Rick. Or should I call you Mr. Assistant Director?" The voice was a purr with a distinct edge to it.

"Summer runs her own business." Agnes pointed to the dress. "Fairy Princess Parties."

"I see." Pretending to be a fairy princess. The idea was laughable. "Well, if the business doesn't make a go of it, you can always get a job at a theme park, right?" Rick thought he'd made a joke, but the blue eyes shot a round of daggers his direction. He tried again. "What's the thing—the, um, wand—made of?"

"The stick's just painted wood, but the star's amber." Summer's voice held a note of pride. "It was a gift from Mom and Dad when I started the business."

Sparkly crowns and amber-tipped wands. He pressed his lips together. *Agnes had called it—spoiled rotten indeed. Mommy and Daddy probably still subsidize the paychecks.*

Summer's indignant eyebrow arch indicated she'd read his thoughts and dared him to say anything snide.

Agnes took the still-shivering Peewee from Summer. "Why don't we all go in and have a snack?"

Following her inside, Rick saw his chance to escape. "Thanks, but I have some things to take care of this afternoon." He picked up the paper he'd left on the table. "Here's the contract, signed and ready."

"And here are those forms you wanted." Herschel handed him a thick folder. "There are also daily itineraries of events we've scheduled. You'll have quite a bit of freedom with that. These are just some basics."

"Thanks." Rick eyed the folder as the four of them headed toward the front door. "And don't worry. I'm sure you're going to locate a girls' head counselor soon." The look of something akin to terror that passed between Herschel and Agnes told him he'd misspoken.

Summer's eyes widened in question, and her gaze darted between her parents.

"Yes, well, we'll be in touch. Thanks again, Rick."

Herschel's slaps on the back pushed Rick out the door.

As he made his way down the sidewalk, he couldn't keep from gawking at the old, gaudily painted purple SUV with Fairy Princess Parties lettered down its side in baby pink.

A grown woman parading around as a fairy princess. Hell-pee-roo.

SUMMER LAUNCHED INTO HER SPIEL as soon as condescending Rick Warren was out of earshot. "You told me the girls' head counselor position was filled."

Her mother swallowed nervously. "Well, it was, dear. But Hannah backed out yesterday."

"So you're going to consider me, after all. Right?" Summer fought to keep the little-girl whine out of her voice—the one that always brought her dad to his knees. The one she'd used to talk them into buying the camp. None of them anticipated the downward turn in the economy—investing in Kentucky Lake real estate should've been a sure thing—or the downward spiral of her dad's health. But her parents were in a financial crisis now, and it was her fault.

Summer had done a lot of soul-searching after her dad's heart attack. She'd been a burden to her parents with her flighty ways, but those days were behind her. She would repay every cent she owed her parents and never disappoint them again. She'd turned over a new leaf, was working hard, making monthly payments. And here was an opportunity to make up for a large chunk of her failures.

Charlie was going to retire soon, which meant they'd be looking for a new camp director. She was determined to earn that position for herself. She could make the camp turn a profit again, she was sure.

The girls' head counselor position wasn't camp director, but it was a start.

"Nubbin." Her dad's arm moved toward her shoulder, but her wing got in the way. Instead, his arm rested heavily around her waist as they walked back to the family room. "We've been through this before. There's a lot at stake here. We just don't think you're ready for—"

"I know I've been irresponsible in the past. The colleges and vocational programs you paid for. But I'm twenty-eight now. My business is doing okay, and I'm making monthly payments to y'all, and I'm really good with kids." She threw a thumb in the direction of the front door. "What about Mr. Stiff Neck? He didn't strike me as the type who would be good with kids. You should have heard how he yelled at Peewee." She plucked the pooch from her mom's arms and nuzzled the top of his head.

"Rick Warren is a fine young man." Her mom washed her hands and busied herself arranging cheese straws on a plate. "He came highly recommended by Gus. He's been a marine and a park ranger, and was the deputy director for the Western Kentucky Division of the Department of Wildlife until just recently."

Impressive, but titles didn't mean the guy wasn't a jerk. "If he's such a great guy, what happened with that job?"

"Politics." Her dad plopped into his chair. "New administration. Bad economy. They're cutting lots of satellite offices, and his was one."

"There wasn't anywhere else for him to go?" Summer thought back to her first impression. Seeing a hunky guy walk out of her parents' house wasn't something she'd expected. "So a handsome, successful guy like that with no job offers? Something's fishy."

"He is handsome, isn't he?" Her mother smiled dreamily.

Summer didn't respond, preferring not to think about Rick's impossibly broad, squared shoulders, or that blond crew cut that showed off pleasant blue-green eyes, or the dimples that were so deep she could see them from yards away.

"Gus told us he was offered a job in Frankfort. A good job." Her dad popped a whole cheese straw in his mouth and reached for another. "But he wouldn't take it and leave his staff here stranded with nothing. He's hoping to get back on as a ranger in the fall, and he's working on his real-estate license just in case."

Summer grimaced at the admiration in her dad's voice.

Rick Warren had already been elevated to hero-worship status while she remained the poster child for People Not to Pin Your Hopes On. A flare of jealousy mixed with embarrassment churned her insides. "Well, he may be a swell guy, but he doesn't love y'all the way I do, and he won't have your best interests at heart. You sank all your money into this—"

"Which is why we need—"

"Me!" Her heart beat faster. "You need someone who knows you and...and your values. Someone who'll keep an eye on Rick Warren to make sure he handles things the way you want and doesn't yell at the kids the way he did poor Peewee."

That drew a frown from her mom. "Surely he wouldn't do that." She chewed on her bottom lip. Not a bad sign.

Summer snorted, making another attempt to drive the point home. "Once a marine, always a marine. And Charlie won't be out with the kids all the time. Most of the time it's only the kids and the counselors."

Her parents' eyes met. They were weakening. If they had more time, she'd lose this one, but the camp was scheduled to open in a few weeks, and plenty of preliminary plans still needed to be taken care of. They needed a head counselor for the girls.

Her mother's eyes widened suddenly. She'd found a loophole. "But what about your business? You can't be away from it the whole summer. Not on such short notice. You've already got parties booked."

Summer had thought that one out some time ago, in case anything like her dad's health ever pulled her away. "Best friend to the rescue. Kate's my fairy-princess-in-waiting. She's already said she'd be glad to be my fill-in if I ever need one, *and* she's looking for a summer job. And no," she countered before they could broach the subject, "she's not interested in the counselor position. She doesn't swim and despises sweating."

Her parents exchanged looks again, and this time things felt positive. Hopelessly resigned for their part, but positive for her. Her mind whirred for the definitive coup de grâce. "I'll work for free."

Two sets of eyes swung toward her.

"I mean it. I don't know what you're planning to pay the counselors, but whatever it is, you can keep my part. It's just another way I can pay you back what I owe." *And show you I'm up to the challenge.*

"Well, you are good with little girls," her dad acquiesced.

"I'm great with little girls! I have all those games and activities from my parties I can use." She did a quick mental inventory of additional items she might need. "Do you still have some of that green granite?"

"In the workshop."

"Can you cut some more stars for me? They'll be perfect for special wands I can use as awards. This is so exciting!" Using her fairy princess persona, she flitted to her mom, then her dad, and planted kisses on each of their cheeks. "I can make the camp a fairy princess dream come true!"

"But remember." Her dad shook his finger in her direction. "Rick's taking Gus's place as assistant director, so he's in charge. Whatever he says, goes."

"Of course!" Summer smiled sweetly, but her insides jumped in a wild dance of victory. Her kid-radar told her Mr. Haughty wouldn't have the vaguest idea how to deal with kids. She'd be surprised if he made it a month. A week might even be pushing it.

But she wouldn't let her parcnts down this time. She'd be there to show them what she was capable of when Mr. Marine hightailed it outta there.

CHAPTER TWO

THE LOGS NEEDED SOME CHINKING, windows needed caulk and the screen door wouldn't close completely. Taking it off the hinges and planing it down would take care of that. Otherwise, the cabin that Summer Delaney would be staying in was structurally sound.

Rick hurried to check the bathroom plumbing and finish up the notes on the cabin Herschel asked him to make for future reference. Summer would be arriving in an hour, and he'd given his word not to let her in on the possibility of selling the camp and the cabins. Evidently, it was Summer who'd talked the Delaneys into buying in the first place, and Herschel didn't want his Nubbin upset by the possibility of the camp property becoming a subdivision. *Hell-pee-roo!* Why didn't they just level with her? Treat her like a grown woman rather than a spoiled child?

Rick blew his breath out in a huff. It was none of his business.

But the camp was his business, literally, for the next two months. He'd seen enough of Summer's ways at the staff meeting to know he and Miss Fairy Princess weren't going to see eye-to-eye. She kept insisting the kids needed more unstructured time—*"time to have fun and just be kids."*

Kids without structure were kids who got into trouble, his dad always said, so Rick and his brothers had daily schedules of chores and lessons, which got checked at the end of each day. If anything was missed, a deduction came out of their weekly allowance. Rick hated it.

But it turned out his dad was right. Rick had learned that lesson the hard way in Afghanistan. Kids with no structure got in trouble…and got hurt. He paused for just a moment before forcing his mind into a U-turn, back to the task at hand.

He made a note the bathroom sink had a slow drip and the toilet stool continued to run when he flushed it. He shook the handle to make it stop. Both easy fixes.

"I thought this was *my* cabin."

Rick spun around to find Summer watching him, a large duffel, a hanging bag and a satchel on the bed behind her.

Damn it! She's early. "I, um…I was just doing a last-minute inspection." His face warmed as he snapped shut the folder he'd been writing in and tucked it under his arm.

Her forehead wrinkled in suspicion as her eyes cut from the folder to his face. "Inspection?"

"Making sure everything's in good working order."

"That's Charlie's job."

Day-to-day operations were Charlie's job, but the old guy was getting up in years. Rick had offered to help get the place ready to sell—if and when it came to that. "Yes, well, Charlie could use a hand."

Summer swung around and moved to the bed, removing a stack of papers from the satchel. She thrust them toward him. "Activity sheets."

So she was still pissed about the forms he'd required her to fill out. Well, too bad. Owners' daughter or not, he intended to keep her accountable for every waking minute these kids spent under his guard. "Thanks." He slid them into the folder, keeping it tilted so she couldn't see the contents, and let his eyes rove over the pieces of luggage on her bed. "You have a lot to unpack." Sarcasm found its way into his tone. "I'll let you get started."

"Don't forget your white gloves. I'm sure they're lying around here somewhere." She turned her back, dismissing him, and unzipped her duffel.

MARY MARGARET AVERY-HENSON's mother handed Summer a list of emergency contacts. Summer scanned it quickly. Mother. Father. Stepfather. Stepmother. Maternal grandparents. Paternal grandparents. Step-maternal grandparents. Step-paternal grandparents.

Piano recitals must be a hoot for this kid.

Mary Margaret peeked out from behind her mom. Chin-length brown hair hung straight, in desperate need of a trim. Large, soulful brown eyes full of fear and apprehension. This child was a prime candidate for some extensive fairy princess training.

Summer held her hand out. "Hi, Mary. I'm Summer."

"It's Mary Margaret," her mother corrected. "My ex-husband and I agreed from the beginning we would call our child by whatever full name we gave her."

Summer tried again. "Well then, hello, Mary Margaret."

"Say hello, Mary Margaret," her mother prompted, and the child's mouth moved in an inaudible "Hi."

Mary Margaret didn't offer to take her hand, so Summer gave her a quick pat on the shoulder.

"She's very shy, which is one of the reasons we thought this would be a good idea. Her father and I agreed some time away might be good for her. Bring her out of some of her reticence, we hope."

"And just have a lot of fun." Summer nodded and winked at Mary Margaret, but the child's expression didn't change. "Well, everyone else is over in the girls' bunkhouse—"

"Oh, dear! They're not sleeping in bunks, are they?" The mother's voice was filled with panic, the same look of fear Summer had seen in the child. "Because her father and I agreed to never have her sleep in an upper bunk. If she fell out, it could—"

"There are no upper bunks," Summer assured her. "All twin beds on the floor. We just call it a bunkhouse because it sounds more rustic than dormitory. More campy."

"Oh. All right, then." The woman's eyes cut nervously toward the bunkhouse, then down to her daughter.

"Well, as I was saying, you can get your stuff put away. Tara, the assistant counselor, is in there helping everybody get settled. We have our first activity planned for an hour from now."

The woman drew a long breath and nodded. With Mary Margaret by one hand and the duffel in the other, she started toward the girls' dorm. "Now, Mary Margaret, your father and I agree that this will be a good experience for you...." Her voice trailed off as they moved away.

Summer couldn't keep from wondering what the trouble in that marriage had been since it seemed Mary Margaret's mother and father agreed on everything.

She glanced toward the boys' side of the camp. Rick Warren still had a couple of people to check in. He stood very straight with his very official clipboard, nodding at a camper and checking things off a list with what she was sure was a military-issue pencil. He didn't seem to notice that the boy's mother was standing closer than was necessary, touching his arm in a flirtatious manner. Obviously, the woman didn't know what a pain in the ass Rick Warren could be.

Nobody seemed to pick up on that except her.

She was still seething about the staff meeting a few weeks ago when Rick's body visibly stiffened at the announcement she'd been hired as the girls' head counselor. And once her dad introduced him as head counselor and assistant director, General Warren just took over, laying out rules and regulations like he was running some kind of POW camp. The audacity of the guy! Seeing her dad pass the responsibility of the camp to a virtual stranger made her heart sink then and every time she'd thought about it since—including now.

She'd tried to show her assertion at the meeting. But when she'd brought up the subject of downtime, Rick had poo-pooed her ideas. To make matters worse, her dad had agreed with him.

Rick Warren put her on edge, made her feel as if he were hiding something. Snooping around her cabin that morning… hiding the file he held. She didn't know what he was up to, but she didn't like it. Or him.

Right at that moment, Rick's face broke into a dazzling smile, directed at the mother who was standing too close, and a flare of anger shot through Summer. *Tsk, tsk. Flirting with the parents. How inappropriate.*

Inappropriate images of Rick Warren had come to her in her sleep the past couple of weeks. Remembering them now caused her cheeks to warm, along with a few other parts of her traitorous body.

"What a piece of work, huh?"

Summer jumped at the voice. She hadn't heard the assistant counselor, Tara O'Malley, approach.

"He sure is," Summer muttered. "We'll just have to make the best of it."

Tara's eyes followed the direction Summer's gaze had gone, and she laughed. "I wasn't talking about Rick. I was talking about Mary Margaret Avery-Henson's mom."

"Oh." Summer's face burned. "Well, it's easy to see why Mary Margaret's so shy. I have a feeling the kid's life is filled with adults telling her what to do and how to feel." She handed Mary Margaret's emergency contact list to Tara.

Tara glanced over it and let out a low whistle. "I think you may be right."

Summer looked forward to getting to know Tara better.

With her bright smile and infectious laugh, the redhead endeared herself to everyone who met her.

"And you're right about him, too." An appreciative gleam sparkled Tara's green eyes. "He is one fine piece of work."

"Yeah," Summer agreed. "Rick's a great-looking guy." The rest of the staff didn't know about her and Rick's mutual dislike, and Summer decided it would be best to keep it that way. No use making everyone uncomfortable and giving them something to gossip about. And kids were very astute. They would pick up on animosity quickly. She wouldn't allow anything to make the kids uncomfortable during their time here. This was going to be the best month they'd ever had.

"Well, I didn't come over here to gawk at the boss, honest." Tara smoothed back a curl of coppery hair that had worked loose from her ponytail. "Some of the girls are a little weepy now that their parents have left. First time away from home."

"Homesickness is to be expected with eight- and nine-year-olds." Summer and Tara fell into step moving toward the girls' bunkhouse. "I remember my first year here."

Tara's eyebrows shot up. "You went to camp here?"

"Six years. I loved every one of them." Summer swept her arms wide. "This is one of my favorite places. I was thrilled when Mom and Dad bought it. My heart broke at the thought that someone would tear it down."

"More reason to see these kids have a great time and want to come back next year."

"Yep." Summer gave an emphatic nod and shot a glance toward Rick, who was checking in the last boy. "I don't intend to let anything stand in the way of this place's success."

HOWIE SQUINTED AND LOOKED RICK up and down. "My dad could beat you up."

"Howard Silas Gerard, Jr.!" Nila Gerard's sharp tone drew

her son's attention. "We don't talk that way. Apologize this instant."

"Sorry." The boy's eyes shifted to the ground at Rick's feet.

"Apology accepted…and I'm sure your dad's very strong." Rick smiled and tried to make light of the situation. The kid was scared, probably the first time away from home. In fact, he and his mother both seemed jittery. She nervously rubbed her cheek. That's when Rick noticed the faint bluish mark tinged in yellow and green below her left eye. It had faded, but careful inspection showed it dropped well below her cheekbone. Combat instinct tightened his gut.

He flipped to the back of his clipboard, wrote a quick note and pulled it free. "Say, sport." He held the note toward the boy. "Would you do me a favor and take this count over to Ms. Ginny, our cook? She should be over there in the dining hall." He indicated the long white building with the large screened-in area.

Howie took the paper and shuffled toward the dining hall.

"Thanks." Nila waited until he got out of hearing distance. "He isn't normally like that. He's usually very sweet, but…" Her voice broke as her eyes clouded with tears.

"Are you okay?" Rick didn't do gentle well, but he gave it his best shot. "Is there anything I can do to help?"

"His dad and I have been going through a hard time lately. I filed for divorce last week, and Howie and I are staying with my sister." Her bottom lip trembled and she caught it between her teeth.

Damn. Seeing a woman cry was a fist in his gut. "It'll be okay, really." He tried to sound reassuring. "Several of our kids are going through or have been through divorce. Howie won't be the only one here. Is his father allowed contact?"

She shook her head, and her gaze cut toward Howie, who disappeared through the screen door. "I have a restraining order against him." She touched her cheek absently and shifted her eyes, shadowed by pain and grief, back to Rick. He knew the look well. As a marine, he'd seen it often.

"We'll see that Howie has a good time. Maybe, by the time the month is over, things will have settled down at home."

Nila nodded, but the way her lips pressed into a thin line told Rick she didn't believe his words any more than he did.

"Maybe you and your sister can use the month to do some fun things together," Rick suggested.

Nila smiled and her shoulders dropped into a more relaxed position as Howie burst through the door and ran back to join them.

"Now, you need to go claim your bunk and get settled in." Rick nodded toward the boys' dorm. "We'll have a briefing to welcome all the campers in—" he checked his watch "—thirty-two minutes." Though his comments were directed to Howie, he hoped Howie's mom would take the hint that it was time to say goodbye.

Nila put her arm around her son's shoulders, walking him toward the boys' barracks. "I want to take a quick look at where you'll be staying, and then I'll head home."

Rick flipped through papers on his clipboard. Everything appeared to be completed.

A flurry of activity erupted from the girls' barracks. Summer burst out, leading a string of girls, giggling and hopping like rabbits.

He rolled his eyes. The first activity on Summer's activity sheet for today. Welcoming Games. *What in the hell were welcoming games?*

He watched as the string of girls hopped into a circle, unable to pull his eyes away from Summer Delaney's tanned and toned legs propelling her across the ground like a gazelle in white shorts.

Once the circle formed, the girls held hands and began swinging their arms in rhythm to the song they belted out. Rick recognized the tune as the same as "Mary Had a Little Lamb."

"Sunny Daze the camp for me," they sang in unison. "Camp for me. Camp for me. Sunny Daze the camp for me. The summer place to be."

How did Summer have time to teach them a song? He hadn't set foot in the boys' barracks yet, and she already had the girls out playing games.

The song started again, but this time the circle moved in slow motion, increasing to a fast trot, faster and faster until the circle whirled as fast as the girls could move and still scream the tune at the top of their lungs. When it ended, they all collapsed in a giggly heap on the ground.

Summer lay back, bright red in the face, and the hand on her chest moved up and down to the rhythm of the body heaving under it.

The sight caught Rick unprepared. Suddenly, in his mind, she was under him, naked, tan legs circling his waist, laughing and heaving from the throes of the climax he'd just brought her to.

He reacted immediately to the image, his erection springing to attention like a marine at the first note of the national anthem.

"Hell-pee-roo." He tried to dismiss the image from his mind as he sauntered toward the barracks. When he reached the door, he recognized the refrain of the song he'd been whistling—"Oh, say, does that star-spangled banner yet wave…"

His face grew hot. He rubbed the tattooed area over his heart and grumbled, "It's gonna be one hell of a long month, Dunk."

SUMMER WATCHED AS NEIL JENKINS, the boys' assistant counselor, held the screen door of the dining hall open and the boys streamed through in single file. They were quiet. Too quiet, considering how the girls had raced in and jockeyed for seats, some of them switching places several times before finally settling down beside a new BFF.

Less than an hour and Rick already had the boys acting like soldiers. One or two would probably want to leave by tonight. She grunted her disapproval.

At precisely ten o'clock, Rick strode through the door. "Good morning!" His cheerful voice boomed through the hall.

Most of the girls gave an answering "Good morning," but the boys remained quiet and those who spoke mumbled.

Rick's hands came together in a loud clap, and everybody jumped, including Summer, who'd been looking around the room to keep from noticing his handsome features.

"Okay, everybody up."

Kids and adults alike scrambled to obey. Summer rose reluctantly.

"Now, I'm going to say good morning again, and this time I want to hear your response. Ready?" He paused and looked around, making a brief eye connect with everyone in the room. "Good morning."

"Good morning." The kids' enthusiasm echoed through the mess hall.

"C'mon, you can do better than that! Good morning," he said again, this time louder.

The kids shouted back, "Good morning!" Then they shouted it louder until they were screeching at the top of their lungs. The action broke the ice, and when they sat down, the boys were smiling and nudging one another along with the girls, red faces broken by bright smiles.

Rick laughed, a deep, masculine sound that vibrated into

the pit of Summer's stomach. She'd never heard him laugh. It was a pleasant sound, but it agitated her a bit nonetheless.

"Okay, let's go over a few ground rules," Rick said, and Summer's inner voice said, *Because Rick's number-one rule is that you can never have too many rules.*

"Welcome to Camp Sunny Daze. We want you to have a great time this month...."

But not too good because what we really want is for you to learn to follow the rules.

"But there are a few things we expect. Rule number one. We always use good manners. We respect one another and ourselves, and we *show* respect for one another and ourselves. As a way of showing respect, you will address the staff as Ms. and Mr."

Oh, for heaven's sake. She and Tara had already introduced themselves to the girls without using titles. *This guy is straight out of the Middle Ages.*

"I'll introduce them to you now, ladies first. Ladies, if you'll please stand up when I introduce you? Ms. Tara is the assistant counselor for the girls, Ms. Summer is the head counselor for the girls and Ms. Ginny is our cook and first-aid counselor."

Summer smiled and waved at Ginny and Charlie Prichard, who stood behind the serving counter. Ginny was a retired school nurse and Charlie a retired electrician. They were her parents' best friends. Summer had known and loved them her whole life, considered them the closest thing she had to godparents. She knew they would side with her against Rick if it came to that.

"That's Mr. Charlie standing next to Ms. Ginny. He's the camp director. Next to him is Mr. Kenny, our security guard. You won't see too much of him because he patrols at night and sleeps most of the day. Over here is Mr. Neil, the boys' assistant counselor. And I'm Mr. Rick, boys' head counselor and assistant director of the camp."

Right. We'll see how long that lasts.

"Rule number two. Never step foot outside the camp without an adult."

Okay, that was a good one.

"And rule number three. Always use the buddy system. Never go anywhere near the woods or the water without a buddy. When we're hiking and swimming, we'll always have a buddy to watch out for. Understood?"

A few of the kids murmured, "Yes," and a few others nodded.

"I can't hear you."

"Yes!" the kids shouted.

"Yes, what?" Rick cupped his hand behind his ear.

A few caught on. "Yes, Mr. Rick."

Rick beamed with pleasure, and Summer's toes curled involuntarily. She looked away, disgusted by her body's reaction.

"Great. Now…do you have any questions?"

"Can I uthe my thell phone?" The question came from a chubby boy with a distinct lisp. Two of the girls giggled and Rick shot them a look that withered them in their seats.

Eight- and nine-year-olds with cell phones? When she'd been here, writing letters home every week was required.

"Yes, Willard." Rick's answer surprised Summer more than the question had. She'd been definite Mr. Nineteenth Century would say no. "But only in the case of an emergency. If there's no emergency, and we don't anticipate there'll be one, it remains in your bunk area and turned off. Got that?"

"Yeth, Mithter Rick."

"Any other questions?"

"What if we don't like what there is to eat? I don't like a lotta things."

Without looking, Summer already could identify the characteristic whine belonging to Lucy.

"Hmm. I guess you'll get hungry."

Summer cringed at Rick's tone, and then smiled to herself. Charlie might want to get rid of this guy immediately.

"But you need to try to eat every meal because you're going to need lots of energy. We have so many fun things planned, and you're going to want to be able to do them all. Any other questions?" No other hands went up. "Well, I'm sure you'll have some eventually, so don't hesitate to ask one of us when you do. Now—" he gave the group a wink "—is everybody ready for a snack?"

"Yes, Mr. Rick!" The answer resounded from both of the long tables.

"Okay then, Ms. Ginny has something ready for us. Line up single file and be sure to tell her thank-you."

Three of the boys jumped up and made a dash for the serving line.

"Uh-uh-uh, gentleman." Rick motioned them back to their seats. "Ladies first."

He'd done that twice, and it was already beginning to get old. Another point of contention to speak with him about.

The girls made a wild dash, flashing one-upping grins at the boys as they picked up their boxes of apple juice and paper plates filled with grapes, carrots and cinnamon graham crackers smeared with peanut butter.

Each of the girls said a polite thank-you to Ginny and Charlie as they took their food.

"Rick's gonna have these kids whipped into shape in no time, Summer." Charlie pushed more plates to the front as he spoke. "That'll sure make our jobs easier."

Irritation burned Summer's throat. Surely, Ginny and Charlie didn't approve of Rick's strong-arm tactics. "Whipped might be one way to describe them, Charlie, but we have to remember they're only eight- and nine-year-olds. We want them to have fun, too."

"They'll have fun." Rick's deep voice right beside her startled her. She stepped back with her plate as the boys hurried through the line and made for the outdoors. "Being well behaved and having fun aren't mutually exclusive."

"I'll bet Summer disagrees with that, Rick. She was a bit of a wild child." Charlie shook his finger her direction. "Herschel and Agnes had their hands full with this one."

"Indeed." Rick's tone implied he was already aware of her past.

Had her parents shared stories with him about her flighty assent to adulthood? The thought made her grit her teeth. Well, she would show them all she was firmly grounded now and that meant she wouldn't be easily pushed around. "Being well behaved doesn't have to mean following stuffy, 'old school' rules."

"Manners aren't 'old school.'"

"But 'ladies first' is. Boys and girls are equal here. We should take turns."

"Duly noted."

Summer pressed for a firmer answer. "Does that mean you agree?"

One end of Rick's mouth twitched. "It means I'll treat *everyone* here fairly."

Once again, Summer felt as though she was the unnamed subject of his sentence. She popped off a quick curtsy. "Then, if you'll excuse me *Mr.* Rick, I'll return to my charges."

Rick bowed gallantly. "Ms. Summer."

With her back turned to him, Summer allowed a smile to play on her lips. She may have been a wild child, but the definitive word was *child.* Rick Warren probably sprang from his mother's womb in dress uniform. He was clueless when it came to kids.

She'd give him a week—tops.

CHAPTER THREE

"OKAY, MEN. HAVE ANY OF YOU ever been in a canoe before?" Rick surveyed the group.

Austin's hand went up. "My grandpa's got a fishing boat. I go with him a lot."

Rick pointed to the boats lined up on the shore. "Is it a canoe?"

"Naw—"

"No, sir," Rick corrected.

"No, sir," Austin repeated. "It has a motor on the back."

"Well, in a canoe, your arms and the paddle are the motor."

He gave each of the boys a paddle and demonstrated how to hold it. They moved into waist-deep water and practiced rowing until he was satisfied they'd all gotten the hang of it. "Today, you men will be in the bow of the boat—that's the front. The counselors will be in the back, which is the stern. The person in the back can guide the canoe by using the paddle like a rudder." He showed them what he meant, then he had the boys stand and walk, practicing using their oars like rudders.

"You never stand up in a canoe," he warned. "It's easy to flip over, but if that happens just swim to the nearest bank. We'll pull the canoe over to that spot and then start again. This cove isn't very big. We'll never be too far from the shore."

"What if somebody's not a good swimmer?"

That Daniel wasn't a swimmer had been noted on his camp

application. Rick read the fear in the boy's eyes and made a mental note to find time to work with him individually on his swimming. "Good question, Daniel. Lots of people who aren't swimmers enjoy canoeing. That's why everybody needs to put on one of the life jackets over there." He pointed to the orange life vests hanging on hooks on the side of the shed. "The life jacket will hold you up, so all you have to do is kick and move your arms to propel yourself through the water. And if anybody would rather not go out in the canoe, that's perfectly acceptable, too. But if you want to give this a try, go get on a life jacket and then line up and we'll divide you up into groups."

All of the boys, including an anxious-looking Daniel, hurried to don the jackets and get in line.

Neil made quick work of grouping them so weight would be more or less evenly distributed among the boats. "Y'all can decide who'll paddle first," he explained, "and that person will be in front. But don't worry. Everybody'll get a chance to be in the front. And we have an hour, so you'll each get a long turn and maybe more than one."

"Willard, Ryan and Daniel will go with Mr. Charlie." Rick pointed to the first canoe. "Evan, Jimbo and Austin will go with Mr. Neil in the second canoe. And Howie, Carlos, Reggie and Mitchell in number three with me."

As the boys rushed to their places, Rick heard the hum of chatter behind him. The girls were coming to the beach area already. He'd hoped to get the boys onto the water before they showed up. He wanted their entire attention without any distractions—or any need to show off.

Summer Delaney in a swimsuit flashed in his mind, and he dared not turn around. *Damn it.* He shook his head, trying ineffectually to rid himself of the image.

"You don't want me to paddle first, Mr. Rick?" A worried frown pinched Carlos's face.

"No, no. You're fine. I was just shooing away a pest. Okay, men." Rick pointed to a large tree stump protruding from the water in the middle of the shallow cove. "We're going to paddle out and around that stump and back to shore, switching front men after each trip. Whoever is in front needs to listen to your instructor. He'll tell you which side of the canoe to paddle on, and he'll be guiding, but turning can be tricky, so listen carefully. Remember, do *not* stand up in the canoe, and men sitting in the middle stay low."

He looked at Charlie and nodded.

Charlie pushed the canoe off the bank, calling directions. "Stroke to the right, Ryan. Right. Right. Now left. Left again. You're doing great."

The first canoe cut smoothly through the water, and the boys in Neil's canoe all turned eager eyes toward Rick, anxious for their chance.

He waited until Charlie's group was almost to the stump and then gave Neil the signal.

Neil eased the canoe off the sandy bottom, and his group was under way…for about three yards. Until someone leaned over too far or moved the wrong way, and then they were sitting on the sandy bottom in waist-deep water.

Girls giggled in the background.

The boys all pointed to someone else to lay the blame on. "It doesn't make any difference," Neil told them. "We're a team." He pulled the canoe back to shore, and they reloaded. Their second attempt went off without a hitch.

"My dad told me he's gonna get us a canoe," Howie said, twisting around toward Rick from his position in the middle of the boat.

I'll bet your dad makes lots of promises, Rick thought, but he said, "That'll be fun. And when he does, you'll know what to do. Now, turn around and stay still. Okay, let's do it."

Rick pushed them off, and the boat glided softly onto the water.

Bass boats passing the cove out in Kentucky Lake caused waves that rocked the canoe gently, but his group instinctively shifted their weight in unison and kept the canoe level. The first and second groups made it around the stump without too much zigzagging.

Charlie and Neil called the orders. The smiles of conquest on the boys' faces as they rounded the stump and headed back toward the shore were priceless.

Carlos was a bit unsure of left and right and had a little trouble keeping a steady rhythm. Rick watched closely, trying to match it so there wouldn't be so much unnecessary drag, but they ended up too far to the right.

"Right, Carlos, right, right, right," Rick called as he shifted his own paddle in the water. The canoe started its arc around the stump.

A flash of red diverted Rick's attention. Summer Delaney stood on the wooden platform that held the slide at the deep end of the beach area. Even the modest cut of the swimsuit couldn't hide the perfect proportions of her petite body. A long, golden braid glistened in the sunlight, looking like a gold arrow pointing directly to the perky, rounded rear below it.

As if his gaze drew her around, she turned toward him, lifting a hand to her brow to shade against the sun. His eyes drifted up her shapely legs, past her flat stomach and tiny waistline, to the small but full breasts molded and sculpted by the spandex in the garment.

"Mr. Rick?"

The panic in Carlos's tone snapped Rick's attention back to the canoe. Damn! They were headed directly for the stump. "Left, Carlos, left." Carlos paddled fast to the right.

Quickly, Rick shifted his paddle flat to the water in an

attempt to slow them down. The technique worked, but not fast enough. The canoe slammed broadside into the stump. A grinding sound against the floor followed by a complete stop told him they were lodged on a submerged limb.

"Okay, men. Sorry. This is my fault. I wasn't paying close enough attention." Rick gave his own ass a mental kick. "Carlos, you paddle. Howie, Reggie and Mitchell—you push against the trunk. Gently."

Using his paddle as a lever beneath the canoe, Rick made contact with the limb and pushed down. Slowly, they started inching away. He could feel the eyes of the entire camp on him…Summer Delaney's more keenly than the others.

They were almost free, when Howie shot up out of his seat and pushed hard against the tree trunk. At the same time, a bass boat's wave caught the canoe from the other side, pushing against Howie's thrust and tipping the canoe precariously. Before the boy could regain his balance, he'd toppled into the water and the shift in the weight flipped the canoe.

Rick gulped in a deep breath as he hit the water. He was only under for a split second, and when he broke the surface, he immediately took a head count. Four small heads bobbed around the canoe, stunned and silent.

But that lasted only for a split second also, before Carlos yelled, "Yeah, man! Whoo-hoo!" and the other three boys joined him in his excitement. They swam toward the shore with wild strokes and spraying kicks while Rick grabbed the overturned canoe and sidestroked behind them.

As they waded onto the shore, applause and catcalls floated across the cove. The boys traded high fives all around and slapped one another on the back, giddy and silly from the attention they'd garnered.

Rick gave in to the excitement of the moment and laughed with them. "Howie, I know you were trying to help, but remember next time that you can't stand up in a canoe. Anyway, I'm proud of you guys and the way you didn't panic. You followed my directions and swam directly to the nearest shore. Great job."

He glanced back toward the opposite shore where Summer still stood on the platform, watching.

He wasn't definite because of the distance, but he thought he could see a delighted smirk on her face.

"SO MR. RICK'S IRON FIST doesn't keep the boys under control, even when they're within arm's reach," Summer muttered under her breath. Her lifeguard training had her ready to dive in, but the boys all appeared to be good swimmers. And Rick—naked back muscles bulging as he paddled the canoe—drew way too much of her attention. The stirring in her body bothered her more than a little.

One unhappy child could spell disaster for the camp, so she'd made it her job to keep a close eye on Rick and stop trouble before it happened. But she had to remind herself that the eye she kept on him couldn't get distracted by his appearance.

Rick Warren, with his military ways, was trouble for Camp Sunny Daze with a capital *T*.

On the opposite shore, the boys climbed back into the canoe, and Rick pushed them off. Satisfied all was well, she turned her attention back to the girls in the roped-off swimming area.

Anne, Becca and the twins, Braelyn and Kaelyn, were excellent swimmers, venturing out into the deeper water near the ropes with Tara watching from close by. Shannon, Lucy, Amanda, Elise and Greta were a little closer to shore and had a game of hot potato going with a small beach ball.

Mary Margaret sat on the sand alone, glumly tossing pebbles into the water.

"Do you want to start your swimming lessons today, Mary Margaret?" Summer waded toward her.

The child shook her head.

"Do you want to get the sand out of your swimsuit?"

Mary Margaret shrugged, which Summer took as a yes since it wasn't a definite no.

She went over to the hooks and picked out one of the smaller life jackets. When she turned back around, Rick and his crew had just beached their canoe and were switching places. Rick flashed a sheepish grin, which immediately made her start to feel all melty inside. She hurried back to Mary Margaret.

"Here, put this on, and you can go in the water with me."

The child stood obediently, and Summer dropped down in the sand to get her buckled in.

Taking the child's hand, she slowly led the way into the water, aware that the little hand inside hers trembled.

"I don't want you to be afraid of the water, but I do want you to respect it." She'd taught lots of children how to swim over the years.

They waded to where the water was knee-deep, and she sat down, letting the water ripple around her chest. Mary Margaret stooped, taking short gulps of air each time a wave passed.

Summer let her get used to the water and then she asked, "Are you good?" Mary Margaret nodded. "Okay then, give me your hands, and we'll go out a little farther."

Little by little, Summer coaxed the child deeper until she could float if she bent her knees.

A look of astonishment passed over Mary Margaret's face when she realized the life jacket would hold her up. "Wow!" she said, which brought a laugh from Summer.

It wasn't long before Mary Margaret instinctively started to dog-paddle, reveling in her newlyfound ability. When

Shannon yelled at her to come join their game, and Mary Margaret did, Summer watched with pride.

The bell sounded, warning lunch was a half hour away. It was time to head back for quick showers.

For the first time, the boys and girls mingled as they headed up the path, most of the conversations centering on the overturned canoe.

"Summer," Rick called, "could I speak to you a minute?"

She waited as he hurried to catch up, relieved he'd put his shirt back on.

"I noticed you were working individually with Mary Margaret."

"She's a nonswimmer, but not for long. She already shows promise." Summer kept her answer short, anxious for the conversation and the close proximity to be over.

"Well, I used to work as a lifeguard, so I taught a lot of swimming lessons, and it's not a good idea to allow her to wear a life jacket in the beach area. You don't want her to get a false sense of security with her ability."

He was trying to tell her how to teach swimming lessons? Summer was incredulous. "I worked as a lifeguard, too, for several years, and I've taught lots of kids to swim. You have to get them over their initial fear of the water before you can make any headway."

Rick's face tightened. "And if they get used to the life jacket keeping them afloat, they won't trust themselves without it. Those damn water wings they put on kids are the absolute worst things ever invented. The kid gets used to them holding him up, and he jumps in the pool the first time without them only to sink immediately to the bottom."

Heat crept into Summer's face. "I always start out the little ones with water wings. It gets them comfortable with the texture of the water. Water in their face. Water in their eyes and ears. Once they get used to all that, then we ditch the wings, and they find out what they can do on their own. I've never had any problem teaching like that."

They reached the clearing where the path separated, leading to opposite sides of the camp.

Summer stopped and faced him, fists on hips and chin jutted toward him in a stance Rick had already grown accustomed to when she was challenged. He was reminded of Charlie's pronouncement that morning. *Wild child.* Willful and used to getting her way, too, Rick concluded.

"Also, I just wanted to mention that I noticed your canoe instruction lacked finesse." Summer arched one golden eyebrow defiantly. "So I'll tell you what. You use your techniques with the boys. I'll use mine with the girls."

Rick could see this was a sticking point with her. He hadn't meant to start an argument, merely to offer some advice, but he'd obviously rankled her. *Choose your battles carefully, man.* "Okay. I suppose that's fair."

Her hands dropped to her sides, though they stayed doubled up into fists. He got the distinct feeling she'd love to punch him right there and then.

"And I really didn't intend to make you mad."

"I'm not mad." She swung around and stomped toward her cabin.

Once she got out of earshot, he allowed himself a disgruntled sigh. He was the assistant director and he wouldn't let her have her way next time…even if she was cute when she was angry.

Damn woman would probably want to dust everybody with magic fairy powder next.

TEACHING THE GIRLS TO CANOE turned out to be easy and uneventful. Tara's group paddled back into the beach three times, and Summer's group got turned around backward, but none of the groups turned over or hit the stump. Summer couldn't have been more proud of them…or relieved, since Rick was on the beach the entire time.

The one disappointment was Mary Margaret, who was too afraid to get into the canoe, even with a life jacket on.

Rick was giving Daniel some individual swimming lessons while the other boys swam supervised but on their own, and he offered to include Mary Margaret.

Summer agreed to the plan but kept a watchful eye from the canoe.

The hour was a complete bust as Rick couldn't get Mary Margaret into the water without a life jacket and obviously wouldn't let her in with one. Daniel, on the other hand, seemed pleased with the dogpaddle Mr. Rick taught him as a first stroke.

After dinner, Rick led both groups on a short nature hike that scored an owl sighting—a first for all the kids. But even their enthusiasm couldn't mask the exhaustion in their eyes.

It had been a very busy first day.

"Nature hike at six-thirty tomorrow morning, so lights out in one hour," he announced, and no one protested, except Lucy, who whined about everything.

"If the girls can be ready for bed in a half hour, we'll have a special treat." Summer had been planning this surprise since she talked her parents into the job.

"Summer and Tara, don't forget the staff meeting after we get the kids down." Rick's reminder caused Summer's teeth to clench. What else had she done today that he would find fault with at the staff meeting?

But she wouldn't let Rick Warren ruin her surprise for the girls. Thank heavens for instant heat hair appliances! She rushed to her cabin and turned on the jumbo wave iron, hastily applied some makeup and made as many waves in her hair as time would allow. Slipping into her fairy princess gown and wings and grabbing her magic wand, she entered the girls' bunkhouse twenty minutes before lights out.

The place erupted into a giant squeal when the girls spotted her, and soon she was surrounded by ten sets of eyes shimmering with excitement. Lucy gushed instead of whining. Even Mary Margaret smiled.

"I need y'all to sit on the floor in a big circle." Summer used her fairy princess voice, and the girls scrambled to get seated. "Now then," she started, like she always started her appearances. "What do you think it is that makes a fairy princess so special?" She looked around the room.

"You're pretty," Elise answered.

"Why, thank you, Elise." The fairy princess smiled and gave an elegant nod. "That's kind of you, and kindness is a big part of being a fairy princess, more important even than being pretty. Everybody's pretty in some way, you know. Some people have pretty eyes or pretty hair. Other people have pretty hearts. And the pretty heart is definitely required to be a true fairy princess." She glanced around. "So what else do you need to be a real fairy princess?"

"A dress!"

"A crown!"

"Wings!"

"A magic wand!"

Answers flooded the room, and Summer waited until they all were finished. "The dress. The crown. The wings. Those are things that can indicate a fairy princess. But did you know that there are a lot of fairy princesses out there who don't show themselves with dresses, or crowns or wings? They're in hiding. *Secret fairy princesses.* And they're all around us. But the one thing every one of them has—" with a dramatic sweep, she pulled the amber-tipped wand from the hidden pocket of her dress "—is a magic wand."

Little eyes widened and mouths opened in awe. "A true fairy princess has a magic wand. Not all are sticks with star tips. A wand might be a piano…a paintbrush or a computer…ballet slippers or a spoon. Every fairy princess gets to choose the wand that wields her magic. So tonight, while you're asleep, I want you to open your heart to your dreams. Allow your dreams to see all the way inside to your pretty heart." She stood and motioned for everyone to do the same.

The girls rose quietly, and Summer glided around the circle, tapping each one on the head gently. "You are now a fairy-princess-in-training, and that makes you special. You need to listen to what your pretty heart tells you because it's going to share a secret with you, maybe tonight. The secret of the special magic only you can give to the world."

When she got back to the starting point, she swept the group with a broad smile. "The next time I visit, we'll talk more about your special magic wand and how you would use it. Now give everybody here a big good-night hug, and it's off to bed."

The girls scurried like ants, bumping into one another as they giggled and hugged and jumped into bed. Summer and Tara tucked everyone in.

"Remember," Summer reminded them, "when it's time for the adults to go to bed, Ms. Tara will come back to sleep in that room over there." She motioned to the private room at the back of the dorm. "She'll be here inside with you all night, and Mr. Kenny will be on guard all night outside."

Summer motioned for Tara to turn out the lights as the two of them slipped out the door. Before closing it, Summer used her fairy princess voice once more. "Good night, everyone."

"Good night, fairy princess!" the little voices sounded in sweet unison, making Tara and Summer laugh as she closed the door.

"An empowerment program for little girls. Great idea." Tara sounded genuinely impressed.

"Thanks." Summer was glad to have Tara as an ally… someone else on her side should the need arise for a hostile takeover.

CHAPTER FOUR

PRANCING AROUND IN PADUCAH, Kentucky, dressed up in fairy garb was one thing, but here where the kids were supposed to be learning new skills while roughing it and getting in touch with nature? The woman was out of her freakin' mind. Even Neil seemed to validate Rick's reaction as they watched Summer and Tara approach.

The assistant counselor pushed his glasses back on his nose and leaned forward for a better look. "What in the hell?"

"Fairy princess."

Neil looked at him with a "you're kiddin' me" glare and burst out laughing.

She's not gonna like that.

Rick could see he was right when the dim bulb illuminated Summer's stern expression.

Their first day was coming to an end, and he was determined to get a fresh start with her tomorrow. He opted for a light mood. "So Toto didn't run off with your wand this time."

"Peewee," she corrected.

"Right."

"You're gonna keep this fairy princess crap confined to the girls' side of the camp, right?" Rick wondered the same thing, but it was Neil who spoke. "'Cause the boys aren't gonna go for it."

"Actually, even the boys could benefit from some fairy prince training," Tara answered.

The defensive tone that resonated in her voice told Rick he

had to do something before this became an us-versus-them issue. "I'm sure they could—whatever that means—but we have a full day ahead of us tomorrow and that's what I'd like to talk about right now."

"Yeah, about that six-thirty nature hike." Summer sat down across from Rick, and he tried hard not to think about the way the silver wings enhanced the golden waves of hair lying on them, or the big blue eyes that were so pretty when they weren't flashing with anger. Well, actually, they were even pretty when they flashed with anger—like right at that moment.

He fumbled with tomorrow's activity sheets, keeping his gaze away from her eyes. "What about it?"

"Are we going to do those every morning? Because they'll have to get up at six o'clock to be ready by six-thirty and that just seems awfully early."

Rick looked back up, but Summer leaned her elbows on the table and the pressure pushed her cleavage against the round neckline of her dress. He dropped his gaze and fumbled with the activity sheets again. "We have to go early. That's when the animals are moving and feeding. Dawn and dusk."

"Well, we'll go tomorrow, but I don't think we'll want to do that every day."

Rick couldn't believe his ears. "Learning about the animals and experiencing nature is what the kids are here for."

"That's only part of what they're here for." Summer cocked her head. "They're also here to have fun. And having to get up at six o'clock every morning for a hike sounds more like basic training than fun."

Rick glanced down at the girls' activity sheets for the next few days. The one-o'clock activity for Thursday caught his eye. "Oh, right. I forgot how much more important things like cookie baking are when compared to something trivial like seeing a bald eagle catching its breakfast."

His sarcastic tone raised Summer's chin like he'd caught her with an uppercut. Her body followed and, when she stood, she leaned forward to get her leg across the bench. The view Rick was treated to caused one of his own parts to rear its head.

"The cookies are..." she said through gritted teeth. "Never mind."

"Well, as the *assistant director* of the camp," Rick emphasized the words, "I'm going to pull rank on you. The hikes will remain at six-thirty *each* morning. Tara and Neil can alternate mornings and have a few hours off duty, not reporting until ten."

The fairy princess's face turned so red, it took on a purple hue. Rick waited for the gasket to blow. Instead, she pinched the bridge of her nose and gave a long blink. "Is there anything else you wanted to talk about? I'd like to get out of this costume."

Rick gave a long blink of his own to try and rid his brain of the image that comment aroused. He looked to Neil and Tara. "Does anybody have any concerns we need to address?"

They both shook their heads.

"Anything else?" Summer asked.

"Nope," Rick answered.

"Then I'll see you at six-thirty, *assistant director.*"

Summer turned on her heels and left, followed by Tara.

Neil waited a minute and then made a "reowr" sound that perfectly mimicked a mad cat. "Marines, one. Fairy princess, zero."

"Got to show her who's boss," Rick growled, frustrated he'd let the woman get to him. "She acts like she already owns the place, but Mommy and Daddy hired *me* to run this show. She was a last resort and probably whined her way onto the staff."

Neil swept his hand through the air as if he could see headlines hanging there. "The Last Resort. Catchy title."

Rick shook his head and chuckled. "I see Kenny's making his rounds. Want a beer? I've got some cold ones in my fridge."

"Now you're talking." Neil clapped his hands. "I'm pleased you remembered to bring the necessities."

"Actually, you can thank Charlie. He's the one who stocked them, saying I'd probably need them. I think he was right." Rick paused, then grinned. "Of course, they're nonalcoholic, but we can pretend."

Neil threw a thumb over his shoulder in the direction the women had gone. "Sounds like something the fairy princess would say. She's not rubbing off on you, is she?"

"Hardly," Rick grunted as he tried to focus away from the image *that* phrase invoked.

"WOULD YOU LIKE SOME LEMONADE before you go back to the girls for the night?" Summer asked as she and Tara strolled the path to the bunkhouse. "I have some fresh-squeezed in my refrigerator, and it's still pretty early." Rick Warren had her so keyed up, sleep was going to be an impossibility for a while. She needed to walk or chat or drink heavily, which wasn't an option—anything but go to bed with him on her mind.

"That sounds great." Tara sounded relieved at the offer. "I'm a night owl, so I'm not at all sleepy."

They eased into the dormitory and made a quick round to check on the girls, who all were sleeping soundly. They eased out just as quietly and made their way to Summer's cabin.

In the vast darkness, away from the lights of any town, the Milky Way spewed boldly across the sky. The sight swept Summer back across the years to her first time at Camp

Sunny Daze and her first sight of her home galaxy. She felt the same awe she'd experienced all those years ago and it warmed her heart. She was so happy to be back here. Even Rick Warren couldn't change that.

The night was warm, not hot, but Tara and Neil had decided to run the air conditioners for the duration of the camp lest the night sounds keep the kids awake. Summer, however, chose to leave hers off. Tree frogs, bullfrogs, cicadas and an occasional heron's call from the lake mixed in a pleasant cacophony while she slipped out of her costume and into a top and shorts. It was music to her ears.

"You squeeze your own lemonade?" Tara eyed the bits of lemon pulp floating in the glass Summer handed her a few minutes later. "I didn't know anybody did that anymore with all the packaged stuff available."

Summer broke an organic chocolate bar into pieces and set it on the couch between them. "I eat fresh and organic all I can. One of the degrees I worked on for a while was in nutrition."

Tara squinted. "One of the degrees? How many did you work on?"

"Several." No point rehashing all of her failed attempts now. They were behind her, and Summer intended to keep them there. "This chocolate is seventy percent cacao and organic, so it's full of antioxidants and good for you. It's perfect with a good pinot noir...." Her sigh completed the thought.

Tara eyed her carefully over the rim of her glass. "It's sexual tension, you know."

"Dark chocolate and pinot noir?"

"This thing between you and Rick. It's classic sexual tension."

"Oh, please. Pfft!" Summer tried to dismiss the subject by taking a long drink, hoping the cool liquid would cool her now-heated face.

"No, it's true." Tara pressed on, unmindful of or ignoring Summer's discomfort with the subject. "Have you seen the way he looks at you when you're not bickering? Well, I mean, you probably haven't, since you're always challenging him, but sometimes he looks at you like *you* just looked at that chocolate."

Summer snorted as she became keenly aware she'd just closed her eyes in ecstasy at the sensation of the bittersweet chocolate melting on her tongue.

"He's obviously a man who's used to calling the shots, and he doesn't know how to handle someone who questions his authority."

His authority—an authority that should have been mine.

Summer chomped down hard on another piece of chocolate. "I want the kids to have a great time so they'll want to come back next year. And I want them to tell all their friends."

"They seemed to enjoy today…mostly." The side of Tara's mouth twitched. "The boys as well as the girls."

"I hope so, but I feel like he's got the boys in military training." A breeze reminded her of the open windows. She lowered her voice. "Did you hear *any* grumbling? It's important for me to preempt any negativity."

Tara hesitated, gnawing her bottom lip. "A couple of boys were complaining."

"About Rick?" Summer's breath hitched. If Rick did a poor job, the camp's success could be jeopardized. If he did a great job, she wouldn't be able to show off her leadership skills. She wasn't sure what she wanted anymore. His presence seemed to assure she was screwed either way.

Tara took a slow drink, eyeing Summer over the rim of the glass. "About having to line up to do everything when the girls don't have to."

Condensation from the glass mixed with the nervous sweat

on Summer's hand. She set the glass down and wiped her hand on her leg. "That's the kind of thing I'm talking about. All that lining-up business makes them look like soldiers."

"I don't know." Tara shrugged. "A lot of schools have the kids line up to move from place to place. Kids like to know their boundaries. They appreciate having limits drawn."

"But this isn't school." Summer paused. Was she off base in her reasoning? "Am I the only one who feels this way… that this is where they should be able to spread their wings and fly without being held back by boundaries we place on them? As long as they're safe, obviously."

"Not at all. I totally see where you're coming from." Tara's lips pursed as she gave it some thought. "And maybe Rick will come around once he sees how the girls responded to the fairy princess stuff."

Summer picked up her drink again and leaned back, relaxed to be once more in a familiar area of conversation. "I wasn't sure about this age group. The younger ones take well to the magic wand idea, so I thought I'd experiment a little and see how this group responded to it."

"I know what I'd wish for if I had a magic wand."

The wistful sound in Tara's voice held an edge that piqued Summer's curiosity. "And what would that be?"

Tara opened her mouth, then closed it again and shrugged. "Maybe an adventure? My life's nothing if not predictable."

The sweet and tangy flavors played on Summer's tongue as she took another sip. "Predictable's not so bad. Maybe it means you've found your equilibrium."

"I'm a preacher's kid from Taylor's Grove." Tara hugged her knees to her chest and rested her chin on her crossed arms. "I've dated the same guy all the way through high school and college. He's studying theology. Plans to go into the ministry, too."

"And...what?" Summer prodded. "He's too much like your father? You regret being with only one guy?"

"No. It's not that. I mean, I love him. It's just..." Tara took another sip and gave her head a shake. "It's nothing. I'm being silly."

There was more to the story, Summer was sure, and the serious look on Tara's face said it wasn't silly at all. She tried a different angle. "Are you two planning on getting married?"

Tara shrugged, and her glance darted away. "He's in Honduras on a mission trip, due home anytime. We're supposed to talk about it when he gets back."

If Summer expected excitement at the announcement, she was wrong. Tara seemed decidedly undecided on the issue. Summer made a hasty choice to share something she rarely admitted to anyone. "Well, take your time and don't rush into anything. I ran off to Vegas with my boyfriend to get married the day after high school graduation."

Shock registered momentarily on Tara's face, but she recouped quickly, eyes dancing with interest. "Really?"

"Yeah, my dad found out what we were up to and followed us out there and stopped everything." Summer could still see the hurt and anger in her father's eyes when he found them in that sleazy hotel. It was a memory she'd give anything to forget, so, of course, it was one that remained etched on her brain. God, she'd put her dad and mom through a lot.

"What happened to the guy? Are you still with him?"

"He dumped me a month later."

Tara gave a knowing snort. "Even smart girls make dumb decisions, huh?"

"Ah!" Summer pointed a philosophical finger skyward. "But we learn from our mistakes, and fairy princesses are born."

Tara's infectious laugh drew Summer in. By the end of camp, they were going to be close. It would be nice to have someone on the premises to confide in. Phone calls to best friend Kate wouldn't always be manageable.

"To fairy princesses everywhere," Tara declared, and they clinked their glasses together in a toast. Tara swigged down the last of her lemonade in one gulp.

"Want some more?"

"No, I better get back to the girls." Tara stood and stretched her lanky frame.

"Yeah, I guess it's time to call it a night." Summer didn't try to hide the sarcasm in her voice. "I didn't actually realize five-thirty in the morning existed."

"Five-thirty?"

"I'll come to the dorm at six and get the girls up so you can sleep a little later."

"That will endear you to me forever. And by the way—" Tara stopped at the door "—I'm an expert on sexual tension, so just remember what I said."

Summer laughed as she picked up Tara's glass and sniffed. "Now I'm gonna worry about what you've been drinking when I thought I served you lemonade."

THE CHILD WAS SPRAWLED IN THE muddy field close to the building, her body contorted, a hideous mass of bloody tissue and bone extending from where a leg had been. She didn't scream. Didn't even cry, really. Just whimpered like a puppy rooted away from the litter. The sound laid Rick's heart wide-open.

There had to be a special section of hell for anyone who would place mines so close to an orphanage. The children had no supervision...spent their days wandering these fields in search of anything they might sell or trade for food.

He watched Dunk lift the child with tender care, staggering under the additional weight that should have been an easy carry.

"Can you make it?"

Dunk nodded, his face etched in determination as he turned and fled.

Another lap around the burned-out shell of a building turned up no survivors, and with every step, a sickening realization coiled Rick's muscles tighter. The child had been left behind to die. A decoy, most likely.

Rage fueled his movement as he sprinted to catch up.

He could hear Dunk's labored breathing.

"Let me have her, Dunk."

Dunk nodded, eyes glassy with fever. "I'll cover you." His words were barely discernible. Rick shook his head, clearing his ears of the sweat that had pooled and filled the cavity like being underwater.

His insides roiled in anguish for the child as they made the switch, a gnarled tree their only protection. He felt eyes watching them out there somewhere in the maddening, stony silence. But she was in his arms, and the choice was made. He ran, determined to get her to the medics...determined not to let her die as a pawn in some merciless bastard's game.

More sweat. Down his face. In his eyes. Blurring his vision.

Sound waves vibrated against his eardrums, throbbing. Too close. Sniper. Oh, God, no! Dunk...down. The scream tore from Rick's lungs.

"Dunk!"

He jerked awake into a seated position, panting, sweat beading down his back and chest. In a scenario he'd long grown used to, he took deep breaths, settling his heart into its regular rhythm, and wiped his face with the sheet, listening all the while for movement. How loud had he screamed this time? Had he woken anyone? Embarrassment flushed him momentarily, and on its heel came the familiar sadness.

The dream, which had lain dormant for a short time, had

returned night after night this week, taking on different forms...always ending the same. Being with the kids here at camp must be triggering something in his subconscious—worry about keeping them safe under his watch, most likely.

A shudder ripped through his body and shook all emotion away, leaving a numbness he regretted and yet embraced.

The nightmares would end...eventually. When he learned to control them. And, damn it all to hell, he *would* learn to control them. "Ooh-rah!" The spirited grunt was all the reminder he needed. He was a marine.

The clock read 4:53. Going back to sleep would be impossible, but it was still early. He stretched out, the damp sheet sticking to his back. *Think about something pleasant to start the day.*

Summer Delaney aka fairy princess danced to the front of his mind. Beautiful? Yes. Pleasant? To everyone but him.

"Nightmares by night, Summer Delaney by day. Maybe Afghanistan wasn't so bad," he growled, pushing out of bed, his body suddenly demanding activity.

THE RADIO BLASTED A BURST of static, and Summer grumbled as she hit the button to turn it off. Five-thirty...three days in a row. Before Tuesday, she hadn't gotten up at five-thirty since...well, never that she could recall. She'd ended a few days at five-thirty, but couldn't remember ever starting one that early.

She shuffled to the bathroom, not coming fully awake until the spray from the shower hit her face. It was still dark outside as she dressed, but when she stepped out into the morning, the black was beginning to give way to a lovely shade of pink. A mist hung over the lake, giving it an ethereal quality that brought a sigh from her lips, just as it had yesterday and the day before. How had she gone her whole life without ever seeing the lake at this time of morning?

An odd, crunching sound broke through the quiet and she turned in time to see Rick Warren, running down the gravel lane. He wore only shoes and running shorts, which hung low around his hips, and he carried what appeared to be a T-shirt gripped in his fist. His broad chest tapered down to a narrow waist and every inch of exposed skin glistened with dampness of sweat or dew. Maybe both.

He surprised her when he didn't veer toward his cabin, but ran past her and on down to the lake. Absorbed in what he was doing, he didn't see her watching him, and she was relieved for that. She'd been gawking in a most *unprincess*-like manner. And it certainly wasn't her pretty heart the sight had been appealing to.

He disappeared, lost in the trees, but soon she heard the splash. In her mind's eye, she could see him cutting through the water effortlessly, the muscles in his back and arms rippling like the early morning waves on the—

"Morning, Summer." Kenny waved from the path that marked the camp boundary, making his morning rounds.

"Morning, Kenny." Her heart beat much faster than could be explained by the startle from Kenny's voice.

"Enjoying the view?" He nodded toward the sliver of red sun barely breaking in the east, but casting a shimmering red reflection across the water.

"Um, yeah," she admitted with more than a little self-deprecation. "But I've got to leave it soon to get the girls up."

"It'll be there again tomorrow." Kenny nodded and continued his rounds.

"Not if Charlie comes to his senses," Summer muttered under her breath as the Rick Warren irritations of the past few days streamed back into her consciousness. She'd had as little contact with him as possible, and he'd stayed out of her way for the most part except to correct her on anything that didn't meet his standards. His enormously *high* standards.

But she'd awakened this morning with a glimmer of hope. Yesterday on the phone, Kate told her about Ron Smithey, who had been cut in the school layoffs and was looking for work. He was a P.E. teacher, would be perfect with the kids and would probably be thrilled to have two months of income this summer.

If Rick Warren did anything else to undermine her, she was going straight to Charlie with her suggestion, which would, of course, include making her assistant director like she should have been all along.

She glanced back toward the lake, soaking up a few more seconds of the beauty to carry with her through the day. Worry darkened her thoughts instead. Rick was swimming alone, and she couldn't hear any movement on the water. He was an excellent swimmer; she'd seen that. Still, sometimes things happened…even to excellent swimmers.

She didn't like the guy, but she didn't want him to drown. That would be a waste of a fine physical specimen of manhood. Just a glimpse would assure her he was okay.

She got all the way to the beach before she saw him. And then it was just a wave of his hand before he disappeared under the water.

CHAPTER FIVE

RICK'S FEET HIT BOTTOM. He gave a push and propelled himself once again to the surface. He'd saluted the four directions and the sun. His final salute was always to Dunk.

He broke the surface, clapped one arm to attention at his side, threw the other straight up beside his ear. Palm out, he made a ninety-degree arc, bringing it back to the surface.

The splashing behind him didn't seem inordinately loud, so the arm circling his neck from behind caught him off guard. "What the he—" A wave filled his mouth with dirty lake water. He spewed it out.

"Don't...panic. I...have...you."

Summer Delaney's voice. What in the hell was going on? He twisted his torso to see what she was up to. Her arm slid under his chin and diagonally across his chest, catching under his armpit. She dragged him backward, giving everything she had to a sidestroke.

"Quit fighting me." She spoke between strokes. "You'll drown us both."

She thought he was drowning? He started to tell her different, but his head was snuggled comfortably between her breasts, and the movement of her body against his was certainly pleasant enough. What the hell? He lay back and relaxed until he felt sand beneath him.

Summer crawled onto her knees, gasping for air, hovering over him. Her hand caught under his chin, tilting his head back. His mouth was already open. With a heave, she rolled him to his side.

He should stop her, but she moved so quickly and so efficiently, he found himself admiring her technique. If this had been a test, she would've aced it.

She'd managed to maneuver an arm under his side and had stretched out full length behind him, fists locked into place under his sternum.

"Are you mounting me, or are you about to perform the Heimlich?" He felt her stiffen.

Unfortunately, he'd done the same.

HIS VOICE DIDN'T SOUND LIKE any of the near-drowning victims she'd encountered. They gasped. They coughed. He… chuckled?

"Oh! You…you…" Her brain wouldn't switch modes fast enough to supply her mouth with an appropriate moniker. She scrambled to her knees, still gasping from exertion, and pulled him onto his back.

His face wore a sober expression, but the side of his mouth twitched, and the twinkle in his eye was unmistakable.

Damn him! He was mocking her. Humiliation stung her cheeks. "You weren't drowning."

"No." He smiled, and the early-morning sunlight brought a burnished glow to his tanned features. "But from the look on your face, you'd rather I had been."

He leaned up and propped himself on his elbows, exposing a tattoo over his heart. Despite her curiosity, she wouldn't allow her eyes to linger.

He didn't feel the same way, apparently. When his gaze dropped from her face to her chest, his grin widened.

Summer followed his gaze. Her wet T-shirt and cotton bra, both white, had molded to her body, leaving very little to the imagination. She bristled. "A gentleman wouldn't gawk."

"My apologies, ma'am." He gave the words an exaggerated drawl and sat all the way up, propping his arms on his bent knees. "That was good work, by the way. You did everything right."

Normally, the praise would have assuaged her anger somewhat, but something about Rick Warren threw her emotional state completely out of whack. Suspicion reared its head. "Didn't know I was being judged." Surely, he wasn't low enough to fake a drowning. Besides, he hadn't been aware she was watching him. "If you weren't drowning, what was with all the waving? What *were* you doing out there?"

He shrugged and cut his eyes away from her. "Just a ritual salute to morning." The response didn't quite ring true.

Damn, she was getting tired of General Warren's secretive ways. Why all the mystery? What was he always writing in that folder, and why did he always close it when she approached? What was he hiding?

Probing would have to wait until she had more time. Right then, she would have to shower again and change clothes. The hair would have to live with the lake water in it until quiet time. And all because Rick Warren didn't play by the rules he'd established.

"You shouldn't be swimming alone for whatever reason." She turned his own tables on him. "Rule number three. Never go anywhere near the water without a buddy." Pulling her shirt away from her body, she stood. "You've broken the camp rules and set a bad example for the kids."

"The kids aren't up yet, and this is the only time I can work out." He cocked his head toward her and raised a challenging eyebrow. "Would you like to be my buddy for the rest of camp?"

"Definitely not."

"Didn't think so."

She heard his snort as she walked away, and her teeth

clenched involuntarily. She stopped and turned back to him. "Hey, Mr. Assistant Director." He swiveled his head toward her. "Can I just call you Ass for short?"

She didn't wait for a response, just made another mental mark on the Problems with Rick Warren side of the board in her mind.

If she had anything to say about it, he would be gone soon…along with his condescension and his secrets.

"WHAT'S THAT SMELL?" JIMBO wrinkled his nose, the crease defined by the smattering of freckles squinched together.

"A skunk's been through here," Rick answered. "May still be somewhere around, so we'll need to keep an eye out."

"My dad shot a skunk once," Howie announced.

"Yeah? Did it spray him?" Rick asked.

"Naw, he's too fast. He runs real fast, my dad does."

Rick was beginning to wonder how many of the Howard, Sr., stories he'd heard were real, how many were fabrications he'd fed to his son and how many were just hero-worship stories Howie made up? Some of them seemed pretty far-fetched.

But this new story caught Jimbo's attention, and he barraged Howie with questions about Howard, Sr.'s, skunk adventure.

The kids were chatterboxes now, which was okay since they were headed back to camp. They'd had to remain silent on the hike out. Any unnecessary noise would've scared the animals away. But their silence had been abundantly rewarded. A doe and her three spotted-coat fawns grazing in a meadow the first morning. A mother raccoon and seven babies washing their breakfast at the edge of the cove on day two. And today…jackpot! Several adult beavers working on a dam. Even Mitchell's sneeze had been a learning experience as the beavers slapped the water with their tails as a warning of nearby danger. But the big reward had been the bald eagle with a fish in its clutches.

Yep…a morning hike these kids would remember the rest of their lives.

Summer Delaney was harder to impress. Although her smile and conversation came easily with the kids, she had scarcely acknowledged his presence the past three days even though he'd tried to engage her in conversation several times. And the episode in the cove this morning had obviously sent her animosity for him soaring even higher…if that was possible.

Her dour expression, which seemed solely reserved for him, grated on his nerves, and it was only the fourth day of camp. He couldn't put up with her prima donna ways for a month. They needed to have a private conversation and get whatever was bugging her off her chest. Her nicely formed chest. He tensed at the thought of her chest with everything off it.

"Ain't there, Mr. Rick?"

The question brought Rick mercifully out of his daydream. "Aren't there," he corrected. "*Ain't* isn't a word."

Austin rolled his eyes. "You sound like my mom, but my dad says *ain't* all the time."

"Mine, too!" Howie piped in.

Rick thought back but couldn't replay the last part of the conversation. "What were you asking me about?"

"Ain't, uh, aren't there such things as white skunks?"

"Yep."

Austin's face broke out in a big told-you-so grin.

"I used to see lots of them when I worked at the Land Between the Lakes," Rick said. "They're beautiful animals. All white with a black stripe down the back instead of the opposite."

"I bet that's the kind my dad shot," Howie bragged.

Summer, who was leading the group back to camp, turned left, onto a narrower path.

"Wrong way, Summer," Rick called.

"I know where I'm going," she answered over her shoulder, never breaking her stride.

Rick looked at his watch. They were a half mile from camp, running a little earlier today. As long as it was only a short diversion, they'd still be on time for breakfast at eight.

Less than a minute of walking brought them to a clearing. An old, ramshackle cabin stood in the middle, surrounded by wildflowers, with a grown-up roadbed leading in from the back. The roof and windows and doors were all gone, and a couple of the walls had rotted and caved in, but despite its decrepit appearance, the place held an aura of serenity.

"This is the old Byassee homestead," Summer explained as the children gathered around her. "The Byassees were the people who owned the land our camp is on. They died a long time ago, but they left all of this land to their family, who eventually left it to a church, which built the first summer camp on it. It's been sold several times since then. I like to come here and say thank-you to the Byassees. If they'd sold it to one of the development companies like a lot of people around here did with their land, this would be a subdivision, and we wouldn't be here today."

Ah! So Herschel Delaney knew his youngest daughter well, it seemed. Rick had to admit she was right, though. What a shame it would be to see the wild beauty of this place replaced by houses and asphalt. And speaking of wild beauty…

Summer's voice and eyes were full of emotion as she talked to the kids. Her passion and loyalty to the camp stirred Rick in a primal sort of way, making him wonder what it would be like to experience her passion firsthand.

"Is it haunted?" Carlos asked, hanging close to Rick's side, and Rick laid a comforting hand on his shoulder.

"Of course not," Summer answered. "But I like to think there might be angels watching over it."

"It has a pretty heart, Ms. Summer," Becca said, bringing a smile to Summer's face that made her look the part of an angel herself. An angelic exterior hiding a wild-child heart.

One of the kids asked, "Can we look inside?"

"You can't go inside, but you can walk around and look."

"Watch for snakes," Rick instructed. As peaceful as it seemed on the outside, the inside looked like a copperhead haven.

Instinctively, the counselors spread out to guard from all angles in case any of the kids decided to disobey instructions and venture inside. Everyone ambled around for a few minutes but soon coalesced back into a large group. Some of the girls picked flowers and gave them to Summer.

"Maybe we can come back to pick enough to make circlets for our hair." Summer made a circle with her fingers and placed it on her head like a cap.

Rick thought a minute, wondering how to make that more educational. "I'll give them a list and description of common wildflowers from around here, and they can see how many they can identify."

"That won't be necessary," Summer said. "This will just be a fun activity." She emphasized *fun*.

"Fun and educational—the best of both worlds."

Summer opened her mouth, and Rick sensed a protest was about to be voiced.

"I insist," he added.

Summer's glare eviscerated him. "Let's go, kids." She waved them forward. "Breakfast will be ready soon."

Rick fumed at the back of the group, as far away from the damn woman as possible. She didn't think it was necessary for these kids to learn anything while they were here. It was all about looking pretty and…and what had Becca said the hut had? A pretty heart? *Hell-pee-roo.*

"Oh, look!" Summer's squeal caught his attention as she bounded off the path toward a group of trees, the girls following at her heels.

"Halt!" Rick shouted, and the boys stopped in their tracks.

"Tree frogs!" Summer pointed out a group of the small creatures clinging to an ancient tulip poplar.

Some of the boys started to move in her direction. "Don't!" Rick ordered. The boys turned back to him, confused. "We need to stay on the path."

"They can't see them from there." Summer's voice held a controlled but angry edge.

"But *I* can see from here." Rick pointed to the thick groundcover. "The poison ivy you're standing in could easily camouflage a copperhead."

Summer's eyes widened. "Run! Everybody run!" She sprinted down the path, followed by the bobbing heads of the girls.

At the head of the boys' line, Neil turned around with a smirk, which faded quickly as his eyes grew wide.

"Skunk," he said quietly, as Rick's olfactory system registered that the odor he'd grown used to had intensified.

Rick turned slightly, and his peripheral vision caught sight of the uplifted tail. "Run!" he shouted. The boys followed directions, except for Willard, who tripped over his own feet in his haste.

Rick became sickeningly aware of the foul-smelling mist that suffused the air as he stopped to help the boy up.

SUMMER STOPPED A LITTLE WAY down the path to let the girls pass. Looking back, she saw the horrific scene play out with Willard's fall and Rick's stopping to help him. She couldn't see the spray, but their reaction and the smell invading her nostrils left little to the imagination.

Neil stopped beside her. “Take the kids on into camp. Get some soap and use the hose behind the kitchen to have the girls wash their ankles and legs off. If they wash within about ten minutes, it should stop the poison ivy from making them break out.” As the assistant counselor took off for the camp, Summer started back to help the two stragglers.

“Stay away, Summer.” Rick squatted beside a now-red-faced, bawling Willard. The boy sat with his legs straight out, pounding the ground in a hissy fit.

Summer ignored the command and continued down the path toward them.

Rick stood. “I said stay away.”

“I heard you.” She continued, determined to console the child who’d just experienced a traumatic occurrence.

“Halt.” His harsh tone tightened Summer’s jaw. “There’s no use getting the oil on you, too.”

That brought her to a stop, although by then she was only a few feet away. The child’s frustrated cry opened her own frustration valve enough to allow a leak. “This could’ve been avoided if you’d listened to me when I warned everybody to run,” she fumed.

“And it wouldn’t have happened *at all* if you hadn’t gone traipsing off the path like I warned everybody *not* to do.”

Summer’s eyes stung from the stench…and the indignation. “You’re going to blame *me* because *you* didn’t have enough sense to get out of the way of a skunk?”

Her attention snapped back to Willard as he began crying louder. In her anger with Rick, she’d forgotten Willard and his part in this.

“I hate thith. I hate thith plathe. I wanna go home!” the child screamed.

His words hit like a punch in Summer’s stomach. An unhappy child covered with skunk spray, wanting to go home. Not good. That kind of thing could make disgruntled talking start, and then it wouldn't take much to get others jumping on the bandwagon…anybody who was homesick or even a little unhappy. The ripple effect personified.

This called for high-stakes damage control. She had to get to Charlie today with her idea about Ron Smithey. These boys had to start having fun, or this whole camp session might be a washout, and that would spell financial disaster.

"C'mon, bud. Let's get back to the camp and get this stuff off us." Rick's hand was under Willard's arm, and he hauled the child to his feet. "Summer, go on ahead and get some dishwashing liquid from Ginny. Then go to my cabin. In the bathroom, you'll find a large bottle of Listerine. Bring them both down to the beach."

Summer spun around and broke into a run.

Charlie met her where the path broke from the woods at the edge of camp. He sniffed and laughed. "You, too?"

She shook her head. "I didn't get any spray on me. This is just from standing near Rick and Willard." The time wasn't right to tell him what Willard said or bring up Ron Smithey. That could wait until this crisis was over.

"Get dishwashing liquid from Ginny and meet us at the beach," she instructed. Charlie nodded and did an about-face. "And send one of the boys to get Willard a change of clothes," she called as she hurried toward Rick's cabin.

Walking into his bedroom was like walking into a military barracks. The bed was perfectly made with perfectly mitered corners, the spread and sheet folded back *perfectly* even.

A guilty urge passed through her to jump on it…or roll around in it…naked…with Rick. Her mouth went dry at the thought—other parts did quite the opposite.

Damn Rick Warren. He made her crazy. If he didn't leave soon, she'd be certifiable.

The Listerine wasn't hard to spot. Two gigantic bottles of it sat on the shelf in his bathroom. Was Rick a halitosis freak or was he drinking the stuff? She shivered at the thought and grabbed them both for good measure.

Passing the bedside table, she noticed Raine Lawson's new thriller. She'd finished it just last week. *Probably the only thing we have in common,* she mused. Under it lay the folder Mr. Assistant Director carried with him, constantly scratching notes in. The one he always closed when she came around. What was in there?

Curiosity got the best of her, and she lifted the corner for a quick peek. Her eyes scanned over the top sheet, which appeared to be an inventory list of items in the dining hall and kitchen. Table, chairs, appliances—nothing of interest and nothing that gave her any clue as to why he would be counting these things.

She gave a frustrated sigh and hurried on to the closet, jerking open the door. A multitude of T-shirts met her eyes, all neatly hung facing the same way, grouped by color. She pulled a gray one off its hanger and opened the top drawer of the chest.

It was full of perfectly creased shorts, folded neatly and again arranged by color. She chose black to go with the gray shirt.

It was then that she paused for a moment and chewed her lip. He was going to need underwear, and the thought of picking out some for him made her belly do a flip. An image ran through her head, and she made a quick bet with herself.

Opening the next drawer brought a chuckle. "Knew it! Mr. Assistant Director has an obsessive-compulsive disorder." That explained his over-the-top need for order and control...why he was always counting things, making notes of stuff that weren't of any importance. She stared at the neatly folded stacks of black and white men's briefs, feeling quite smug at her discovery.

The next drawer held socks. All white and already secured into pairs. She stuffed socks into one pocket of the shorts and the underwear into another.

Running shoes sat by the door. She grabbed them on her way out.

By the time she got to the beach, Charlie, Rick and Willard were there along with the awful smell. Rick was helping the boy out of his shirt. Willard had stopped crying but looked miserable.

"Here's the Listerine." She handed him both bottles, getting a good look at the tattoo over his heart this time. Dog tags—in addition to the ones he wore on the chain. He really was eaten up with military. "And I brought you some more clothes." Pulling her eyes back up to his face, she held them out.

"Would you set them over there? I don't want to touch them." He motioned to a pile of towels and clothes lying in the sand. "We'll probably just wrap ourselves in towels and go shower afterward, but thanks for bringing everything." The gratitude in his eyes was genuine.

"I've never seen so much Listerine." Oddly, she wanted to hold on to the moment a bit longer.

One side of his mouth rose. "Not my first rodeo." He turned to the boy and handed him the opened bottle. "Okay, Willard, we're going to strip off the rest of our clothes and pour this brown stuff all over us because it'll cut the oil. Keep your eyes closed tightly—we don't want to get any in them."

Willard sniffled and nodded.

"We'll rinse off in the lake and then we'll take a bath with dishwashing liquid, which should get rid of any of the remaining oil—" he looked at the squeeze bottle and laughed "—and leave us with a pleasant, lemony scent."

"Can't we jutht take a thower?" Willard's breathing caught a couple of times. "And what about my clotheth?"

Rick shook his head. "If we did that, we'd carry the stench into the bunkhouse. We have to get the oily stuff off first. Then we'll go take a real shower and get dressed."

"I'll burn your clothes," Charlie said, and Willard's bottom lip quivered like he was going to cry again. "Go on, Summer." Charlie turned and shooed her away. "They can't get on with this process while you're here."

Summer nodded and started up the path. Behind her, she could hear Willard's plaintive cry loud and clear, and her stomach rolled with every word.

"I wanna go home. I hate thith plathe. I hate thith plathe."

"AND WE'RE USING TWO KINDS of flour." Summer motioned for Greta and Anne to pour their ingredients into the giant bowl. "Greta has whole grain oat flour, and Anne has whole grain graham flour."

"Mmm, will the cookies taste like graham crackers?" Amanda asked.

"Better." Summer nodded toward Lucy. "And Lucy's going to add cinnamon." She stopped and looked around. "Is anybody allergic to cinnamon?" No hands went up. "Okay then, Lucy's going to add cinnamon, milled flax seed and wheat germ."

Lucy's nose crinkled in distaste. "Ew, I don't want to add germs to it!"

That made Summer laugh. "It's not that kind of germ, Lucy. Not the kind that makes you sick. This kind of germ is what *germinates.*" She stressed the word. "It's where the piece of wheat starts its growing cycle. It has lots of vitamins in it, so it makes us healthy, not sick. It's the heart of the wheat."

"The pretty heart?" Mary Margaret asked.

"Precisely, M&M," Tara answered, using the nickname the girls had come up with.

Summer turned the giant mixer on, and the blades incorporated the dry ingredients into the liquids. Her belly churned along with the machine as she thought about what she was going to do after the cookies were done.

When a dough formed, she stopped the mixer and cued Shannon and Kaelyn. "Now, we add vanilla flavoring and…?"

"Chocolate chips!" the girls answered.

"Correct. But not just any chocolate chips." Kaelyn poured the dark morsels in as Summer stirred the heavy concoction. "These are organic, dark chocolate chips, so they're full of antioxidants and are good for you." Her arm tired, and she let Tara finish the mixture as she supplied the girls with spoons. "But even though these cookies are good for you, you only want to eat them as a special treat after you've eaten your fruits and vegetables and proteins. You shouldn't ever let sweets take the place of food that's better for you."

As the girls filled the baking sheets with mounds of cookie dough, Ginny placed them in the oven. "Thanks for making my job easier today," she told them. "These will be a delicious bedtime snack tonight."

After they'd cleaned up the work space and washed their hands, Tara announced, "It's time for quiet time."

The girls laughed, leaving Summer to wonder what was so funny about the announcement. She shot a questioning look at Tara, but the young woman was busy answering questions and herding the girls out the door.

The next hour wasn't going to be so quiet for Summer, but it was time to do what she had to do. "Is Charlie around?" she asked Ginny.

"Maybe in his office. I don't think I've seen him since

right after lunch." The woman's chin wrinkled in concern. "Everything okay?"

No use trying to pretend with Ginny—the woman had changed Summer's diapers. "I just have some concerns about the camp I'd like to discuss with him."

Ginny gave her a knowing smile. "About the camp or Rick Warren?"

"You know me too well, Ginny."

"Charlie said yesterday he was surprised you hadn't been in to talk to him yet." Ginny bent down and peered through the oven window to check on the baking cookies, the yummy scent of which had already started to permeate the air. "You and Rick are like oil and water. Not a bad combination, but it takes some shaking up to get it to mix."

"I'd like to shake him up, all right. He's so…so…" Summer groped for the appropriate word.

"Take charge?" Ginny offered.

"Bossy," Summer spewed. "And rigid and cocky. And he doesn't know beans about kids, or fun, or what summer camp is supposed to be like."

Ginny had pulled the binder of handwritten recipes from the shelf, and started leafing through it. "Maybe you could teach him. But he does come across a bit stodgy, so you'd have to make him think it's his idea."

"That wouldn't be hard since everything is his idea." Summer stalked off, Ginny's chuckle echoing behind her.

Charlie's office door was closed, so she gave a couple of light raps with her knuckles.

"Come in."

Not Charlie's voice, and she tensed. If she hadn't already pushed the door open a little, she would've left.

Rick sat at Charlie's desk. He glanced up. "Hey, Summer. Charlie's not here." He went back to writing.

His dismissive attitude toward her once again caused her

to see red. She closed the door and walked to the desk, planting herself in front of it. "I guess it was you I was meant to talk to, then."

Rick laid the pen down. "Okay." He leaned back in the chair, giving her his full attention. "Talk."

Even in the closed room, not the slightest hint of skunk odor hung in the air. She sniffed again. "Listerine and dishwashing liquid, huh?"

"An old park ranger trick." Rick regarded her warily. "But something tells me you didn't come here to discuss trade secrets."

"No, you're right. I, um…" She cleared her throat. "Rick, I don't know you very well, and it was very nice of you to take this job on such short notice and help my parents out." His enormous shoulders fell as he relaxed. "But—" she took a deep breath, determined to say what was on her mind "—I don't think you're cut out to be a camp counselor, and I think it would be better for everyone if you let me, um, Charlie, find someone who's better suited to working with kids."

One eyebrow shot up and his face reddened slightly as if the act had taken some exertion. "Why? You missing your boyfriend? Gonna talk Mommy and Daddy into letting him take my place?"

She rolled her eyes in exasperation. "Hardly. I would never run to my parents with anything that might worry them. In fact, I'm doing the opposite. They've invested everything they have in this place, and they can't afford to have even a single kid talking about what a horrible place it is and how much he hates it. What if he wants to go home, and what if that causes others to start thinking the same thing?"

"You're referring to Willard."

Summer's pulse swished through her ears. "Yeah, but not just Willard. You've got all the boys marching around like little wooden soldiers—"

"Instead of dancing around like little fairy princesses."

"The girls are having fun, and they're learning things in the process."

"Because circlet making—" he made a circle with his fingers and set them on his head, mimicking her gesture from that morning "—is such an important thing for girls to know how to do in this day and age."

"There's more to life than learning the scientific names of a region's flora and fauna." She ground the words out.

He stood, leaning on his fists over the desk. "There's more to life than being beautiful."

She paused. Had he just inferred he thought she was beautiful? Butterflies fluttered in her stomach, then just as quickly swarmed in an angry mass. "I'm not teaching them to be beautiful." She was shaking, anyway, so she released the energy by punching a finger in his direction.

"I know. You're throwing in extra lessons. How to be a wild child in four short weeks."

"I'm teaching them to find their own beauty and, by extension, the beauty in others, so maybe when they grow up and can think on their own, they won't listen to the violence mongers who'll try to tell them war is the road that leads to world peace."

"And while you're at it, teach them to grab their fairy wands the next time terrorists use planes to target our country's capitol." He flicked his fingers above her head. "They can sprinkle them with pixie dust and make all the mean people disappear."

Summer's ears were burning now. She leaned closer, bringing her nose within inches of his. "Behind that mannerly exterior, Rick Warren, beats the heart of a cad. An extremely anal cad, whose life is all neatly folded and color-coded because he can't stand to have things mixed up a little. Everything, all the way down to his briefs, is black and white."

"Or maybe he's a marine—" his voice was a low growl "—who found it easier to organize the little mundane things so he didn't have to think about them and could concentrate on the big things like how to keep his and his buddies' asses from being shot off…not that it always worked."

Summer swallowed as his words stuffed her own comment back into her throat. His blue-green eyes were sending out sparks like she'd never seen, and they were causing a fire in her belly. Some of it was anger, but part of it was the sheer excitement of being near him.

Just then, the door swung open to reveal the surprised face of Willard with the more surprised face of Charlie behind.

Rick and Summer jerked up to a standing position, and Summer cringed, realizing the position they'd been in probably looked as though they were either in a heated argument or about to kiss. It somehow felt like both.

Willard removed his baseball cap and shuffled into the room with downcast eyes.

"I didn't know you were here, Summer, but I'm glad you are." Charlie's face held an expression she couldn't read. "Willard has something he'd like to say."

Willard looked up and bravely locked eyes with Rick. "I'm thorry for acting like a baby thith morning, Mithter Rick."

"It's okay, Willard." Rick pointed to the paper he'd been working on. "I filled out the accident report so your parents will understand you didn't do anything to cause this."

The boy's honesty was touching. "I'm sorry, too, Willard." Summer patted his arm. "It was my fault for stopping the group. It was probably my squeal that stirred up the skunk."

"Nonsense," Rick said. "The stench should've warned me to watch more closely—"

Charlie's impatient wave cut Rick's speech short. "That's neither here nor there. Willard and I have just talked to his mom, and she's fine with it. She said not to worry about the clothes."

"So is she coming to pick you up?" Summer's lunch threatened to come back up.

"No, Mith Thummer." Willard shook his head. "I don't really want to go home. I wath jutht upthet when I thaid that."

Charlie laid a gentle hand on Willard's shoulder. "Go on, son. Tell them what you told me about why you were upset."

Willard's glance bounced from Summer to Rick before landing back down at his feet. He sniffed. "I wath afraid that the kidth would make fun of me and call me 'thkunk boy' and thingth like that."

Kids could be cruel. Even good-natured kidding sometimes went too far, and this poor kid had the extra worry of a lisp. "We won't allow any bullying, Willard," she assured him. "Pretty soon, they'll have forgotten all about the skunk, you mark my words."

Willard nodded.

"Willard, tell them the rest now." Charlie nudged the boy with his elbow.

Willard blew out a long breath. "When y'all were arguing, you thounded jutht like my mom and dad did before they thplit up." His eyes teared up, and he blinked several times. "It thcared me."

His words gripped Summer's lunch and squeezed. "Oh, Willard, I'm so…so sorry. We should never have argued in front of you like that. We were acting childish."

"Yeah, bud, I'm sorry, too." Rick's low tone was filled with regret. "We weren't being very good role models. It won't happen again, I can assure you."

Rick's eyes met Summer's on the last four words, like he was assuring her at the same time. Did he really think that *poof!* they would just start to get along all of a sudden? Or…

could it be he had listened to her, after all, and was considering leaving?

"I'm really enjoying the camp, Mithter Rick. You've taught uth lotth of cool thtuff already."

"Thanks, Willard." Rick's triumphant smile made Summer's jaw tighten. Guess she had her answer.

"You can go now, son." Charlie patted Willard on the back as he directed him to the door. "Remember, it takes a big man to say 'I'm sorry.'"

"Yeth, Mithter Charlie."

Charlie closed the door behind the boy and then turned toward Summer and Rick, his scowl easy to read this time. Pure aggravation etched lines all over his face. "Now." He shook his finger at the two of them. "I don't know what this spat between the two of you evolved from, or maybe it's just an innate dislike for each other, but either way, I don't give a tinker's dam. We're here for one reason and one reason only, and that's to make this camp a success. These kids are going to have a summer to remember, and it isn't going to be remembered as the summer the assistant director and the girls' head counselor raised a ruckus." He moved behind the desk, and Rick shifted around to stand by Summer. Charlie shooed them with a hand gesture toward the door. "Go kiss and make up or whatever you need to do to get along for the rest of the time 'cause I won't tolerate any more of this nonsense. You understand?"

Summer nodded. "Yes, Charlie."

"Yes, sir."

"Now get out of here." Charlie sat down in his chair and leaned back. "I've got work to do." He propped his feet on the desk and popped the newspaper open.

Summer and Rick left the office in silence. She didn't know what Rick was thinking, but she felt a pout coming on. For the first time in her life, Charlie had uttered a cross word to her.

What made it worse was that she deserved it.

CHAPTER SIX

RICK PULLED HIS T-SHIRT OVER his head as soon as he walked into the cabin. He threw it and the folder over the end of the couch and marched straight to the kitchen for a bottle of water from the fridge, rubbing it across his chest and the back of his neck before opening it and downing its entire contents in a couple of swigs.

Damn! Summer Delaney had a knack for making him angry. The little spitfire seemed determined to make his time at Sunny Daze as miserable as possible. She'd gone to Charlie to complain about him, he was sure. What had he done this time to irritate her so? Well, whatever it was, at least she'd gotten her own ass chewed out, as well. He tossed the empty bottle into the trash can.

Speaking of ass-chewing… He pulled out his phone and punched his dad's number.

"Nolan Warren speaking."

"Hey, Dad."

"Oh, hello, Rick. Thanks for calling back. From the sound of things, you had your hands full when I called earlier."

"A skunk took perfect aim at one of the campers and me, and it's been downhill since then."

His dad gave a grunt of disapproval. "That is unfortunate indeed. But you've lived through worse."

"Yes, sir. That I have." He paused. Not one for idle chitchat—or idle anything—his dad wouldn't have called for no reason. Rick was relatively sure he knew what it was.

"How are the nightmares?"

Yep, there it was. The inevitable discussion about his post-traumatic stress disorder that always left him feeling like he had a hideous flaw in his character. "Not nearly as aggravating as the girls' head counselor I'm having to work with," Rick answered. "Who happens to be the owners' daughter," he added in an effort to redirect the conversation.

"Yes, your mother said something about that." His dad cleared his throat, the signal he really wasn't interested and was getting down to the important business that warranted the call. "But I didn't call to talk about trivial matters. I mentioned your continuing bouts with PTSD to Vance Leighton at the club last night. He told me about a therapy he's had quite good success with. It's called— Do you have a pen to write this down?"

"Yes, sir." Rick walked over to the folder he'd dropped on the couch and flipped it open.

"It's called EMDR. Eye movement desensitization and reprocessing. I've been reading about it on the internet, and I'm very impressed with the results I'm seeing. I want you to look into it. Paducah has a Dr. Enlow who's trained in it."

"I've got my hands pretty full right now, sir."

"Bullshit. Twenty kids and a feisty woman does not add up to full hands. Get your priorities straight."

"I have the information." Therapy was a waste of time, and Rick wasn't about to make a promise he wouldn't keep.

Warren senior gave a long sigh. "I guess Luke told you he signed on for another tour of duty?"

"Yes, sir. I spoke with him a few days ago." The idea of his little brother going to Syria made Rick's skin crawl, but he didn't bring that up. It was just one more thing he and his dad had opposing views on. "How's Mom doing with it?"

"As always," his dad answered crisply. "No news from

Jack since we last reported to you." Calls from the oldest Warren son in Lebanon were rare occurrences.

"Well, I have a few things to get done here, if there's nothing else." Rick stretched out on the couch, hoping for a few minutes to himself before quiet time was over.

"No, I've accomplished what I called for."

"Give Mom a hug for me and tell her I'll call this weekend."

"Will do, son. Goodbye."

"Goodbye, Dad." Rick set the phone on the table and picked up the sheet of paper he'd written on.

EMDR.

He wadded up the paper and tossed it into the trash.

SUMMER HUNG UP THE PHONE after her conversation with Kate, satisfied that Fairy Princess Parties was in good hands.

Twenty minutes of quiet time remained, but the events of the day had her restless and edgy. Maybe a short walk in the woods would calm her down before the geocaching adventure, which was planned for the rest of the afternoon.

The path took her by the girls' bunkhouse and, as she neared, screams and sounds of general chaos filled the air. She sprinted across the distance, bursting through the door, expecting to find a wild creature had made its way into the building. Surely, they couldn't have two skunk episodes in one day.

A pillow smacked her upside the head as soon as she walked in the door. The girls were running amok, jumping on beds, over beds, slamming one another with pillows, squealing with laughter. The floor was littered with clothes, shoes, socks, books.

"Hey!" Her voice couldn't make it over the din. She jerked the whistle out of her shirt and let go with an ear-piercing trill.

All activity in the room came to a stop as the girls turned their attention toward the sound. “This is supposed to be quiet time.” Jaws dropped and eyes grew wide at her harsh tone.

In the corner, Tara laid down the book she’d been reading and pulled the earbuds out of her ears.

“Get this place cleaned up. Now!” Summer cut a path through the debris back to Tara. The girls scurried to the task.

“What’s going on?” she asked under her breath as she neared Tara. “This is quiet time.”

Tara’s face filled with contrition. “I’m sorry. I thought quiet time was Rick’s idea, and you’d just want to use it as free time, you know, to allow the girls to do what they wanted.”

Summer looked at the mess around the room. For four days, she’d assumed the girls were napping, or at least resting. Instead, they’d been having a free-for-all? “Well, I don’t mind them having free time, but this looks like somebody could get hurt.”

Tara surveyed the room. “It *has* sort of escalated. The first two days it was just running around and talking. Getting to know one another. Yesterday, they started jumping on the beds a little. Today—” she waved a finger toward the strewn clothes “—it started out as a fashion show….”

“Well, no harm done, I guess.” Rick Warren’s comment about what she was teaching the girls ran through her thoughts. She tried to shrug off the ominous feeling in the pit of her stomach that he could be right. “But no more pillow fights,” she announced to the group. “Something will get broken or somebody will get hurt. Quiet time is to be quiet from now on. Got that?”

The girls nodded glumly as they folded clothes and put things away.

“Okay then, ladies, finish cleaning up this mess and line

up so we can go for our geocaching adventure." The girls stopped what they were doing and looked at her strangely.

"Line up?" Anne voiced the question they obviously were all thinking.

"You sound like Mr. Rick!" Becca laughed.

Oh, no, that was one comparison Summer wouldn't allow to go any deeper.

Hopscotching her way back toward the door, she made a game of leaping over the items remaining on the floor. "The first person to get her area clean and neat and get in line gets to carry the GPS." She held up the small, computerized compass containing the coordinates for the treasure they would seek today.

As the girls' actions became frenzied, she exchanged smiles with Tara.

Even cleaning the dorm and lining up could be made into a fun game with the right incentive.

Rick Warren would never be able to get that through his handsome but thick head.

WHEN THE CHANGE HAD OCCURRED, Summer wasn't entirely sure. Had it been subtle, or had she just not been paying close enough attention, too caught up in watching Rick and not paying enough attention to her own charges?

Earlier she'd tried to dismiss the tightening in her gut caused by the pillow fight, telling herself it was leftover anxiety from the scene with Rick and Charlie.

But the feeling had returned at dinner with more intensity. The girls had run into the dining hall, pushing and shoving and jockeying to be in the front of the line. The boys had entered quietly a few minutes later, removing their caps as they entered the building and staying in perfect order as they thanked Ginny.

Throughout dinner, the girls had laughed loudly, even

emitting a couple of shrieks just before Tara brought the soon-to-be food fight under control before it started.

A hum of low modulated voices had surrounded the boys' table—nothing notable that stood out or called attention to their area.

Now, sitting around the fire pit, listening to Rick tell the story of Perseus and Andromeda, she kept telling herself the girls were having fun and the boys were miserable, only the boys didn't look miserable. The truth be told, everybody else seemed to be having a fantastic time. Why was she feeling so miserable?

"But Queen Cassiopeia—" Rick outlined the W-shaped constellation with his flashlight beam "—had angered the goddesses by bragging about how much more beautiful she was than they were. So as punishment, she spends part of every year sitting in her chair, but turned upside down so she's on her head."

The kids laughed and applauded Rick's story. Teaching them Greek mythology and astronomy at the same time was a great idea. Summer wished she'd thought of it.

"Can we do this every night?" Lucy asked.

"Not every night," Rick answered. "But we can do it several more times. There are a lot of stories up there in the night sky."

Reggie raised his hand and Rick pointed to him. "Are we ever gonna get to have a campfire, Mr. Rick?"

Rick laughed and shrugged. "If we ever get a rain, it might cool things off enough to have a campfire. So far, the nights have been too hot and things are too dry to risk it. We'll have to wait and see."

"If we do get to have a fire, we'll make s'mores," Summer promised.

Ginny showed up with a large tray of the cookies the girls had made and announced, "Snack time."

Summer watched, horrified, as the girls stampeded Ginny like a herd of wild elephants. They snatched and grabbed at cookies as though they hadn't had a meal in days.

"Girls!" Summer shouted, but they were too busy shoving to be next in line to pay her much attention. She moved toward the horde. "Girls, mind your manners!"

A cookie got knocked out of someone's hand, and it came hurtling toward Summer. She instinctively ducked and stumbled backward. Something hard caught her at midcalf, causing her to lose her balance. She fell backward and to the side, landing with a soft thud on her hip, directly in the middle of the cold fire pit.

Ashes billowed around her, filling her nostrils and sending her into coughing spasms. Her eyes and throat burned as the tiny flakes settled into every open orifice in her body.

As she scrambled to get up, strong hands caught under her arms and lifted her from the sooty debris, setting her on her feet.

"Sit down!" Rick bellowed, and the place came to an agitated silence around them. He swiveled her toward him. "Are you okay?"

Her eyes were too blurred to see his, but the tone was one she recognized. She'd heard it often from her dad—a mixture of anger and relief after what could have been a disaster. She nodded, unable to stop coughing long enough to answer.

He wrapped her fingers around a water bottle. "Rinse your mouth first a couple of times, and then try to drink." Summer took a gulp. The cool water was welcomed.

"I've got eyewash in the first-aid kit." Charlie's voice faded in the distance.

With one hand enclosing hers and the other arm around her shoulder, Rick guided her out of the group. "You can spit behind this tree."

She rinsed her mouth a couple of times, and after a few

tentative sips assured her she wouldn't get choked, she took a drink, and then another and another. The water calmed the irritation until she was able, at last, to croak out a "thanks."

"No problem. I'll help you to your cabin."

The weight of Rick's arm around her shoulders and the strong grip on her hand sent a familiar, pleasant sensation rippling through her. Letting her body associate *that* sensation with Rick Warren would be a major blunder. She practically jerked her hand from his grasp.

Her eyes still burned, but the tears began to cleanse away the debris enough to allow forms to take shape. "I can see well enough to make it by myself. Thanks." His disgruntled sigh followed her as she stumbled toward her cabin.

Charlie met her at her door and followed her to the bathroom with the eyewash. "You know how to use this stuff?" She nodded and filled the cup with liquid, rinsing each eye repeatedly until her vision was, at last, restored enough to make her gasp at the hideous mess she saw in the mirror. Restored enough to see Charlie's face contorted by worry.

"Quit worrying, Charlie. I'm fine."

"I'm not worried about the ashes, sugar." His mouth drooped farther at the corners.

"What, then?"

"Well, I'm not so sure this is gonna work out." He lowered his voice, confiding in her. "I know how much you want the camp to continue."

At last! When he'd yelled at the kids, Rick Warren had finally shown his true colors to everyone—including Charlie. Her heart leaped at the thought. "More than anything," she said.

"You're trying hard. I know you are."

A bubble of pride swelled in her chest.

"But you just don't seem to know how to keep the girls under control."

"What?" Had she heard him correctly? Charlie was questioning *her* ability? The bubble burst and rushed out of her lungs.

"Rick got them under control, but he shouldn't have to do that. They're always running around, pushing and shoving and loud." He waved his hand as his eyes skimmed her from top to bottom. "What if there'd been a fire in that pit?"

"But there wasn't."

"But what if there had been? We would've had a tragedy on our hands. One I never could've forgiven myself for."

His words weighed down her heart, sinking it to the bottom of her stomach. "You're right, Charlie. I'm sorry. I've been way too lax. It won't happen again."

"I don't know, Summer. The children's safety is at stake." Charlie let out a deep breath and rubbed his hand down his face. "Your mom and dad are coming down Saturday...."

A surge of panic coursed down her spine. She'd promised herself no more strain on her dad because of her. "Please, Charlie. One more chance. I can do this. I know I can."

"Nadine might still be willing...."

"No! Don't call her yet. Please?" She laid a hand on his arm. "Give me tomorrow to try and make things right?"

Charlie's chin wrinkled as his lips pressed together tightly. He shook his finger at her in warning. "Tomorrow. That's it."

Summer swallowed hard as she watched him leave.

Twenty-four hours to get the girls under control. That feat would take some real fairy princess magic.

"MMM. THESE COOKIES ARE fantastic." The tension had finally left Rick's jaws enough to let him take the first bite out of the cookie in his hand.

He shouldn't have held on to Summer that way. His brain kept telling him to let go, but she felt so good that his arms wouldn't obey. Obviously, it didn't feel good to her. The way she'd jerked away…

"We put germs in them." Lucy's comment brought him back to the present.

Tara laughed. "Wheat germ," she explained. "Summer's fairy princess recipes are all made with organic ingredients. She teaches kids how to eat healthy at her parties." She pointed to the tray, still piled high. "As cookies go, these are about as healthy as you can get."

Rick took another bite, chewing carefully as he thought about what Tara just said.

"For the parties," Tara continued, "she makes carrot cake and zucchini cake for the cupcakes. All organic, of course. And her brownie recipe even has broccoli in it, if you can imagine such a thing."

The admiration in Tara's voice flavored Rick's next bite. He'd assumed Summer's parties were just frivolous fun. He hadn't considered there could be any meaningful agenda.

Could it be he'd underestimated her?

Maybe, but the revelation still didn't take away his annoyance from their meeting that afternoon. Sure as hell, she'd gone to the office to talk to Charlie about him. One thing about her—she didn't try to hide anything. She'd been quite blatant and unapologetic about her dislike for him.

"Can we play hide-and-seek?" Howie asked the same question every night.

Rick looked at his watch. They had about fifteen minutes to kill. "Yep. Tonight we have time for some hide-and-seek."

"Yeah!" Howie pumped his fisted hand in a triumphant gesture. "The girls have to be 'it' this time."

The girls huddled in a circle with their eyes closed as the boys scurried to hide.

Rick enjoyed a few more cookies while the kids played.

When he saw Charlie veer off the path from Summer's cabin toward his office, he hurried to catch up. "How's Summer?"

"Oh, she'll be fine…but I'm not sure I'll be okay." The grimace on Charlie's face made the words seem painful.

"What do you mean?"

Charlie shook his head. "I'm not sure she's cut out to do this kind of work, Rick. She doesn't have any control over the girls. She lets 'em run wild, just like she's always done."

"She's good with the kids, Charlie." Rick could hardly believe those words came out of his mouth after the fast one she'd tried to pull this afternoon. But it was true. She *was* good with the kids—just not much of a disciplinarian. Maybe she could learn. "She has some great ideas and imaginative activities."

Charlie peered at him through half-closed eyes as though he didn't recognize who he was talking to.

"I believe I can help her in the discipline department."

Charlie's lips pulled into a wry half smile. "She doesn't know the meaning of the word."

"I'll work with her." Rick wasn't sure why this was suddenly so important to him. Perhaps it was the challenge involved. Or maybe he wanted to believe that second chances made a difference. If he'd had a second chance with Dunk…

"I tell ya, Rick. I love Summer like a daughter, but I'm not sure Herschel and Agnes did her any favors supporting her every whim." Charlie gave a sad shrug and continued on his way to his office.

Rick turned back to Summer's cabin, trying to imagine the conversation that had just taken place inside those walls. What could he do to help her? Would she even accept any help he offered?

"We can't find Howie."

Rick's attention snapped back at the sound of Neil's voice.

"All the rest of the boys have been found, but Howie's still hiding, and it's time to go in."

Rick walked back to the circle. "Any of you guys see which direction Howie went?" All the heads shook in unison.

Rick felt a tug on his sleeve. He looked down into the large, brown eyes of M&M.

"Just call 'Olly, Olly, in come free,' Mr. Rick."

The words drifted back to him from summer nights of his childhood. "Olly, Olly, in come free!" he called. "That means you win, Howie. Come on in."

A delighted war whoop floated down from somewhere up above.

Rick felt his jaw drop as Howie came clambering down from the top of a nearby pine tree. He'd have to give the little twerp another lecture on safety.

And he'd have to convince Spitfire Summer to accept his help.

Of the two, the former sounded more doable.

CHAPTER SEVEN

SUMMER SAT AT THE TOP OF THE circle dressed as her fairy princess persona. The girls had been inordinately quiet since she came in, although a couple found the voice to apologize for the incident at the fire pit.

While she cleaned herself up, she'd tried to come up with a strategy that might turn the girls' behavior around in one day. There was no guarantee it would work, but she had nothing to lose.

"So." She moved her eyes slowly around the group, making direct eye contact with each girl. "An hour ago, I was poor Cinderella, and now I'm ready for the ball."

A ripple of giggles passed through the group, and the wide-eyed stares relaxed, relieved she wasn't angry.

"The last time I was here, we discussed our pretty hearts and what they tell us about our own special magic wands." She paused. "Would anyone like to share something her pretty heart has told her?"

Greta's hand drifted up slowly. "My pretty heart tells me we should be nicer to one another."

Summer felt the smile break out on her face. She had so hoped someone's conscience would make her feel bad about the boisterous behavior. She glanced around the room again. "And how can we be nicer to one another?"

Almost everyone's hand went up and a flurry of answers ensued.

"We can take turns better."

"We can be more careful not to step on people smaller than us."

"We can share stuff."

"All wonderful ideas," Summer said. "We certainly have to learn to be careful when we're in large groups in small spaces. I wasn't hurt tonight, but think about what might've happened if there had been a fire in the fire pit."

M&M raised her hand hesitantly. "You would've been hurt really bad."

"That's right. No one meant for it to happen, but it did happen. So what can we do to be more careful so another preventable accident doesn't occur?"

Greta spoke up. "The boys are always in line. Maybe we need to line up more."

Summer could hardly believe her ears. They *wanted* to line up? Maybe Tara was right about giving them some limits.

"And we could take turns being the first in line," Braelyn offered, "so everybody would get a turn. That way the little ones won't always get pushed to the back."

Summer well remembered what that was like.

Although she hadn't expected it, this was exactly how she'd hoped the discussion would go. She could feel her face beaming. "Great ideas. All of them. So how do we start?"

"We start with M&M because she's the smallest." Amanda seemed to be giving this some analytical thought. "We line up in the morning, smallest to tallest. And then we change each time until everybody's gone first, and then we decide on a new way to line up."

"Super!" Tara applauded. "And what about watching our manners like Mr. Rick said the first day? I think we need to be quieter when we're indoors."

"I think so, too," Summer agreed.

While the other girls seemed agreeable, Shannon sat with her arms folded, frowning. She wasn't buying any of this.

"Shannon," Summer addressed her directly, "you aren't happy about these plans?"

"It sounds like school," Shannon huffed. "Line up. Be quiet. Don't do anything fun."

"We'll still have lots of free time to play and have fun," Summer assured her. "That's not going to change. But we need to concentrate more on our fairy princess training. Sunday will be the end of our first week. So Sunday night, we're going to choose which camper has made the most progress toward becoming a fairy princess by listening to her pretty heart. That person will get a special prize."

Tara threw her a questioning look, and Summer winked in response.

"Now, to bed all of you. Dream about your pretty heart and listen to what it tells you."

As the girls climbed into their bunks, Tara sauntered over. "Good job, but do you really have a surprise in mind?"

Summer kept her voice low. "My dad's making some wands I was going to give out at the end of camp. But maybe doling them out one at a time will be a better incentive. I'll ask him to bring a couple when they come up Saturday."

Tara nodded. "No staff meeting tonight, by the way. Rick didn't think you'd be cleaned up so fast."

"I rushed. I had to start tonight trying to straighten up this mess I've created."

"It's not that bad...." Tara reassured her.

"Yes, it is. And I've got to rectify things before my parents get here."

Tara gave a resolute nod. "We can do this."

"Well, let's hope so." Summer looked around to find all the girls in bed. "Want to come over for some lemonade?"

"Thanks, but I think I'll pass tonight. I'm beat, and I just want to go straight to bed."

They tucked the girls in, and Summer left the bunkhouse.

Sleep wouldn't come easily tonight. Too many things happened today, and she still had a lot to think about concerning tomorrow. She needed something to make her worries more palatable, and she knew just the thing.

A healthy, organic chocolate chip cookie was calling her name.

RICK WAITED UNTIL ALL WAS quiet before he grabbed his folder. Tonight, he would make his notes about the kitchen. He took the shortcut through the dining hall.

Although the emergency light put out a glow, the kitchen at the back of the building would be too dark to see the numbers on his measuring tape, so he flipped the light on as he passed through the open door. His movement was met by a startled "Eek!" The wide-eyed fairy princess was caught literally with her hand in the proverbial cookie jar.

"Oh, my God, Rick. You scared me." A becoming blush crept from the rounded neckline of Summer's gown into her cheeks.

He had to think fast, hiding the measuring tape in the back pocket of his cargo shorts. "I had a hankering for some more cookies." He had a hankering, all right, but Summer was by far the most delectable morsel around.

Her eyes cut to the file folder and narrowed. "You always bring inspection sheets with you to get a snack?"

He laid the folder casually on the shelf above the microwave and above her line of sight. "Just notes on some activities Neil and I discussed." He shifted the conversation away from his lie. "You couldn't resist, either?"

"I didn't get any earlier." She stepped away from the gigantic jar on the counter to give him access…or maybe to gain some distance from *him*. Again.

That little flicker of irritation he always felt when she was around flared. He'd told Charlie he would help her, and if he was going to do that, he had to get past his anger…and whatever the hell else it was that distanced them. He opted for a light approach. Looking her over thoroughly, he saw no sign of the soot that covered her earlier. "You cleaned up fast."

"Fairy magic." She pulled her wand from her pocket and he noticed a slight tremble when she held it up. Was she nervous? Because of him?

Nibbling on her cookie, she reminded him of some wild, skittish woodland creature, ready to bolt at any second. He had the urge to calm her by reaching out and brushing his fingers across her face. Or his lips across her mouth.

Damn it, this woman vexed him. Her presence turned him into a fickle lunatic…from Jekyll to Hyde in a matter of seconds. If there was ever going to be even a modicum of peace between them, he had to get something off his chest. He took a determined breath and tried to ignore the luscious, clean scent that filled the small space between them. "Summer, this afternoon when you came to Charlie's office, you didn't know I was there, did you?"

"No." She fumbled with her skirt, unable to find the pocket for the wand.

"So you'd gone to Charlie to talk about me."

She straightened and looked him directly in the eye. "To talk to him about replacing you."

Her honesty took him aback, scraping off the protective layer of lust and exposing his aggravation again. "Why? What have I done that's made you dislike me so?"

"I could ask you the same thing." Her head tilted back, lifting her chin. "But since you asked first, I'll tell you." She swallowed the bite of cookie. "I thought you were too hard on the boys, and you were going to make them hate being here. If anybody wants to go home it could start a chain reaction and then my parents are going to suffer. When I heard Willard saying he hated this place, it was like confirmation of my worst fears coming true."

"But he told us why he said those things."

"I didn't know that when I went to talk to Charlie." She glanced down at the cookie, seeming to contemplate another bite, but laid it on the counter instead. "Anyway, it doesn't make any difference now because it turns out I'm the screwup, not you. The girls are out of control, and I have tomorrow to get them turned around, or I'm the one who's history."

Her frankness doused his anger somewhat, but he stirred it, anyway. "Why didn't you come directly to me?"

"Because you're unapproachable. You're evasive…like you've got some big secret you're hiding." She flicked her hand in the direction of the folder. "And you don't seem to like me very much because…?" Her head tilted.

Hard as it was for him to admit it, the woman was extremely perceptive. Rick shrugged. At least her doubts about him were backed by her concern for her parents. His were pure prejudice. "Well, you're the owners' daughter, but not their first choice for the job, and you do have that wild-child image." He waved his hand toward the costume she wore. "I mean, a grown woman pretending to be a fairy princess. It seems a bit bizarre to me."

Her cheeks blazed a hot pink, which made her blue eyes deepen. "You don't know anything about my business."

Despite her pissy-ass answer, Rick's gut told him they were making progress and he sure as hell didn't want to screw it up now. He smiled. "I *didn't* know anything about it until Tara shared a little about your healthy recipes." He took a quick bite "Damn fine cookies, by the way"—and was rewarded by a hint of a grin that made his breath catch. "She says, at your parties, you teach kids about eating healthy."

Summer braced her hands on the counter and weightlessly

hopped up to sit on it. "It's not just about eating right, though. It's all about empowerment for girls. Making good choices. The fairy princess shtick is just the gimmick I came up with."

"Empowerment and fairy princess? The terms hardly seem appropriate in the same sentence. Why a fairy princess?"

"I'm the baby of the family and, as you and Charlie so aptly put it, a wild one...."

Rick's body stirred as his mind played with new images related to the term.

"And I've always been small," she added, which gave a dimension to his images that made him shift his weight to relieve the growing pressure. "So it's harder to get people to take me seriously. I decided to use that to my advantage. Be the fairy princess that my size and voice are suited for, but—" her eyes twinkled, pulling him with their magic "—give them a message they don't expect, and let the dichotomy work like a surprise attack."

Hellfire and damnation. The little minx spoke with the spirit of a seasoned soldier. "And what's the message?"

She pursed her lips in thought before she spoke. "As females, we're taught we have to take care of everything and everybody, and sometimes it seems like the only way to do that is with the wave of a magic wand. But when we discover the magic within us—our wand is our talent, if you will—then we realize we can only do so much. We begin to accept the world and our limitations and keep the faith that other wands will take care of the things we can't."

The depth of her words left Rick intrigued and speechless for a few seconds. He wanted to keep her talking—about anything. "So tell me about the recipes. How did you come up with something this good yet still healthy?"

"There was a time I thought I wanted to be a nutritionist, so I started a major in that." She seemed about to say something, but changed her mind and gave a shrug. "I lost interest. But later on, I took some classes under a pastry chef, and learned the basics. I combined what I learned and started coming up with my own recipes."

A seed of admiration had been sown. Rick took in the tiara, the silvery wings, the pink dress. If the effect worked on him, a hardened marine—and he was definitely hardened at the moment—he imagined little girls would follow her without ever knowing they'd been recruited. "Well, it all works together nicely for you," he said. "You're enchanting."

The twinkle in her eyes began transforming into a bewitching smolder before she glanced away. "Thanks." She reclaimed her cookie. "And what about you?" She crunched off a bite. "Why all the macho stuff?"

Rick smiled. Her use of the term twenty minutes ago would have irritated him but now seemed to be part of her charm. "Discipline's all I know. My dad was a marine. I'm the middle child and was a marine. Both of my brothers are still active-duty marines. Organization, discipline—they're all I've ever known."

Her head tilted in question. "How come you left? I mean, if your brothers are still in active duty..."

"I..." Rick wasn't about to get into his personal issues. He shrugged. "I'd had enough."

She seemed to ponder that—and him—as she swallowed the last bite of her cookie. Then, placing her hands to each side of her on the counter, she shifted her weight, leaning toward him slightly. Her pink tongue darted out to swipe the last crumbs from her lips, leaving behind a glistening trail of moisture that Rick had a hard time tearing his eyes away from. The air around them pulsed with an electrical charge, and his heartbeat took up the rhythm.

"It must be hard, living with all that pressure to be perfect," she said quietly. He watched her eyes deepen again, and it wasn't embarrassment that darkened their hue this time. "Don't you ever just let go and do whatever you…um, whatever you want to do?"

Her eyes. Her lips. The way she leaned forward. Everything screamed of invitation. But in his thirty-four years, Rick had never kissed a woman the first time without asking. It was something a gentleman didn't do. He leaned forward, his eyes locking with hers. "Summer, I'd like very much to—"

A whistled tune. Close by. Someone in the dining hall was headed their way.

Rick straightened and cleared his throat. "I'd like to help you get the girls under control."

She drew back, looking like he'd slapped her. "Thanks," she said curtly, and the irritation he'd grown familiar with returned. "But I think Tara and I will be able to handle it by ourselves." She rubbed her hands together briskly as if demonstrating how finished she was with the conversation—and him—just as Kenny strolled into the kitchen.

"Caught ya," the guard announced with a broad grin. "I saw the light and knew somebody was after cookies."

Rick consciously unclenched his fists, which had tightened at the interruption. Sure as hell, what he'd almost gotten a taste of would've been sweeter than any cookie.

SUMMER'S HEART POUNDED a strange nonrhythm. Rick had been about to kiss her, she was sure. What she *wasn't* sure of was if she wanted to thank Kenny or throttle him. Feuding parts of her cheered for both.

The grown-up part she'd been trying so hard to cultivate these past couple of years told her that kissing a guy she'd considered the enemy just a few hours ago was capricious and wouldn't lead anywhere she needed to go.

The wild child was totally miffed, though. A good kiss—

and she sensed this would've been on the superlative end of the scale—was one of the things that should never be passed up, provided it was between two people who had no other commitments.

Did Rick have a girlfriend? She hadn't thought much about that—hadn't allowed herself to think about him in terms of any kind of relationship. And just the idea she was thinking about it now scattered her thoughts willy-nilly.

Rick and Kenny began discussing the morning's skunk encounter, and somewhere between the polar extremes of her thoughts, her mediator said to get out of there while things were in neutral.

"I'm going to leave the cookies with y'all," she said when Kenny hesitated in his own skunk tale for a moment. "If I stay, I'll only want more."

"Yeah, me, too." Something in Rick's tone fractured the reserve she'd momentarily gained. Was he insinuating something, or was her imagination running away with her? Either way, she needed to get out of there. Immediately. She scooted to the edge of the counter to jump down.

Rick's hands flew to her waist, lifting her. Involuntarily, her eyes swept up to meet his, and she saw her own frustration mirrored there. Time seemed to slow down as the press of his thumbs along her rib cage imprinted on her consciousness. She was still aware of where they'd been long after they were gone and he'd set her on her feet.

"Some for the road." Kenny grabbed a handful of cookies and screwed the lid back onto the enormous jar before they all left the kitchen.

Her irritation and frustration coalesced into one manageable, meaningful mass, which grew with every step back to her cabin.

By the time she reached her door, she was carrying a weighted balloon in her chest cavity, and though she tried to mollify it, her “Good night” to Kenny and Rick was expelled on a petulant huff.

She closed the door, aching for the kiss that had been thwarted by Kenny, who’d made it his job—intentional or not—to be their chaperone…all the way back to her cabin.

CHAPTER EIGHT

BY NOON FRIDAY, SOMETHING was in the air—and it didn't look or feel normal. An eerie yellow tinge clung to everything, turning Kentucky Lake an ominous shade of green. The surrounding trees looked as though an artist had flecked them with a neon hue.

Sometime during the night, Summer awoke from a fitful, sweat-drenched sleep and turned her air conditioner on for the first time.

The morning broke oppressively hot with humidity and temperature both hovering close to one hundred. The nature hike before breakfast had been like herding slugs.

True to their word, the girls lined up throughout the day with Greta emerging as an obvious leader, always making sure everyone was in the proper place.

A couple of tiffs broke out. One between Kaelyn and Braelyn, which seemed to be just normal sibling bickering. The other was a bit of a surprise when M&M told Lucy to "Shut up" after a particularly long whine about the heat.

Summer corrected both of the girls, secretly delighting in M&M's spunk. She tried not to overreact when the verbal exchange took place right in front of Charlie. Some testiness was to be expected in a group of girls living in such close proximity...at any age. And the oppressive heat was enough to make even a hardened soldier—like Rick—grouchy. Charlie smiled at her afterward, though. That was a good sign.

She'd done a fair job of keeping her mind off the almost-kiss with Rick the night before. But the current situation had her shivering in anticipation despite the heat.

Rick stood behind her with his hands on her shoulders, and while she was trying to concentrate on his words, his voice kept getting lost in the sensations zinging through her as his breath feathered down the back of her neck.

"Are you ready?" he asked, and she nodded, tightening her grip on the bow. "Okay, nock the arrow." Her hands shook, and it took a couple of tries to get the bowstring to stay within the slit. His hand closed around hers, helping her keep it in place. Large and warm, it engulfed hers with its size.

"Now, bring the bow up and pull back the arrow with the string in one easy motion." His voice caressed the area behind her ear as he bent lower to help her aim.

She did as she was instructed, but the hard plane of his chest pressing against her shoulder blade made her pulse accelerate. The tip of the arrow wobbled all over the place.

"Just relax," Rick whispered as the arrowhead zigzagged back and forth across the intended target. His low chuckle only made the movement worse, until finally Summer just closed her eyes and let it fly.

A gale of laughter erupted from the group behind them. She opened her eyes to see the arrow sticking in the ground about fifteen feet away…a good thirty-five feet short of the target.

"Okay," Rick said. "Not a bad first try."

"Whoo, that poor mole never knew what hit him," Neil joked.

"Don't you mean *Talpidae,* Mr. Neil?" Reggie had proven to be a whiz kid at remembering scientific names.

Summer laughed and handed the bow to Rick, grateful to gain some distance from the heat he'd stirred inside her.

Out of nowhere, a clap of thunder rumbled as a strong

wind whipped simultaneously through the surrounding trees. A black front headed in from the southwest corner of the archery range.

"Everybody to the dining hall." She pulled the arrow from the hole it had created. "And don't forget your water bottles."

Jimbo stood near her, but he looked to Rick for confirmation. "Us, too, Mr. Rick?"

"Ms. Summer said 'everybody,' Jimbo. That means the boys as well as the girls. And don't worry about lining up."

Finally! Summer smiled at Rick's underlying message of support. If he really was trying to make things better between them, she supposed the next move was up to her.

As the kids took off with Tara and Neil, she turned to him. "Rick, I'm sorry about the warmonger crack yesterday. I didn't really mean it. I'm thankful for our men and women who serve in the military." She held out the arrow. "I don't have an olive branch, but I'm hoping this can have the same effect."

His chin buckled in question, then he took it from her and held it up solemnly. "I humbly accept this token. May your people and my people live in peace from this day forward."

A loud, unexpected snicker bubbled out of her chest, and the surprise on Rick's face transformed it into a full-blown laugh. The force behind it became uncontrollable, and the more she tried to stifle it, the harder she laughed. Tears streamed down her face, and her breathing came in spurts.

His laughter joined hers and built into a loud bellow. "What…are we…laughing at?" he gasped between guffaws.

"Us and our silliness."

Another warning rumble of thunder sounded closer than the first, sobering them both. Their laughter gave way to broad smiles, and then softened as their gazes locked for a long moment.

Rick's mouth twitched at one corner. "Was it just me, or was Kenny's timing last night as terrible as I thought?"

"That depends." Summer raised an eyebrow. "Were you about to kiss me when he came in?"

"I was."

She grinned up at him and nodded. "Then his timing was terrible." A large drop of rain plopped on top of her head, followed by another and another.

"Good to know." Rick gave her a wink and slung the quiver over his shoulder as the sky opened up.

With a squeal, Summer took off in a run, Rick right behind her. Exhilaration pumped through her, propelling her across the field.

The slower kids had fallen behind, and she and Rick caught up easily. They slowed their pace to stay in the rear, encouraging the kids to hurry, but Summer found it difficult to hold back. She wasn't worried about getting wet, but rather her heart was skipping in her chest, and she had the most remarkable urge to skip along to the beat.

By the time they reached the dining hall, everyone was drenched. The yellow in the air had shifted to a green hue that made the hairs on Summer's neck rise. The barometric pressure was dropping fast.

"We need to get to the storm shelter," she said to Rick just as Charlie came charging from the back of the building.

He visibly caught himself and cleared his throat before he spoke. "Weather radio just went off. Everybody to the storm shelter for a little while. Ginny's already got the door open." He motioned to Rick to join him in the kitchen.

Summer saw fear register in some of the kids' eyes. This was a time when they needed the assurance of order and control. "Everybody line up…quietly. Girls behind Ms. Tara. Boys behind Mr. Neil."

Wordlessly, the kids followed orders. Tara and Neil led them through the kitchen and out the back door.

Rick and Charlie grabbed a couple of boxes, and Summer stopped to see if she could help.

Charlie shook his head. "Go on. We've got these."

"What's the report?" she asked.

"Tornado warning for the county. Funnel cloud spotted near Benton."

Ten miles away wasn't very far. Summer's stomach twisted as she recalled the marina that had been virtually destroyed when a tornado touched down two years ago only three miles from here.

When she opened the back door for Rick and Charlie, a gust of wind jerked it from her hold, slamming it against the building. Stinging rain pelted her face, making it difficult to keep her eyes open. More by feel and instinct than sight, she forced the door closed and made a blind dash for the safety of the underground shelter a few yards away. Rick caught her hand as she reached the steps and guided her in. She heard him throw the bolt behind her.

The rain had broken the heat and the thick concrete walls were damp with condensation. A musty, earthy scent permeated the air. Although the room was built for double the number of people, the kids huddled against one another, cold and scared, on the wooden benches that lined the walls.

"Whew! I feel like a drowned rat!" Summer forced a bright smile as she made a mental head count but felt it fade as her heart leaped into her throat. Something was wrong. Someone was missing. Her chest tightened as she counted the kids again. Twenty. Rick. Ginny. Charlie. Tara. Neil. "Oh, my God! Kenny!" The name exploded from her lips.

Before she could reach the door, Rick already had it opened and was outside. "Bolt it back!" he shouted as he forced it closed against the wind.

RICK RAN, TRYING TO KEEP HIS concentration on Kenny and not the trees whipping ominously around him…or the rain blowing straight-line into his face…or the lightning that every few seconds edged his surroundings in opalescent blue and brought a crackle of static with it.

As he ran, he scanned his memory. He hadn't seen Kenny out today. Maybe the weather had kept the security guard from his normal afternoon activity, which was fishing. Was it possible he was sleeping through this? The wind had to be giving his travel trailer quite a buffeting.

A cold shudder passed through Rick, propelling him faster. Living in Arkansas, he'd seen the remnants of mobile homes demolished by tornadoes. That dilapidated camper of Kenny's wouldn't stand a chance.

Relief flooded him when the trailer came into view with the security guard's old Jeep parked beside it.

Rick pounded on the door with his fist. "Kenny!" he shouted. "Kenny!" He waited a few seconds, but the door didn't open. He ran around to the back, beating a staccato rhythm hard against the metal walls. He covered the entire length, around the end, and back around to the front. As he reached the window, the door flew open.

Rick lunged, grabbed the door and used his momentum to leap into the camper and close the door behind him.

Kenny stood wide-eyed and openmouthed, shirtless and grasping a throw around his middle.

"Get dressed. Quick! Tornado." Rick kept his words to a minimum.

They had the desired effect.

"Shitfire!" Kenny exploded, and hightailed it to the bedroom end of the trailer.

The door handle jerked in Rick's hand as the camper swayed menacingly. The metal shuddered and creaked, and a foreboding tremor passed through him. "Hurry!" He felt the movement of the air outside change directions.

Kenny came running, pulling a T-shirt over his head. His flip-flops were a mistake, but there was no time to change.

"Storm shelter," Rick yelled, trying to be heard over the roar as they jumped off the steps and slammed the door.

With the wind now at his back, Rick was being pushed by an unseen hand into a swirling blackness. He fought to stay upright as the force threatened to topple him forward. Tree limbs twisted in a frightful, otherworldly dance. A cry brought him to a stop and he whirled around.

Kenny was on the ground, holding the back of his head, a dazed expression on his face.

Combat training sprang to the forefront of Rick's brain when he saw the fallen comrade. In an instant, Kenny was Dunk and the lightning cracking around him was sniper fire. He rushed to the security guard and slung him over his shoulder as a deafening crack splintered the air around them.

Blocking out everything else, Rick focused on breathing, on keeping enough air to sustain him as his lungs protested the additional burden. "Not far now," he reminded himself, concentrating on the placement of one foot in front of the other time and time again, until at last he found Charlie blocking the door of the shelter open against the raging wind.

Rick gave his charge over to the helping hands that reached through the door, and the door slammed shut of its own accord as soon as his foot hit the steps.

Cries of relief filled the air. The warming presence of Summer's body hugging him tightly grounded him back in the moment. More hands, more bodies joined hers, all exuberant with joy, as everyone rushed to greet him and Kenny.

Ginny immediately started checking Kenny's head, which he'd bumped hard when his flip-flop broke and sent him sprawling. He kept insisting he was fine, and finally she agreed.

When the initial excitement was over, it was Summer who took the lead in calming the kids, diverting their attention with some group games and the snacks Rick and Charlie had carried over in the boxes. Then Neil took over, showing off some remarkable shadow hands with the help of a flashlight.

Rick smiled at the kids' absorption in the activity, their fears of the raging storm outside sidelined by a few emergency flashlights. His smile grew wider when Summer came to settle beside him on the bench.

"I'm glad you and Kenny are okay." In the dim light he could see tears brimming in her eyes.

This time yesterday, he'd been ready to sign her discharge papers. Today, she was a caring person who could calm twenty children—and several adults—with the flash of a smile and a few words. What a difference twenty-four hours could make…especially now that he knew she'd wanted him to kiss her.

He gave her a smile. "Another good thing to know."

EXHAUSTION DESCENDED ON SUMMER like the rainstorm from earlier, and her thoughts started to blur.

They'd spent three hours in the storm shelter as wave upon wave of severe storms passed through the area.

Once the storms were over, everyone had exited the shelter to find the entire camp littered with limbs and branches ripped from the trees by the wind.

Kenny's worst fears had been confirmed. The cracking sound he and Rick heard had been a downed tree that toppled directly across his trailer, effectively demolishing it and most everything he'd moved in for the month.

Rick was vaulted to reluctant hero status since Kenny

would likely have been killed as the bulk of the tree tore through the bedroom end of the camper.

The remainder of the night had been spent letting the kids call their parents to let them know they were okay, salvaging anything of Kenny's that could be saved from the debris left behind in the wreckage and dragging the fallen limbs and branches into piles.

A cold supper of sandwiches and chips seemed to satisfy the kids, who appeared to be walking in their sleep by lights-out. They'd cheered, though, when Rick announced no nature hike for Saturday morning and Ginny pushed breakfast up to nine so everybody could sleep in.

Despite her fatigue, Summer wasn't sleepy. She'd hoped for a little time alone with Rick this evening, mainly to satisfy her curiosity, but Mother Nature had effectively squelched that.

She'd also heard Kenny and Rick discussing Kenny's new living arrangements. He was going to share Rick's cabin until insurance paid for him to get a new camper.

She thought back through the day, to Rick's acts of selfless behavior. That she'd been wrong about him was obvious. She had a lot of making up to do and wasn't even sure where to start.

A knock on her door startled her.

Please don't be anybody needing anything else done tonight. She swung it open.

Rick met her startled gaze.

Without a word, he stepped into her cabin and swept her into his arms. His mouth closed down on hers, which was already open, and she found she hadn't the slightest desire to close it. Instead, she brushed her tongue softly against his in invitation, feeling his muffled groan as he tightened his arms around her. Her arm slid across his shoulder and her fingers played in the hair at the nape of his neck.

His lips pressed firmly as his tongue swept into her mouth, releasing a need deep within her, making her breathing erratic.

His tongue retreated and his lips closed slowly, guiding hers closed as his hands glided from her back to cup the sides of her face. He placed two or three soft kisses on her still-puckered lips and then stepped back, leaving her in a blissfully dazed stupor.

"Good night," he whispered before he disappeared into the darkness.

Summer stood watching for a few seconds, willing him to come back for a repeat performance.

When it was clear he was really gone, she closed the door and leaned heavily against it.

"Oh, my!" Her chest heaved in a contented sigh.

CHAPTER NINE

"SO...ANY INEXPENSIVE BUT fabulous ideas on ways to give this place more eye-appeal?"

His mom's laugh on the other end of the line made Rick smile. "The place is really dated. It needs color," she answered. "All that white and gray is...blah."

Rick looked around and noticed for the first time the lack of color. Camp Sunny Daze *was* drab. It looked like the military barracks he was used to rather than a summer camp for kids. "What would you suggest?" he asked.

"I'd start with painting the buildings different colors. The colors wouldn't have to be bright. Organic greens, rust tones, corals." Rick scribbled the ideas into his folder as she talked. "Flower beds would add color and vibrancy, and they wouldn't cost much because perennials go on sale for next to nothing in July. Window boxes would look great. Oh, and striped awnings would really spiff things up, but they'd be expensive."

"I'm sure expense will be key in what gets done."

"I can't tell a lot about the property from the pictures you emailed, but it looks like it has plenty of potential and would be a great investment. It just needs to be brought back to life."

Rick visualized how the place might look if his mom's ideas were implemented. "Paint and flowers sound easy enough. I have that week off between sessions, so I could stay here in the cabin and work on that project myself." Would Herschel and Agnes be interested in putting in a week of work? Or Summer? If she stayed and helped, maybe he wouldn't need her parents. The thought of Summer and him alone at the camp for a week stirred up various and sundry ideas that were indeed colorful. Mostly red hot.

"I was hoping you'd come home that week." When did his parents become so predictable? He knew his Mom would want him to come home. She never missed a chance to try to get the family together. "We haven't seen you in a month."

"Or maybe you could all come here and help." Rick cringed. Had he really just suggested a week with his dad? The elder Warren would pull him off work detail and insist he go see that shrink in Paducah, sure as hell.

"Sorry, sweetheart, but we have a couples' tournament at the club that week."

Whew! Dodged that bullet.

"Well, I'll come home sometime in August. I promise."

"I'll think some more on the project you have there. You know, I love that you're taking the Realtor role more seriously. You haven't shown much enthusiasm toward it until now."

"The Delaneys are nice people. They helped me when I needed it. I want to return the favor."

"And what about the daughter? Summer, isn't it? Made any progress there toward getting along?"

"Um, yeah, you could say that." Rick felt his face heat.

"Oh, my goodness! I hear the smile in your voice from here."

Rick gave an embarrassed laugh. "We've made peace. We'll leave it at that."

"Oh, no, we won't leave it at that. But we'll have to leave it at that for right now because I'm showing the Eldrige place in twenty minutes." Rick heard the door to the garage close and a car door open. "You call me back when we both have time to talk, you hear?"

"Yes, ma'am," Rick answered. "Love you, Mom."

"Love you, too, sweetheart."

As he hung up, a sound from behind alerted him that someone was approaching. He closed the folder quickly, lest it be the fairy princess herself. But it turned out to be Kenny.

"You need to get some rest." He gave the security guard a once-over, taking in the heavy eyelids and dark circles. "You've had a long night."

Did his own eyes look as tired as Kenny's? Last night, the nightmare had been especially vicious. What started out as Kenny over his shoulder soon became his brother Luke before morphing into Dunk. Like being with the kids, carrying Kenny through the storm had triggered strong memories—and fears. He blinked to clear his thoughts and finished off the coffee in his cup.

It was almost noon on Saturday. The insurance adjuster had just left, and even the woman's promise to get Kenny a check "very soon" couldn't shake the security guard's glum mood.

"Go on," Rick urged. "A good, long sleep will help you more than anything."

Kenny yawned, his whole body shuddering in response. "Maybe you're right."

He sauntered away toward Rick's cabin as the sheriff's car pulled in.

Sheriff Buck Blaine ambled out of the car, adjusting his holster belt, which anchored his pants firmly beneath the roll of his large belly. "Well, if it isn't Rick Warren as I live and breathe."

Rick's mood lightened when he shook the hand of his old friend. "How you doing, Buck? It's good to see you."

"Good to see you, too." Buck clapped him on the back as they exchanged their handshake. "Heard you was stickin' around these parts for a while, and I was sure proud to hear it. Paducah would do well to hang on to the likes of you."

Ever since they'd worked together on the Brennans' cave rescue operation a few years ago, Buck had treated Rick like he hung the moon. Rick found it embarrassing but tolerated it because he knew Buck's praise was genuine and not given lightly.

"I'm glad to still be here," Rick answered. "I actually hope something opens up soon that'll allow me to stay for good."

Paducah, Kentucky, *had* been a good match for him. It reminded him of his home in Arkansas—he noticed Summer watching him and Buck from a short distance away—and the saying about Kentucky's fast horses and pretty women seemed to be more truth than tale. "Summer—" he motioned her over "—this is Buck Blaine, the Marshall County sheriff."

"Hi, Buck." Summer extended her hand and flashed a disarming smile.

"Glad to meet you, little lady." Buck looked around, his eyebrows drawing together in feigned concern. "Rumor has it y'all have a camp for kids going here. You got 'em stashed away in a closet?"

Summer didn't miss a beat. Her face grew somber, but a telltale, mischievous glint appeared in her eye. "Yeah." She shrugged. "But the sleeping bags add an authentic camping experience. We open the door and throw in some trail mix every six hours."

Buck popped his chewing gum and gave Rick a lopsided grin. "Got your hands full with this one, huh?"

Summer's laugh tinkled pleasantly in Rick's ear. It was a nice sound—soft and feminine—and the memory of his hands full of her last night stampeded southward from his brain. "You know it. I had to send the kids fishing. I couldn't keep an eye on them and her, too." He said it only half in jest. Despite the mess and the work, the past couple of hours with Summer had been fun. Flirting. Teasing. The occasional "come-on" look that placed a repeat of last night's kiss high on today's agenda. If his woman radar wasn't totally off-kilter, the little lady wanted a repeat performance, too. He'd be more than happy to oblige when the right time came.

"You ended up on the best end of *that* stick." Buck gave Summer a wink before his manner became all business. He eyed what was left of Kenny's camper with the tree still slicing through it. "Looks like y'all had a little trouble here last night."

Rick's gaze followed the sheriff's. "That we did, but this is the worst of it. The rest was just downed limbs, most of which we've taken care of."

"Nobody was hurt," Summer added. "That's the important thing."

"You got that right." Buck took a deep breath, and Rick noticed that he, like Kenny, had dark circles under his eyes. No doubt, the sheriff had had a long night, too. "We had twenty-two from Marshall County taken to the hospital. Some broken bones. A couple of concussions. This county's huge…covers a wide area. But nobody died, thank the Lord."

Summer's face went serious again, but this time she wasn't faking. "Our security guard would've been goners if Rick hadn't woke him up."

Buck gave a knowing nod and his hand clapped heavily on Rick's back again. "Rick's a true hero. Savin' lives is what he does best."

Rick flinched. *Everybody but my best friend.*

Buck meant it as a compliment, but his words stung just the same.

Summer tilted her head, regarding Rick closely, and it would be only a second before she started interrogating him about things he would rather not discuss right then…or ever. "Summer's the lifesaver." He shifted the focus away from himself. “She’s the one who realized Kenny wasn’t in the storm shelter with us.”

“Well, I’d say having the two of y’all around makes Kenny one lucky son of a bitch,” Buck concluded. “’Course, it could just be that Mr. Warren here has a nose for trouble. Seems like he manages to sniff it out no matter where he is.”

Summer snorted. “Well, it’ll have to smell worse than a skunk for Rick to catch a whiff of it,” she drawled.

Buck’s brows furrowed, and his glance bounced between them, demanding details until Rick finally threw up his hands in surrender.

Oh, his friend the sheriff was going to *love* this.

SUMMER HAD DRAGGED THIS STORY out as long as she could. Time to let Tara in on the best details… “And then he kissed me,” she sang in a whisper.

Tara let out a surprised shriek in response, then covered her mouth quickly. Easing the door of her bedroom open, she glanced around and quietly closed it all the way. “All still asleep. He kissed you? How was it?”

Summer’s stomach did a quick-step and she chuckled that a sixteen-hour-old memory could still bring on such a response. “Hmm.” She searched for the most appropriate term. “I’d rate it as the best first kiss since Adam and Eve.”

“Oh, wow! I want one like that.” Tara’s voice sounded dreamy. “And I also want a week like this has been for you.”

“This week wasn’t that great until last night,” Summer reminded her.

“Yeah, it was. You just haven’t been listening to yourself talk about it. There’s been fun and excitement…”

“And way too much drama.”

“But look what it’s all led to.” Tara’s eyes glistened with excitement. “Charlie went from wanting to fire you to praising how you handled the kids in a crisis situation. You went from gnashing your teeth about Rick Warren to licking your lips—"

Summer chuckled when she realized she'd licked her lips just as Tara said that.

"—and we still have three more weeks of this session, and then another whole month—"

"During which anything can happen," Summer inserted.

Tara smiled and sighed. "Precisely."

"You're letting your imagination run away with you, Tara. It was just a kiss."

Her friend gave a knowing laugh. "That's how it always starts. With 'just a kiss.'"

Summer noted the time. "And that's how this conversation's gotta end. My parents are due here any minute. I'd better finish straightening up my cabin."

Tara gave her a quick hug. "This is so exciting! Keep me informed?"

"Always, girlfriend."

Summer hurried through the dorm, careful not to awaken the napping girls. The conversation with Tara had her giddy. She was so glad the young woman had taken the job as assistant counselor. Of all the friends she'd made at this camp over the years, Tara was turning out to be the one she most wanted to keep in her life.

On the way to her cabin, a quick phone call to Kate assured her that Fairy Princess Parties wasn't going broke without her—in fact, five more parties were booked into August and the first of September. That was a good thing, but time allowed for so many more. The small ad running in the local paper was garnering some attention, though most of the business seemed to be coming purely by word of mouth. Someday, she would be able to pay for an expensive, eye-catching color ad, but until then, she'd have to be contented to do what she could afford and keep customers happy.

Happy. The word seemed to sum up most of what she was feeling today despite the unusual morning.

She closed her eyes and again imagined the kiss with Rick, wondering if it was really *that* good, or if her imagination had embellished it. She replayed it in her mind several times and concluded she'd have to experience another to know with any certainty. Last night's surprise element had added to the excitement. She'd be ready for the next one when it came… tonight, she hoped.

She continued tidying her cabin and thinking about the kiss until car doors slamming brought her back to the present. Through the window, she saw that her mom and dad had arrived. There was a time when they'd made these visits to the camp weekly, but with the decline in her dad's health, the visits had become sporadic.

The happy glow she'd been enjoying dissipated as her stomach twisted into a knot. Even though she'd received praise from Charlie for her handling of the kids yesterday, she still didn't know how he would respond to her parents when they asked how the week had gone. Her dad didn't need any anxiety, and she especially didn't want to be the cause.

Rather than rushing out to greet them, she stayed in her cabin for the rest of quiet time. Charlie would have fifteen minutes alone with them to report what he wanted…good or bad.

She lay across her bed and tried to concentrate on the book she was reading, but her mind kept wandering to Charlie and her parents. What was he telling them? Was her dad getting upset?

When quiet time was over, she hurried to the girls' dorm, expecting to be met by Charlie and her parents, but the trio was nowhere to be seen.

The day's nature hike had been shifted to the late-afternoon activity slot, which turned out to be a blessing in disguise. Not only did it give the campers a different perspective on the animals' activities, but it also shoved her mom and dad's presence into second place. The knowledge they were at the camp still niggled at her, but she didn't have time to brood…much.

On the return hike, the closer she got to camp the more her pace slowed as though her feet were practicing avoidance behavior and overriding her brain's commands. Before long, she found herself at the back of the group.

Rick dropped back to fall into step beside her. "You okay? You seem a little preoccupied."

She nodded. "I'm okay. Just worried about what Charlie's telling Mom and Dad about me."

"I'll bet he's filling their ears with how you saved the day yesterday by keeping the kids occupied during the storm." He trailed a finger down her arm.

It was barely even a touch, but her brain understood the message. He *wanted* to touch her, and suddenly the discussion going on at the camp didn't seem nearly so threatening.

"I watched how you kept them calm," Rick went on. "You would have been a good soldier if you'd been a little bigger," he added, regarding her size. "You're good under pressure."

It was a strange compliment, but she could tell he was sincere. "Thanks," she answered. She smiled, and the way he smiled back unleashed a flurry of butterflies in her stomach. Her temperature rose and she wasn't sure if it was from his smile, his words, his touch…or the sight of her parents standing with Charlie at the point where the path broke out of the trees.

Neil stopped the kids and had them line up single file. They introduced themselves and shook hands with her parents as they walked by. Summer giggled softly at the stunned look of surprise on her parents' faces.

When she and Rick got to them, he stepped behind her.

He's got my back, she thought. And whether it was the marine or the Southern gentleman, she wasn't sure, but the idea relaxed her shoulders either way.

"Nubbin!" Her dad's hug was followed by one from her mom. The greeting and the warmth of the hugs told her she had nothing to worry about.

"Charlie's been telling us what a great job you two have been doing." Her dad's smile was as broad as she'd ever seen it. Knowing that his smile meant he was proud of her made her giddy, but only momentarily. Three more weeks of camp remained. She couldn't get overconfident and let her guard down yet.

Her mom's eyes glistened with what Summer assumed was probably relief. "He says y'all have made a good team."

Dad motioned toward the kids, still in single file as they headed to dinner. "I'm impressed. Really impressed."

"Thank you, sir." Rick shook her dad's hand and nodded. "It's been a good week." His glance shifted to Summer, and he gave her a smile that brought the butterflies to flight in her stomach again. "Actually, it's been a great week."

"Well, I hope we won't upset your schedule too much, but..." A hint of mystery accompanied her mom's smile. "We've arranged for a surprise activity tonight."

Summer didn't know what her parents had planned, but she'd bet her last dime it wouldn't compare with the surprise activity she'd received last night.

"I DON'T WANT TO SQUARE DANCE. I don't know how."

Lucy's whiny complaints had become so habitual, Summer often ignored them—like now.

When her parents announced at dinner they'd hired a square dance caller for the night, she'd wondered if they were both becoming senile at the same time. What were they thinking? Eight- and nine-year-old boys didn't dance with girls. They would all spend the entire evening standing around looking at one another.

"Ms. Agnes said the man would teach us how." It was Amanda who spoke. What a super kid. She had a great attitude about everything. If she ever had a daughter someday, Summer hoped she turned out like Amanda.

Summer looped a bright blue ponytail holder around the base of Lucy's braid. "All done." She gave the child a pat to send her on her way. "Anybody else need help?" She looked around. While all the other girls were busy changing clothes or fixing their hair, M&M sat quietly on her bed, taking it all in.

Summer felt in her pocket for another ponytail holder, and pulled out a pink metallic one. She held it up as enticement. "Want me to fix your hair, M&M?"

The little girl's eyes went wide and she bobbed her head.

Summer stood back and regarded the brown locks, calling upon her one semester of cosmetology training. Not enough length for a braid or a ponytail. Hmm, but maybe... She swept the front and sides up and back into a high ponytail, but left the back down. Fussing a bit brought out some funky, little spikes in the front of the tail, which she sprayed to maintain the hold, while the back fluffed out nicely. The pink holder jazzed up the child's mundane tan T-shirt and brown shorts, and Summer made a mental note to add tie-dying T-shirts to the activity list this week.

"Wow, you look cute!"

Was that Lucy talking? Summer could hardly believe her ears. M&M's face flushed bright pink, which added to her adorable glow, while Summer rushed to give the other child positive reinforcement that might encourage recurrent behavior. "What a nice thing to say, Lucy."

Too late. The corners of Lucy's mouth had already settled

in the downward position. Her upper teeth worried her bottom lip. “Ms. Summer, what if nobody asks me to dance?”

The room grew quiet, and Summer realized every little girl in the room was worried about that very thing. She remembered sitting at dances, waiting for somebody—anybody—to ask for a dance. And she realized this was an empowering moment.

“Well,” she spoke loud enough to be heard all around, “you don’t have to wait for someone to ask you. If you want to dance, there’s no law that says you can’t ask one of the boys to dance with you.”

“But what if he says no?” Though the voice was a tad whiny, Lucy’s question was asked in earnest.

“Then you can ask somebody else, maybe somebody who really looks like he wants to. Or ask me. I’ll dance with you.” Another thought occurred to her. “But while we’re talking about this, let’s listen to what our pretty hearts tell us. Would it hurt your feelings a little if you asked someone to dance and he said no?”

Lucy nodded.

“Yeah, I’d want to punch him.” Greta spoke up from across the room.

“We’re not going to punch anybody,” Summer warned, but pressed on to make her point. “But the boys here are all our friends, right?” She looked around at the nodding heads. “Soooo, if one of the boys asks you to dance—” which she doubted was ever going to happen “—what does your pretty heart tell you to do?”

“Say yes,” M&M answered quietly.

“That’s right. We should accept because we wouldn’t want anybody to hurt our feelings, and we don’t want to hurt anybody else’s feelings. These guys are our buddies. And remember that tomorrow night we vote on who gets this week’s special prize.” She smiled, remembering the lovely little wands her dad brought this afternoon. She looked around. Everybody seemed ready. "Okay, let's go. Since this is a party, we won't line up."

When they exited the bunkhouse, a lively jig wafted from the dining hall, causing a ripple of anxious giggles to pass through the group. Strummed on a banjo, the catchy music had a strong beat that had some of the girls skipping and hopping in rhythm before they'd even taken a few steps.

Through the screens, Summer could see the boys sitting in chairs placed along the wall. The tables had been moved back to create a huge space in the middle of the dining floor.

As if on cue, as soon as the girls stepped inside, the boys rose from their chairs.

The move seemed like something straight out of the nineteenth century. Summer rolled her eyes and gave Rick a resigned shake of her head, which he answered with a smug grin. Trying to impress her parents, was he?

Well, this could be her chance to shine, too.

"Okay, ladies," she said loud enough for her mom and dad to hear. "We're in a public situation," she continued, reminding them of the talk Tara had given. The girls looked at her and nodded, giggling softly. They found their way to chairs and sat down as demurely as could be expected of eight- and nine-year-olds.

The caller, an elderly man dressed in Western attire that included cowboy boots and a bolo tie, spoke into his microphone. "All right, you young whippersnappers," he addressed the boys. "The ladies are here, so it's time to kick up our heels. Go grab yourselves a partner and form two groups."

A trace of anxiety tightened Summer's chest, and she recognized it reflected on the tense faces of the girls. Who would be asked? Who would have to do her own asking? She wanted them to know it was okay either way. "Remember to listen to your pretty hearts," she said in her fairy princess voice. "And it's okay for you to ask, too."

Some of the girls nodded. But before any of them could make a move, the boys, who'd all been looking at Rick, took a step forward in unison. Rick gave the order. "It's time, men."

Looking like soldiers going into their first battle, the troops marched across the open space. Although they had to shift positions as they got closer, each boy went directly to a specific girl. When they got there, they bowed, asked the girls to dance and held out their hands to escort their partners to the floor.

Summer watched, astonished and speechless. While one part of her completely rebelled at the forced nature of the act, it had been executed flawlessly, and the smiles on the girls' faces were genuine with relief. The whole spectacle, obviously choreographed and rehearsed, could only have been the brainchild of one person.

Rick.

She turned to find him standing in front of her, blue-green eyes flashing in silent humor and something else that made her insides twirl in a different kind of rebellion. His wide smile showed white teeth that glowed against his tanned face, and at that moment, she decided he might be the most handsome man she'd ever laid eyes on…and he was asking her to dance.

He bowed elegantly. "Ms. Summer," he drawled, "might I have the pleasure of this dance?"

When he held out his hand, her heart took on the pounding rhythm of the music. They were Rhett Butler and Scarlett O'Hara in the flesh. "Well, fiddle-dee-dee, Mr. Warren." She glanced coyly away and saw her mom and dad, Tara and Neil and Charlie and Ginny all making their way to the dance floor. "I thought you'd never ask."

His large, warm hand enveloped hers, and her heart lost

its steady rhythm, plunging into its own wild dance, taking her along for the ride like a loose roller coaster careening out of control.

They joined one of the groups, and the caller directed them to form two lines facing each other, men in one line, ladies in the other. Reluctantly, she let go of Rick's hand to take her place, but his smoldering gaze held her across the small distance that separated them.

"Before we break into squares, we want to get everybody warmed up," the caller explained. "We're gonna start with the Virginia Reel."

Summer decided he couldn't have started with a more appropriate dance; her head was already reeling.

For the next two hours, she and Rick danced every dance. They held hands, held waists, locked arms, locked eyes, smiled, laughed and had the time of their lives.

Sometime during the first few do-si-dos, she lost herself. She was no longer Summer Delaney…or even the fairy princess.

She was Cinderella. And she was having a ball.

RICK WONDERED IF THERE WAS more to the fairy princess thing than met the eye. Magic? Maybe. He certainly felt like he was under some kind of spell.

The square dance had been fun, although being so near Summer and not being able to kiss her again had been torture. Even now, he could smell her faint perfume where she'd brushed so often against his shirt and just the scent was conjuring images in his mind that had nothing to do with dancing—unless it was the kind that happened between the sheets.

He glanced out the window again. Yeah, Agnes and Herschel were still visiting at her cabin.

His meeting with them while everyone was getting ready

for the dance had gone well. The notes he'd taken so far pleased them, but he promised to get measurements and make scaled sketches of all the buildings. Agnes especially liked his mom's idea of painting and adding flowers. Herschel wasn't as enthused, seeing it as an unnecessary expense, even when Rick volunteered his time. But they both seemed genuinely interested in his mom's opinion that they could make a profit if they could catch the real-estate market at the right time.

Herschel was uneasy about what Summer's reaction would be to such news, but Rick assured him, based on conversations he'd had with her, Summer's top priority was their well-being. Her dad wasn't so sure. He continued to insist they needed to stay mum on the selling option until they'd made a decision. And Rick continued to remind himself that what they did with their property was their business, and he certainly didn't want to get involved with their family matters. If he could only give them a glimpse of the woman, Summer, whom he was getting to know.

"Summer's got a good head on her shoulders," he assured them.

"Sometimes," Agnes answered.

"And sometimes, you can't tell her anything. You have to just stand back and let her flounder in her own mire."

Herschel's face had reddened when he made that remark, and Rick had chosen to let the conversation die there.

Now, he jerked the T-shirt over his head in frustration, taking one last whiff before tossing it into his duffel of dirty laundry. He'd hoped for some one-on-one time with the wild child tonight. Had counted on it all day long.

Although another kiss—or two or three—admittedly had been part of the Summer scenarios playing on a continuous loop in his mind, mostly he wanted to talk, wanted to get to know this woman who was capturing his…thoughts.

He jumped into the shower and scrubbed away the last of the pleasant scent, and then doused himself with a hard spray of icy water for good measure.

As he turned off the water, the sound he'd been waiting for echoed in his ears—car tires crunching down the gravel road. The Delaneys were leaving.

He scrambled to get dressed, grabbed the other things he'd laid out and made a beeline for Summer's cabin, undeterred even though he watched her lights blink out when he was a few yards from her door.

He leaped up on the porch and knocked quietly, waiting breathlessly until he heard her soft approach on the other side.

The door swung open, bringing a fresh breeze of the Summer scent he'd worked so hard to rid himself of just moments ago. He breathed it in, and felt the magic bringing his body to life again.

"Rick." Her tone sounded surprised…and maybe a little relieved. "I was afraid you weren't coming tonight." The teasing lilt of her voice emphasized the open look of pleasure glinting from her eyes in the moonlight.

He let out the breath he'd been holding and held up the towel in his hand. "Want to go for a moonlight swim?"

CHAPTER TEN

SUMMER HURRIED TO CHANGE INTO her swimsuit and work her hair into a braid. She wasn't sure if she was hurrying because of excitement, nerves or fear Rick would change his mind. After all, if she was Cinderella, this magic would end in an hour and thirty-seven minutes.

Rick stood up as she came back into the front room. "Ready?"

Her body's response confirmed she was indeed ready—for much more than a swim in the moonlight.

"Not quite." She held his gaze as she made a pass around the couch and came to stand in front of him. "If you don't kiss me again pretty soon, I think I might scream."

Desire was evident in Rick's eyes as he leaned close. "Well, we wouldn't want to wake the kids." He leaned closer.

In an English lit class, she once heard that the most blissful moments in life occurred the split second before being touched by someone we care for. If all those moments were totaled, they would only add up to approximately seven minutes out of an entire lifetime. The people depicted in Keats's "Ode on a Grecian Urn" were fortunate to have been captured in that moment forever.

She closed her eyes in anticipation, wishing this moment, with the warmth of Rick's breath on her lips and the sound of it in her ears and her heart threatening to gallop away, could be captured forever.

His mouth brushed against hers in just a whisper of a

touch that caused her breath to stutter in her chest. She inched closer as his fingertips feathered up her arms, and the pressure of his lips increased ever so slightly. Her arms slid around his waist as his hands moved up to cup the sides of her face. The strength in the muscles she could feel beneath her palms was such a contrast to his soft and tender caress, an urgent need to respond to both tugged and coiled inside her. He captured her whimper with a delicate sweep of his tongue before he broke away.

When she opened her eyes, he was still holding her face close to his. The heat in his gaze zinged through her, down to her toes. "Now, you have to promise not to scream before I can let you go."

Faced with such a compelling decision, her brain whirred, trying to decide on the best course of action. Finally, she smiled. "Then I think I *want* to scream, but I'm too weak."

He laughed and gave her another quick kiss before he loosened his grip.

They were leaving her cabin when Kenny came strolling along the path from the dining hall on his nightly rounds.

"We're going for a swim, Kenny." Rick held up the towel as apparent proof of their intentions.

A sarcastic chuckle pierced the air as Kenny passed them. "Call it whatever you want. You're on your own time."

Rick's hand reached for hers as they wandered down the path to the beach, and she relinquished it gladly. This entire night had been a reminder of how romantic holding hands could be.

"So, you've been practicing some fairy princess magic on the sly, haven't you?" She punched a playful elbow to his ribs.

"Me?" The trees along the path obscured the light enough that she couldn't see his eyes.

"How else can you explain ten eight- and nine-year-old boys asking ten girls to dance and not a complainer in the bunch?" For hours, she'd been wondering how he'd accomplished such a feat. Now another possibility came to her. "Or did you threaten them with some especially heinous KP duty?"

He waved his hand nonchalantly. "Oh, *that?* That didn't take a threat or magic. That took good old-fashioned bribery." He grinned, and she could see the line of his white teeth break across his shadowed face. "Did I mention that Charlie's rounding up some hand-crank freezers for homemade ice cream tomorrow night?"

"Food! I should have known." When they laughed together, he squeezed her hand, and the butterflies materialized in her stomach again and took flight.

For several nights, the moon had been approaching full. As they broke through the stand of trees and onto the beach, the sight stopped them in their tracks.

A full moon floated in a cloudless sky above them. Its reflection cut a swath across the cove directly in front of them.

Without hesitation, they ran hand in hand, plunging headlong into the moon glade.

RICK WAS IMPRESSED WITH THE way Summer kept up to him. He was a stronger swimmer and didn't give it his all, but she didn't lag too far behind.

Kentucky Lake's temperature had reached bathwater stage, perfect for night swims. They swam across the cove and back.

"Want to go again?" he asked.

"No way. Gotta rest." Hard breathing cut the ends of her words. He tried not to focus on the way the sound excited him or how the lake surrounding him warmed even more because of it.

He reached shallow water first and waded over to wait for her, offering his hand to help her up. With one arm, he lifted her to a standing position, then kept it around her for support—and because it felt so damn good to have it there. He could feel her muscles quivering with fatigue as they stumbled to the towels they'd dropped. She plopped down on the towel he'd spread out while he fetched a couple of the life jackets to use as pillows.

When he stretched out beside her, she rolled over on her stomach and tucked her hands under the life preserver, turning her face toward him. She closed her eyes dreamily. "If I weren't so excited, I think I could sleep right here."

"Why are you excited?" He needed to hear her say it.

"Tonight with the dancing. Being here in the moonlight." She paused and opened her eyes. "You."

Had a word ever sounded so sexy before? Breathy and hot and… His wet swimsuit molded to him, making an embarrassing spectacle of the word's effect. He started to roll onto his stomach, but Summer's knuckles brushed his arm. He remained on his side, enjoying her touch and what it was doing to him.

Her gaze slid down him boldly as her finger drew a light pattern on his bicep. "You really are quite a hunk, you know that?"

The flush her words caused didn't stop at his face. His entire body suffused with warmth. "And you're very beautiful…and very direct."

She grinned. "You're very diplomatic, too…which is a genteel way of saying 'a tight ass.'"

The unexpected twist in the conversation jarred a chuckle loose from Rick. He relaxed and shook his head. "Gotta love Southern women and their gentility."

"Yeah, we learn early that we can get by with most any comment if we add a 'bless your heart.'" She paused, and a gleam lit her eyes. "You can be a real pain in the ass, bless your heart."

Rick didn't try to contain his laughter. Summer had such a cute way about her. "You are a mischievous little imp."

Their smiles collided and Rick noticed the way the moonlight glinted from the braid that curved off her back and curled under her arm. He couldn't resist touching it. Catching the end, he gave it a soft tug. She responded, rising up on an elbow and leaning closer. He wound the braid around his hand, reeling her in like a mermaid out of the depths until their lips locked in a kiss that was anything but genteel.

Their tongues entwined and he rolled her onto her back, sliding an arm under her neck and the other around her tiny waist. She shifted against him and the kiss deepened, lasting until they were panting so hard they had to come up for air.

Her hand brushed his cheek. "We have a lot of getting to know each other to catch up on."

He nodded. "I agree. Getting to know more about Summer Delaney is high on my list. Especially that wild-child part I keep hearing about." He grinned and was rewarded with a poke in his ribs.

Her mouth pursed, and then her bottom lip dropped into a sensuous pout that Rick couldn't pull his eyes away from. She sighed. "But we'll have to get back in the water."

The woman was a master of the unexpected. "Why?"

"Because talking is going to be the farthest thing from my mind if we stay here."

Rick protested her logic. "Mine, too, but we can't talk if we're swimming."

She pushed out of his arms, and he groaned at the loss. "But we can talk if we float." Grabbing her life jacket, she rose to her feet and held her hand for him. "C'mon. I've got plenty to tell you. And maybe the water will cool you off." She cocked her head with a look of feigned sympathy. "Bless your heart."

"SEVEN." SUMMER COUNTED the flash that emanated from the lightning bug's tail as it moseyed its way across her bedroom ceiling. She'd taken to counting them instead of sheep as a means of calming her mind enough to fall asleep. So far it hadn't helped.

Every time she closed her eyes, Rick Warren filled her brain. She could still feel the scorching heat of his goodnight kiss, although almost an hour had passed since he'd walked her back to her cabin. The vibrant sound of his laughter still danced in her ears, and the breath from his whispers still crept down her spine. Every part of her was filled with him, it seemed—every part except the part that *needed* to be filled with him.

The lightning bug flashed. "Eight." She sighed and punched her pillow to fluff it up a bit from where she'd been wallowing.

She shouldn't even be thinking about sleeping with Rick. They'd just scratched the surface of getting to know each other. A few kisses—even extremely hot kisses—a night of dancing, two hours of talking. None of that constituted a romp in the sack anymore.

A couple of years ago, she wouldn't have thought twice. But she was beyond that now, and she marveled a bit at her growth in character. The aching need at her core said it sucked, but the bubble of pride in her chest reminded her that the first two letters in idiot were *id.*

"We're within view of twenty kids, my godparents and a night watchman," she confided to the lightning bug, who flashed his tail in response. "Nine," she counted, which also reminded her of the number of times she and Rick had kissed. "And he is my boss, technically." That thought might sting more tomorrow, but tonight his kisses had been a balm that soothed that particular pain.

He'd listened to the story of her five colleges and eight majors with impeccable diplomacy, barely even cracking a smile as she'd confessed to her worthless degree in philosophy.

But getting him to talk about his years as a marine was like pulling teeth. That haunted look when she asked about his tattoo? She shuddered again thinking about it. His best friend's dog tags. What kind of person carried around a constant reminder like that?

Of course, he'd been just as reticent to say much about his ex-girlfriend. He wasn't one who would kiss and tell. But, wow! Could he kiss!

Rick was an enigma. "Ten." A deliciously, intriguing enigma. The quintessential Southern gentleman. The heroic marine. The oh-so-politically-correct diplomat. So many layers of shellac—such a polished exterior.

She'd seen the flame in his eyes, however. Experienced the heat in his kiss. Felt the pounding beat of his heart when he held her close. She recognized the rhythm…the same wild beat her heart danced to.

If they ever slept together, which she shouldn't even be thinking about, but since she was, she might as well let her brain complete the thought… "Eleven, or was that twelve?" She gave up on the lightning bug and closed her eyes.

If Rick ever ended up in her bed, she would break his wild side out of his shell to come play with hers, and they would dance to the pounding rhythm of their hearts.

Sort of like they'd square danced tonight except that this kind of dancing would be far, far from square. And it would happen so naturally, Rick wouldn't know his guard was down until it was too late…bless his heart.

"ONE TWENTY-THREE, one twenty-four, one twenty-five." Rick eased his weight off his arms, enjoying the feel of the cool wood floor against his stomach. The push-ups exhausted his body, but still his mind wouldn't let go.

Kissing Summer was a mistake.

After dropping her off at her place, he'd come straight to his cabin and taken a cold shower. That had helped ease his physical discomfort some, but as soon as he'd lain on his bed, she was there with him in his imagination.

He'd gone for a two-mile run, which required a second cold shower. Hell, he'd never been so clean. After an hour or so of reading, he realized he was merely scanning words and had no idea what had occurred in those chapters.

A hundred and twenty-five push-ups and all he could think about was how it would feel to be performing a different kind of push-up with Summer beneath him.

He rolled over and sat up. Hmm. Sit-ups, maybe? He shook his head, disgusted with his lack of self-control, and finally surrendered to the call of his bed.

Three weeks. He could do this. He'd gone without sex for two years when he was on tours of duty. He could certainly survive three weeks. And if this budding relationship with Summer continued to thrive, it would be good for them to wait. It would be a character-building exercise.

He wouldn't entertain the possibility of making love to Summer here at camp. It wouldn't be prudent and certainly wouldn't be proper. He needed to remain focused on the kids. *They* were the reason he was here…*they* were the reason for this tour of duty.

But how was he going to keep his upper brain focused on the kids when his lower brain stayed focused on Summer? The feel of her body pressed against him had imprinted on *both* of his brains, it seemed.

Would it be better to go ahead and make love to her? Maybe that would get it out of his system for a little while.

Hell, who was he kidding? If just kissing her was doing this to him, what would sleeping with her do? Her kisses were so hot. Holding her was like pulling the pin on a live grenade. Only he was the one who was about to explode.

A lightning bug landed on his ceiling, flashing its tail to call a mate…or maybe prey.

Poor bastard. I know exactly how you feel. “Two,” he counted aloud as the soft green light blinked again.

The obvious solution to this dilemma was to stop kissing Summer and avoid being alone with her.

So do I want to avoid being alone with her?

“Nope.”

Then am I going to keep kissing her, knowing the state it's going to put me in?

“Absolutely…every chance I get.”

The lightning bug's beacon glowed.

“Three. So I have your approval, then?”

It flashed again in affirmation.

“Four.” Rick smiled. “That's good to know.”

CHAPTER ELEVEN

"BY USING APPLESAUCE INSTEAD of vegetable oil, we still have moist and tender zucchini bread but without all the icky fats." Summer cut the slices into fourths and offered each of the girls a piece to taste. "Tell me what you think."

She watched closely for the reactions. Lucy scrunched her nose up, but eventually nibbled a bite. M&M gobbled hers down like she did everything. Greta took a bite and contemplated her answer.

It was interesting how well Summer had gotten to know these kids. She knew exactly what the reactions were going to be before they indicated them. They'd become predictable, although she still couldn't figure out who the winner of tonight's wand was going to be.

Shannon had the twins' backing, but Amanda had a following of her own. Summer was anxious to see who carried the most clout because determining who held the most respect or perhaps power would tell her a lot about thc valucs and personality of the group as a whole. She would gain insights on where to go from here in their fairy princess training.

"Do you like it?" Tara asked.

Most nodded, a couple gave thumbs-ups, some remained more guarded, but none openly objected.

Summer took that to mean it was a hit. "I'll take some out to the boys. If they like it, too, Ms. Ginny said she'll use it to make a special French toast for breakfast tomorrow."

"Who's ready for a swim?" Tara asked, and was met by

an exuberant cheer. "Let's go get changed, then." She herded the girls out of the dining hall just as Rick finished up the tae kwon do with the boys.

Summer made quick work of cutting more zucchini bread and getting it on the tray. Rick was almost to his cabin by the time she got outside, but she called to Neil, "I want the boys to try this, then I'll send them on in."

Neil nodded and went ahead into the dorm. The boys gathered around as Summer offered the pieces. "Zucchini bread. What do you think?"

The pieces disappeared quickly until Howie spoke up. "Who made this?"

"The girls," Summer answered.

"Ewww." Howie made a retching sound and pulled his hand away from the piece he was about to pick up. "Girls touched it means it's got cooties."

"Oh, Howie, don't be silly." Summer rolled her eyes. "You touched a girl when you danced last night."

Howie stuck out his tongue and exaggerated a shiver. "And I had to take a shower as soon as I got back to the bunkhouse to wash all the cooties off."

"That's not very nice, Howie." Summer didn't want to make too big a deal of this, but she also didn't want him to think this behavior was okay.

"I'll take his piece if he ain't gonna eat it," Austin volunteered.

"Isn't going to eat it," Summer corrected.

Howie leaned toward Jimbo, making his voice high and girlish. "Isn't going to eat it," he mocked.

"Howie." Summer used a warning tone.

The boy whispered something too low for her to hear it.

"What was that?" she asked.

Howie pointed at her and cackled. "Ms. Summer used the *W-H-A-T* word. That's the nerd word."

The boys fell into a fit of laughter.

"Oo-rah!" Howie yelled, and pumped his fist, which made the boys laugh louder.

"Howie, stop with the disrespect." Summer's face heated. She was about to demand an apology when Neil let loose with a whistle and the boys scattered in his direction.

She watched them leave, her mind whirring. The other day Tara had mentioned Howie's escalating disrespect, and that it always seemed to happen when the men weren't around.

Well, the boy's father had probably given him permission to act this way, but it was time he learned some new lessons. He needed fairy princess training in the worst way.

She would bring it up at tonight's staff meeting, and she'd be watching very closely to Rick's reaction. That would be the perfect way of judging whether he really *got* her, or if he just *wanted* her.

"SHE SOUNDS BRAND-NEW, Charlie." Summer gave a thumbs-up to the steady purr of the old bus's motor.

Charlie nodded. "Told ya. Ginny's nephew might not be the sharpest tack in the box, but he's a top-notch mechanic. We'll get her painted before next year. He says he can do that, too."

When her parents told her they'd purchased an old school bus for the camp, Summer thought it was a frivolous expense. But now she had to admit, it was a great idea. The area around Kentucky Lake was teeming with educational experiences for the kids, and the field trips they'd planned would be nice breaks from the same old surroundings.

Rick had arranged this first one. Some friends of his who lived not too far away—the same people Sheriff Blaine had referred to yesterday morning—owned a piece of land that contained a cave inhabited by some rare kind of bat. The

Brennans agreed to host the camp kids for the evening on a bat-sighting adventure.

Summer swung the door open as the boys approached the bus.

Neil got on first. "Huhh!" He grabbed his chest in feigned terror when he saw Summer at the wheel.

"Don't." She gave him a no-nonsense look. The male counselors needed to be careful of the messages they were sending, too.

Carlos and Jimbo got on after Neil, and then Howie came up the steps. "Ick! A girl bus driver?"

"Girls can do anything boys can, Howie, and I'm not a girl. I'm a woman." Summer flipped her thumb over her shoulder. "You're holding up the line. Keep moving. All the way to the back."

The rest of the boys found seats quickly. Rick was the last one to get on.

His shocked look wasn't faked. His eyes went big, and jumped from Summer to Charlie and back. "You're driving us?" His tone echoed disbelief.

"Oh, for heaven's sake." Summer raised an indignant eyebrow and nodded. "Y'all could all use some serious fairy princess training."

"Here, Rick." Charlie vacated the seat behind the driver and moved across the aisle to sit with Ginny. "You sit there, so you can give Summer directions."

Rick leaned forward, keeping his voice low. "You really know how to drive one of these?"

Summer rolled her eyes and slipped the gearshift to Reverse. "I drove an old school bus for a tour company on Cape Cod for two summers. This one's a Cadillac compared to those."

As the girls started a loud rendition of the Sunny Daze camp song, she made eye contact with Rick in the rearview mirror and watched his mouth rise at one end. He leaned closer. "Something you left out last night?"

"Oh, I left out a lot last night." She backed up enough to get out of the parking space, shifted into First and eased the bus down the drive. "Now, which way do I turn?"

The girls continued to sing, but the boys didn't join in. She couldn't lay all the blame on the men. It was probably as much her fault as it was theirs since she and Rick had gotten off to such a bad start. But this group needed more cohesion. The boy-versus-girl mentality had gone too far.

Rick's friends' house was only a few miles away, and the trip took much less time than Summer had expected. Before she knew it, Rick directed her up a gravel lane that wound through a stand of ancient trees and eventually opened in front of a beautiful old farmhouse.

When the bus appeared, a man and woman stood and waved from the shady porch. The man lunged to grab up a little boy who was about to make a dash toward the bus. The little boy wiggled in protest, but a chocolate Lab came running from behind the house, wagging her tail and barking an enthusiastic greeting.

"That's Chesney," Rick told the excited kids. "She'll stay out of the way, Summer. Just pull the bus on around the drive."

"Amanda's allergic to dogs," Summer reminded him.

"So is Jimbo. I called Chance yesterday and told him. He's putting Ches in the garage."

Even as Rick spoke, Summer could see the dark-haired man pulling the reluctant dog by the collar toward a large garage.

She brought the bus to a stop, and Rick led the kids off in single file. Summer brought up the rear. By the time she got out, the man named Chance had successfully sequestered the dog and was headed toward the group. The little boy, who looked to be about three, wiggled around in his father's arms and held his own arms out toward Rick. "Rick! I want Rick!" he cried. When his father put him down, he headed straight for Rick's waiting arms.

Rick scooped him up and gave him a hug that was so sweet to watch a lump of emotion clogged Summer's throat. This was a side of him she hadn't seen. Gone was the soldier, replaced by a man capable of showing affection in front of a large crowd without any qualms.

"Everybody, this is Hank," Rick said. The little boy gave the group a wave.

The man had made it to Rick's side by then, and they shook hands warmly. "And this is Hank's dad, Chance Brennan. You can call him Mr. Chance."

By Summer's standards, Chance Brennan was handsome—devastatingly so. Dark hair. Black eyes. About the same height as Rick, but a bit leaner. A physique to match Rick's…almost. Looking at them standing side by side was like being at a fantasy smorgasbord. Something for everybody.

Chance welcomed the group and told the kids they could mill around for a few minutes until his wife returned. "Our nine-month-old twin girls just went down for a nap. Kyndal's checking on them," he explained.

Rick made individual introductions between Chance and the adults in the group while the kids played a game of freeze tag.

Was it Summer's imagination that a flash of recognition lit Chance's eyes when Rick introduced her? "I'm glad to meet you, Summer." Chance's low voice was warm and mellow like his handshake, and Summer liked him immediately. "Your parents own the camp, right?"

"That's right." What else had Rick told him about her? "Thank you so much for having us."

"It's our pleasure." His glance shifted above her head. "There's Kyndal."

Kyndal Brennan's long black hair was pulled back into a ponytail that swung from side to side as she made her way quickly to Rick's side, welcoming him with a bear hug around his waist. He shifted Hank to one side and squeezed Kyndal about the shoulders with his free arm, planting a kiss on the top of her head.

The ease with which Rick showed affection to these people was certainly an eye-opener. Summer had wondered if his gentle side only came out when he was pursuing a female, but obviously he wasn't nearly the hard-ass she had him pegged as. He smiled and her breath, which she hadn't realized she'd been holding, left her in a rush.

Once again, Rick made the introductions and when he got to Summer, Kyndal's head tilted momentarily in question. "You're the fairy princess?"

"That's me." So Rick *had* told them some things about her. Was it about the Summer he couldn't stand or the one he'd grown to like?

"I think our girls—" Kyndal pointed to the baby monitor attached to her belt "—are going to love you in a few years." She flashed Summer a genuine smile that made Summer feel like they'd known each other a long time…and gave her the answer to how she'd been portrayed to them by Rick.

"I hope so," Summer answered.

Just then, a heavy arm slid across her shoulders and Rick spoke low in her ear. "Let's get the kids rounded up, okay? I'd like to get started."

Summer nodded and his arm dropped away. But when she looked back at Kyndal, the young woman's face broke into a wide, knowing grin, and she gave Summer a wink.

Summer winked back, feeling like they'd shared some secret. She liked this woman. She believed they could become good friends if given the opportunity.

After a few calls and whistles, they had the kids seated in a semicircle on the grass in the Brennans' backyard. A concrete structure jutted out of the ground with a door built on a slant into it.

The campers had spent so much time Friday night in the storm shelter at the camp, showing them another one seemed silly. "Another storm cellar?" she whispered to Rick, wrinkling her nose.

"Trust me," he whispered back.

"Does anybody know what this is?" Chance asked, pointing to the structure. His dark eyes scanned the crowd and a grin illuminated his face when everyone's hand went up.

Howie waved his hand frantically and was rewarded when Chance pointed to him. "It's a storm shelter. We were in one of those during the storm the other night." The boy sat back with a look of satisfaction on his face before blurting, "My dad's going to build us one of those."

"We need to talk about Howie," she whispered, and Rick's eyebrow shot up in question. She shook her head. "Not now."

"You're right. It is a storm shelter," Chance was saying, and the boy's face beamed with smug satisfaction. "But this isn't an average storm shelter. This door also leads into an underground cave."

A collective gasp of surprise moved through the group.

"Have any of you ever been in a cave?" Chance asked, and three hands went up, including Howie's, which was once again waving.

Before Chance could call on him, Howie was already talking. "My dad says he's gonna take me to some cave that's big and famous and has snowballs in it!"

"He's talking about Mammoth Cave. It's only a couple of hours from here," Chance explained. "It doesn't really have snowballs, but there is a huge room called the Snowball Dining Room that's covered in white quartz crystals, so it looks like snowballs are stuck to the walls and ceiling."

Howie's hand shot up again, but Neil leaned down and said something to him and the boy dropped his hand, disappointment etched on his face.

The look weighed on Summer's heart.

"Well, caves can be dangerous." Chance's face grew serious. "My wife and I got lost in this cave a few years ago. We entered the cave about a quarter mile from here, not planning on going very deeply into it. But a piece of the floor broke, and Kyndal and I fell into a subterranean passage. Do you know what that means?"

"A path that's underground," M&M said.

"That's right." Chance nodded. "And Kyndal broke her ankle in the fall."

Hank squirmed in his mother's arms and she put the child down. He ran to Rick, who picked him up. "We have to be quiet while Daddy's talking, bud," Rick whispered, and the child nodded.

Summer smiled to herself, noticing how her once-frosty attitude toward him had melted into a warm puddle that seemed to linger in her belly now.

"Beneath where we're standing is a little room that was built a long, long time ago by the Native Americans who lived in this area."

"My dad says we're part Indian," Howie said.

Chance smiled patiently. "A lot of people around here are, and that makes the little room very special. Mr. Rick led the rescue team that found us and saved our lives."

Another gasp of surprise moved through the group and all eyes turned to look at Rick. He shifted uncomfortably. A spontaneous round of applause caused his face to blush redder than Summer thought possible. This was the same rescue Sheriff Blaine mentioned yesterday—and Rick had been embarrassed then, too.

When the applause quieted down, Chance finished his story. "Kyndal and I want to keep this ancient room safe, so we don't allow many people to see it. But we're going to take you all down a few at a time to look at it." An excited titter passed through the campers.

"You won't be allowed to go into the room," Kyndal added. "But you can stick your head in the opening, and look around. We've put some lanterns in there so you can see."

"Okay, y'all, let's line up," Rick said, and the kids scrambled into two lines. Summer watched with pride as the girls lined up alphabetically, just as quickly as the boys did.

Chance opened the door, which revealed a set of concrete steps descending into the subterranean cavern. He motioned to Neil and Tara, and the three of them went down first, while Summer and Rick stayed near the back of the lines.

Kyndal came over to them. "Hank, did you show Rick the surprise you found this afternoon?"

"No, Mommy. I go get it!" The three-year-old zoomed off on his errand.

Summer squeezed Rick's hand. "That was some story."

He gave a modest shrug and pointed to his friend. "Kyndal's a photographer. She captured the entire event with her camera, and then she and Chance wrote a book about it. It's fascinating."

"And available at all the local bookstores." Kyndal laughed. "I've become an expert at shameless self-promotion."

Summer vaguely remembered hearing about the story around town a few years back. "I'll have to get a copy. I'd love to read it."

"I'll give you a copy," Rick offered. "I've got five signed by the authors."

Hank came running up, proudly gripping a box turtle,

and Rick sat down on the lawn to hear the little boy's story of its capture. A squawk from the monitor on Kyndal's hip sent her scurrying into the house.

Summer moved around the group of campers, listening to the exuberant chatter from the kids as they emerged from the dark hole in the ground. The ancient room was a hit. The anticipation of seeing it herself made her heart beat a bit faster.

When everyone had a turn, she and Rick were the only ones left.

Rick had Hank in his arms again as they descended into the dimly lit cavern where Chance waited. With each step, the scent of damp earth became more pronounced, and the temperature dipped a few degrees. Summer moved slowly, allowing her eyes to adjust from the twilight outside to the near-dark inside.

As they got to the bottom of the steps, the child started to wail. "No, Daddy. I don't want to. I want to pway wif de kids. Pwease, Daddy?"

Chance took his son into his arms and raised an eyebrow toward Rick. "I'll take Hank back up. Think you two can find your way around by yourselves?"

Rick laughed and nodded. "I know my way around this place pretty well."

Chance clapped him on the shoulder with a broad grin. "Take your time, and go on in the room. We've got a half hour still before it's time for the bats."

As Chance ascended the steps, Rick reached out to Summer and pulled her to him. His mouth pressed hers, kissing her thoroughly and leaving her breathless.

While she brought her respiration under control, he pointed to a small opening in the side wall of the cave that glowed from the lantern light within. "There are paintings on the walls and animal pelts cover the floors. We suspect the Native Americans used it for fertility rites."

Summer was shocked by his words. "A room for making love?"

He nodded and the thought sent her heart into overdrive. She looked at him and saw her own reaction reflected in his eyes.

"Um..." Rick cleared his throat. "Maybe I'll just mosey on back upstairs. You take as long as you want."

She nodded. "Good idea." Her pulse didn't return to normal until he was completely out of sight.

RICK SAW JUPITER emerging as the first object in the night sky. "Won't be long now," he told the group.

"They're not as predictable as Old Faithful," Chance said. "But they have to eat, and they do that as soon as it gets dark." He took the few spare minutes to tell the kids about the vandalism the cave had received.

It was a good lesson for the kids to hear. It might keep them from defacing property in the disgraceful way Chance and Kyndal's cave had suffered a few years back when it was a prime party place for local teens bent on drinking and mischief.

Rick watched Summer's face, intent on Chance's words. Her eyes flashed with anger as Chance relayed the story of the names scrawled in spray paint on the walls just inside the entrance.

Her face was so expressive. He swallowed hard, remembering the heat that registered in her eyes outside the ancient room. He would have given his right arm to have had a couple of hours to remove her clothing one item at a time and slowly explore each area as it was exposed.

An odd rumbling sound—thunder forced through a giant sieve until it shattered—filled the air, jerking his thoughts out of their delightful reverie.

"Here they come," Chance called, and at that moment

the entrance to the cave blackened with a mass that moved as one entity across the open space, then broke into what seemed like millions of pieces as they reached the tree line and scattered.

Though he'd seen it many times, the sight of the bats never ceased to fill Rick with a sense of awe, which made him appreciate Summer's reaction even more. She squeezed his hand, and her breast brushed the back of his arm as she bounced up and down with excitement.

The turbulent breeze from the beating of the bats' wings seemed to suck the air from everyone's lungs, but it returned just as quickly. Shouts and squeals reverberated from the group, with Summer's louder than everyone else's.

She clutched her chest like her heart might escape and swiped at tears streaming freely from her eyes.

Shannon put an arm around her waist. "Why are you crying, Ms. Summer?"

Summer laughed, pulling the hem of her T-shirt up to wipe her nose and eyes. "It's so…so magnificent. It's even better than a rock concert!"

A woman who found bats magnificent? More enjoyable than a rock concert? Summer's words drove through the spot her kisses had burned in his thickened hide. It nicked at his heart, this vulnerability. He was falling for this woman. Falling hard and fast.

Hell-pee-roo! His breath froze in his lungs. *A marine and a fairy princess. What am I getting myself into?*

CHAPTER TWELVE

"I'VE LECTURED HIM SEVERAL times about safety. He's promised not to go anywhere dangerous," Rick said. He and Neil were once again on their nightly search for Howie. The kid was a master at hide-and-seek. So good, in fact, Rick made it a point to search for him, trying to learn his strategy. It was kind of fun—a real challenge. Neil found it beyond annoying and showed no remorse about voicing that opinion.

"Well, if you ask me, the kid's as loopy as my mom's chenille robe." An irritated grunt pushed through Neil's bared teeth. "Just call him in free again."

Rick shook his head. "Not yet. This is the thing he does really well that sets him apart from the others. His time to shine. It won't hurt to give him a few more minutes."

"Very touchy-feely of you." Neil shot him a quizzical glance. "You going soft on us, Mr. Rick?"

"Nope." The near-constant erection caused from being around Summer was a good indicator he was being honest with his answer, but he couldn't share that bit of information. "The kid's begging for male attention, and this strikes me as an innocuous means of getting it. You have to agree that, except for all the wild stories, he's pretty well-behaved."

Neil scratched his head. "He's got one hell of an imagination, all right."

Rick couldn't hold back the chuckle. "Which makes him think of hiding places that wouldn't enter the other kids' minds."

"Um, speaking of imagination." Neil lifted the lid on a trash can and peered inside. "Is mine working overtime, or have you and Summer managed to put your differences behind you?"

The question wasn't much of a surprise. The staff surely noticed the warming climate surrounding him and Summer, and he'd suspected there might already be some talk. "We're making a concerted effort to get along." He shrugged nonchalantly.

"Get along or get it on?"

"We don't want to be a distraction." Rick scanned the roof of the dining hall. Would Howie consider a rooftop dangerous? Limbs from overhanging trees would give access, and Howie certainly had proven his climbing agility. Hell, the kid was part monkey. Thankfully, nothing on the roof looked suspicious. Rick dropped his gaze to the ground. "But as long as you brought up the subject." He'd been curious and now seemed a good time to ask. "Did I notice some interest in Tara on your part?"

Neil gave a lopsided grin. "Strictly one-sided. She evidently has eyes for only one guy, and it's not me. They've been together for, like, eight years."

"Too bad."

"Yeah, her loss." Neil punctuated his remark by pushing his glasses farther back on his nose.

Rick spotted fresh footprints in the mud left behind from Friday's deluge. They led behind the building. Putting a finger to his lips, he jerked his head in that direction.

Drawing on the infinite hours they'd both pretended to be ninjas during childhood, the two men stealthily followed the footprints to the door of the storm cellar. On the pantomimed count of three, Rick jerked the door open as Neil did his best imitation of a lion's roar.

Howie's startled shriek evaporated into a hoot of relieved

laughter. "You found me! But I hid great, didn't I? Am I the last one again?"

Neil tousled the kid's hair. "You're the last one. You win again."

"Ooh-rah!" Howie jumped and punched the air.

The marine slang coming from the boy's mouth dropped Rick's jaw. Summer had mentioned it when they talked, but he hadn't realized how much he had become a role model. The responsibility overwhelmed him momentarily. How many *bad* habits was he teaching these kids without even being aware? He'd have to be more careful.

The three of them started back around the building to join the others. "How'd you manage to become so good at this?" Rick asked.

The child's face lost its glee and took on the somber look of someone five times his age. "I hide at home…sometimes."

Aw, hell. Rick clenched, then unclenched, his fists. What he'd give for one round with Howard Gerard, Sr. It might change the son of a bitch's tune if he had to stand up to a real man. "Well, we might have to let you start giving lessons." The boy's ready smile returned. "Go on, now." He started to swat Howie's butt locker-room style, but thought better of it. He tousled his hair instead. "Get your bragging over with so everyone can get to bed."

Cheers greeted them as they rounded the corner, and Howie broke into his victory run, high-fiving all his fellow campers.

"Okay, you're right," Neil admitted as they watched the boy revel in his moment of fame. "And, for the record, his dad needs his ass kicked up around his shoulders."

Rick nodded. "I just wish I could be the one to do the kicking." He clapped his hands to get the kids' attention. "Okay, everybody. Let's call it a night."

"Y'all get ready for bed," Summer called after the girls.

"I'll be there in a few minutes. We've got some fairy princess business to take care of."

The girls took off at a run toward the bunkhouse with Tara. Summer started down the path to her cabin but veered off to meet Rick and Neil as they followed the boys.

"Staff meeting tonight?" she asked.

Rick nodded. "Whenever you get finished. No hurry."

She waved and her accompanying smile made Rick hope the next hour would fly by fast. They'd get the kids to bed and have the staff meeting. Then she and Tara would spend about thirty minutes together. After Tara went back to the girls, maybe they'd have some time alone tonight…and every night.

"Man, I hope Howie doesn't run out of hiding places." Neil rubbed the back of his neck as they watched Summer walk away.

"Why the change of heart?"

Neil grinned. "Because now that you and Summer aren't at each other's throats, Howie's hiding places are about the only excitement we have left."

"SO WHAT WAS YOUR FAVORITE thing this week?"

Summer had made a hasty change into her fairy princess costume while the girls readied for bed. Now they all sat in a circle, primed for the vote that would grant one of them their very own wand. But first, Summer wanted to know what activities to keep for week two and which to discard.

"The bats."

"The bats."

"The bats."

Shannon, Braelyn and Kaelyn had become inseparable in almost everything.

"The storm." Elise's answer to Summer's question came as a surprise until she added, "I mean, I didn't like the part about Mr. Kenny's camper getting messed up. But being in the shelter with all of us together was exciting."

"Yeah, that was fun," Amanda agreed. "And I liked the bats, too…and the dance."

"I liked the dance." Lucy giggled.

Word around the camp was that Carlos had written Lucy a love note after being her dance partner. She'd actually seemed upbeat today, so maybe a camp romance would give everybody a reprieve from the girl's whining for a while. Until the romance ended, which summer camp romances were destined to do.

Not wanting to let her brain settle on that thought, Summer moved on to M&M.

The child pursed her lips in thought before she answered. "I liked sort of learning to swim best."

While it was true Rick already had Daniel swimming, Summer was convinced that peer pressure from the boys played a greater role in his success than teaching style. M&M hadn't conquered her fear of the water yet, but she got a little braver every day. "I'm proud of the progress you've made," Summer said. "You'll be swimming before the week's out."

She couldn't help but notice the hopeful timbre of M&M's answering sigh.

The dance received one more vote and the bats got two before Summer asked the second part of her question. "What was your least favorite thing?"

The skunk and going to bed garnered all of the votes except one—Becca missed her dog.

Not much there she could change.

Summer pulled the new fairy princess wand from her pocket and held it up proudly. Her dad had become quite a craftsman during his retirement. The small piece of green granite thrown away by the grave marker company had been a booger to cut, but somehow he'd managed to do it and to polish the pieces into lovely little stars that topped a metallic gold dowel rod.

"As promised, somebody's going to earn her wand tonight," she said. The girls exchanged quick looks that melted into grins and a couple of snickers.

Summer picked up on the unspoken message. The winner had been predetermined. Which girl impressed them enough to bring about such a response? She hoped intimidation didn't have a hand in this, but most likely, the winner's name would let her confirm or deny that.

Tara handed out the pencils and small slips of paper. Summer watched the girls scribble their choices. There was no thought. No hesitation for anyone that she could see.

Tara had all the slips back and went to count them. Within a couple of minutes, she reappeared, a wide smile spread across her face.

"And the new fairy princess is…" She laughed and shook her head in disbelief. "Mr. Rick!"

RICK SAT AT THE PICNIC TABLE beneath the pavilion, waiting for the other counselors to finish with the kids. Who was he kidding? He was waiting for Summer. Tonight began week two of camp, and his outlook had pivoted a hundred and eighty degrees since a week ago. Camp Sunny Daze was precisely where he wanted to be right now.

An unexpected noise put him on alert, and he swiveled in his seat to locate the source.

He could make out the ten pajama-clad girls heading down the path toward him, Summer and Tara in the rear. *Hell-pee-roo!* What was Summer thinking? Letting the girls come out of the dorm after lights-out was a disturbing breach in protocol.

But if he'd learned anything this week about Summer, it was to not jump to conclusions. She generally had a good excuse when she broke the rules—at least, good by her reasoning. They had T-shirts over their pajama tops, so they were quite properly covered. Since he seemed to be their destination, he held his tongue as the giggling mass of girls gathered around him.

Summer's mischievous smile gave him no indication of what was in store.

Amanda stepped from the middle of the group and cleared her throat. "Mr. Rick, this week during our bedtime chats, we've talked about how a true fairy princess finds out what makes her special."

Ah, a lecture on fairy princess-ship.

She looked at Becca, who glanced down at her palm and said, "Then she uses whatever it is that makes her special to help other people."

Becca poked Elise with her elbow, prompting her. Elise took the cue. "A true fairy princess listens to her pretty heart."

The speeches moved on down the line with each of the girls saying an obviously rehearsed part.

"And her pretty heart tells her what makes her special."

"Tonight we voted on who from the camp should get the first fairy princess wand."

"We decided that you listen to your pretty heart."

"The special thing you do to help other people is you save people's lives."

Oh, hell.

"You saved Mr. Kenny, Mr. Chance and Ms. Kyndal."

But not my best friend.

"And we know you were a soldier and probably saved lots more."

Damn! Rick pressed his lips together, keeping the tortuous emotion hidden.

M&M stepped forward from the end of the line and held

out a star-tipped stick. "We know you're not a girl, but you are like a true fairy princess, and we want you to have the first wand."

A battering ram hit his gut. He didn't deserve this… didn't deserve any of the medals tucked away in his mom's cedar chest. Dunk was the one who deserved the medals… the wand.

He hesitated, looking down the line of girls. Reverence… eagerness…excitement. Their sweet faces were filled with emotions, and the sight touched his heart. Undeserved or not, he couldn't refuse their gift.

"Thank you very much." Smiling, he took the wand and waved it over their heads. "This is one of the most meaningful things I've ever received. I'll keep it with me all the time."

He slipped it into his pocket, but the stick protruded awkwardly. He pulled it out and contemplated it for a moment.

Reaching in his shirt, he pulled out the dog tags ever-present around his neck. "These are my dog tags from when I was an active-duty marine. I don't ever take them off, either." He grasped the back of his T-shirt, pulling it over his head, and pointed to the dog tags tattooed over his heart. "These are the dog tags of my best friend, Lt. Duncan Ballard. He died in Afghanistan."

He scanned the wide eyes of the group. "Would it be okay with y'all if I wore the star on the chain with my dog tags instead of keeping it on the stick? Maybe some of the magic will absorb into my pretty heart…that's where Dunk continues to live, so maybe he'll feel it."

All the heads nodded vigorously, including Summer's.

Amanda stepped up to give him a hug, but she paused and pointed to the words tattooed under the dog tags. "What's that say, Mr. Rick?"

"*Semper fi.* That's short for *Semper fidelis.*" He found

Summer's eyes, and locked his gaze with hers. "It means 'always faithful.'"

He watched a shadow pass over Summer's face. Was she doubting whether or not he could be faithful? Obviously, there was still more about him she needed to get to know.

All the girls fell into line and gave him a hug one by one.

Summer was last. "Thank you. That was beautiful."

As she turned away to follow the girls to the bunkhouse, he looked back down at the polished granite star. He imagined Summer's look of admiration reflecting back at him.

What a treasure!

It wasn't just a magic wand. He'd been given the key to Summer's heart.

"WE WERE BEGINNING TO THINK you gals had fallen asleep," Neil said when Summer and Tara finally showed up at the staff meeting.

"You can thank Tara," Summer answered. "If it wasn't for her resourcefulness, and her magical CD, we'd still be trying to quiet them down."

After the presentation of the wand, the girls had been pretty keyed up. Tara had come up with the brilliant idea of putting a relaxation CD in the player and turning it up loud enough to be heard all over the room. The gentle sound of rain with Native American flute music in the background had calmed the girls to sleep.

Summer took the seat next to Rick, who shuffled the papers in front of him. He glanced up to give her a smile before turning his attention back to the activity sheets. Even the quick look spiked her temperature.

Tara slid onto the opposite bench. "This job makes good use of my teacher training. Next time the kids get too rowdy in class, I'll put that same CD on and give them nap time."

"I'm ready for nap time." Neil didn't try to cover his noisy yawn.

"Okay, let's make this fast before Neil falls asleep." Rick used his authoritative tone. "Any concerns?"

"Yeah." Summer gave Neil an apologetic shrug. "I'm worried about Howie. He's a bit of a smart mouth with Tara and me. We've both noticed it."

Tara nodded. "Yesterday morning, I heard him refer to me as 'that Tara chick' to Jimbo. But he did apologize when I called him on it."

"And today, he was very disrespectful to me," Summer continued.

Rick's eyebrow quirked. "I'll talk to him," he answered.

"I don't want you to talk to him," Summer shot back. This was the telling moment. Rick's reaction to the wand had her hopes soaring, but this would give her a definite answer. "I want to be more proactive than that. His dad's obviously got issues with women, and boys with dads like his are the ones who grow up to be abusive toward women."

Neil perked up enough to comment. "No argument there. What do you propose we do about it?"

"I'm hoping we can break the cycle for him. Convince him girls are his equals."

Rick's eyebrows drew together. "How do we do that in three weeks' time?"

"We start mixing the groups with both sexes." Summer used her most confident tone. "Like this morning, instead of the girls cooking and the boys doing tae kwon do, we could've mixed the groups with five of each. That would make them think of themselves as one group instead of two." She paused for a reaction. Neither of the guys seemed too off-put by her suggestion, so she went on. "The first week was all about respect. Now we'll concentrate on accepting differences and developing unity. What do you think?"

Neil shrugged. “Sounds okay to me.”

“I think it’s brilliant,” Rick said.

The compliment made bubbles rise in Summer’s stomach, and her heart danced. Rick got her! It wasn’t an act to get her into bed. He understood what she was about. The realization left her momentarily speechless.

Tara’s head tilted in thought. “Almost everything in the schools is coed. I can’t think of any reason why it shouldn’t work here. But the girls get their wands as rewards. Will we give the boys wands, as well?”

“What about stars hanging on chains, like Rick’s?” Summer’s insides were still melty, thinking about how he’d handled that situation.

A yawn slipped from Neil as he tried to stifle it. “What are y’all talking about?”

Rick pulled his dog tag chain out of his shirt and the wand from his pocket. “I’m going to have a hole drilled in it so I can wear it on the chain. Without the stick.”

Neil squinted. “Cool.”

Summer’s breathing came easier. She hadn’t been sure Neil would go along, but since he had, she could throw out her other idea. “I can ask my dad to make some more. We’ll give the kids a choice of either a wand or a star on a chain.”

“Oh!” Tara applauded. “I like that.”

“Me, too,” Rick agreed, and Neil mumbled a sleepy assent.

“Okay, then…” Rick directed them to the week’s activities, pushing through each item so fast it became almost comical.

Summer knew the reason for his fired-up agenda, but she wondered if the others suspected he had plans with her for later.

And while she looked forward to their time alone to talk, she wasn’t so sure Rick would be thrilled with what she planned to say…what she’d thought about during her alone time in the fertility room.

"So, I guess that's it," Rick was saying, and she hadn't even heard the last item he'd brought up.

Rick whisked the papers off the table. "Good night, everyone." He was gone before they could get out their responses.

Neil looked at the two women over the rim of his glasses. "Either of you ladies want to carry me?" Summer and Tara shook their heads, and he blew out a dramatic sigh. "I guess I'll just stumble my way home, then." He got up and tripped over his first step, seeming bent on proving his words. He caught his balance, though, and managed to make progress up the hill.

"Do you want me to go on to bed, too?" Tara asked, and Summer heard in her tone that she was asking about Rick.

Tara and Summer had gotten to know each other pretty well over the first part of the week with their nightly tête-à-têtes, and Summer looked forward to their chats. But then the storm had happened and her parents had come, so she and Tara had a lot of catching up to do. In the absence of Kate, Summer had come to think of Tara as a trusted girlfriend—and she needed some girl talk tonight.

"No way," she answered. "I need you to keep me sane."

A few minutes later, when Summer had changed out of her costume, Tara was waiting with lemonade in hand and a plate with two oatmeal raisin cookies Summer's mom had provided from the organic bakery in Paducah.

"So what happened after the dance?" was Tara's first question.

"We went for a moonlight swim." Summer closed her eyes, feeling again the heat generated by the kisses on the beach. "It was so romantic." She caught herself and forced her eyes open.

"Tonight was great, watching you two." Tara grinned. "When the girls gave him the wand, there was something in his expression, and then I looked at you, and the look on your face seemed to mirror his. It was—" she seemed to search for the word, but settled for "—cool."

They sipped the lemonade, quiet for a moment, and then Tara waved her hand toward the bedroom. "It's nice that you have your own cabin. Y'all can, um, have some privacy."

"Actually, that makes everything more difficult."

A crease appeared between Tara's copper eyebrows. "Because…?"

"Because even though it's possible, it's not the right thing to do. I don't want these weeks to be about anything but the kids and keeping the camp going. And I have no doubt sex with Rick would shift my focus."

"That's very noble of you."

"Pfft." Summer shrugged off the compliment. "I'm not trying to be noble. I just know me. Sex with the right guy is capable of giving me tunnel vision for a while. You know how it is."

Tara's eyes broke contact. "Actually, I don't."

The wistfulness in her friend's voice pushed an alert button in Summer's brain. Things must not be too great in the lovemaking department. "Well, you and Louis have been together for a long time, but remember how it was in the beginning when you first started having sex?"

"We've never had sex." Tara took a small sip of her lemonade. "I'm still a virgin."

The announcement stopped the forward motion in Summer's brain. "You're still a virgin at twenty-three?" The question made it sound like there was something wrong with virginity. She pulled her foot out of her mouth and tried again. "What I mean to say is, how've you held out so long?"

Tara's shrug suggested it was no huge deal, and maybe it wasn't in her world, but it certainly was in Summer's. She and all her friends had lost their virginity by the time they were seventeen.

"When we were in high school," Tara said, "our church sponsored one of those save-yourself-for-marriage campaigns. We signed cards, vowing chastity until marriage, and we've managed to stay true to that vow." The young woman nibbled thoughtfully on a bite of cookie. "In some ways, it's made things easier by taking away the choice. And it's given us time to focus on building a strong bond without having the confusion of sex thrown in."

"But eight years." Summer drew a long breath, the length of time seeming incomprehensible to her. "So how do you stand it?" It was possible Tara could give her some pointers about the celibacy thing. "I mean, do you have any tricks I could use to keep from thinking about...well, about *it*."

Tara laughed. "There's no magic wand, if that's what you mean—unless it would be the kind you buy at adult toy stores. And no, I don't use one." Her eyes squinted in contemplation as she washed down the last of her cookie. "Louis goes on a lot of mission trips, so he's gone most of the time. I think that helps. When we're together, it is definitely harder."

Summer raised her eyebrows. "That doesn't help me much here. Rick and I are together a lot."

"I know, and the celibacy thing isn't for everybody." She looked Summer squarely in the eye. "If you and Rick sleep together, it's okay with me. I don't judge people about that kind of thing. What you do when the kids aren't around is your business. Their parents have sex after the kids go to bed. I mean, that's been going on since the beginning of time." Tara looked around the cabin as she finished off her lemonade. "Back in the pioneer days, huge families lived in cabins very much like this one."

"Ack!" Summer banged her head on the back of the couch. "You're messing up my rationalizations."

Tara laughed. "You just have to be discreet." She wiped her mouth and tossed the napkin on her plate. "And with those sage words as my parting message, I need to get back to the girls." She stood up to go, motioning for Summer to keep her seat. "I know the way out."

Summer drew her knees up to her chest and rested her chin on them, thinking about what Tara had told her.

"Maybe," Tara said, her voice trailing off. "You can just keep telling yourself that it's only for three more weeks. After that, you'll have all the time you want…if you want it."

"I've never been very good at waiting," Summer called over her shoulder as she heard the screen door slam.

RICK'S TIMING WAS OFF. He thought Tara would be gone by now, and he had one foot on Summer's porch before he saw the young woman standing at the door.

Damn! He stepped back into the shadows at the side of the cabin. He'd rather the staff not know about his private time with Summer. He and Kenny had an understanding, but too many tongues were sure to start wagging, and then it would be an easy jump to conclusions.

Of course, the conclusions would be wrong. He'd made up his mind. No matter how much he wanted Summer, this was not the time nor the place to begin a physical relationship.

It wasn't going to be easy to keep a lid on his desire. The kisses they'd already shared nearly sent him careening over the edge.

He'd come prepared to talk with her about it now, before things went any further.

"If you want it," Tara said as she came out the door, and Summer called after her, "I've never been very good at waiting."

The exact words Rick did *not* need to hear when *waiting* was exactly what he was about to propose. That this thing with Summer might grind to a halt a few minutes from now came like a punch to his gut, which bothered him more than a little. But he'd set his course, and he would see it through and face the consequences of his actions.

He waited until Tara was definitely gone, then he stepped up on the porch and rapped softly on the door.

Summer leaped up from the couch to meet him, smiling and breathless. "Hi." She glanced down and laughed. "You glad to see me or is that a magic wand in your pants?"

He followed her eyes, surprised by the bulge created by the wand in his pocket. "Both." He chuckled. "Reason number two I need to wear the star around my neck." He kissed her lightly. Her lips were soft and met his eagerly, but she broke off quickly and slid her hand into his, tugging him toward the couch.

They'd no more than gotten seated before they were both speaking. "We need to talk," they said simultaneously.

Their gazes locked and Rick felt an "oh, hell" reaction in the pit of his stomach when he saw the heat registering in her look. She was ready to take it to the next level. Pulling one knee onto the couch, he rested his elbow on the back cushion, and turned fully toward her. "You first."

She nodded, drew in a long breath and let it out slowly. "We haven't known each other very long, and we've only liked each other for a few days." She paused and gnawed on her bottom lip, obviously thinking about how to say it.

But you're not good at waiting, and I'm about to make you very annoyed with me.

"But I'm already feeling a strong connection with you." She turned and mirrored him in her position.

He took the hand she laid on the back of the couch. "Probably the strongest connection I've ever felt in so short a time." *Keep driving home the message that's it's only been a short time.*

She nodded and gave him a small smile before she continued. "I want you, Rick. I would love to move into a physical relationship with you."

Gotta be strong. He gave her hand a squeeze and saw her wince. *But not that strong. Tell her how you feel.* "That's been in the front of my mind since the first time I kissed you."

She nodded. "Me, too."

He took over. "But here, with everything else going on… this doesn't seem to me to be the best time or place to move a new relationship to the physical level."

"Exactly!" Her voice was breathless with relief.

"You agree?"

"Yeah, I mean, it's hard for me to resist the idea of going to bed with you right here and now."

"Same here," he said, and her knee pressing against his made him do a quick scan of the couch to see if it could take his length.

"And we would be *really* great in bed together. I just know it." She kissed his hand, and her lips made a tiny sucking sound against his fingers that made his breath catch.

"We'd be the best…the best ever." Words weren't downloading from his brain to his tongue as effortlessly as usual.

Her gaze dropped to his mouth. "I want to stay focused on the kids." When she licked her lips, the blood flowed southward from his brain. "And I don't think I can stay focused on the kids if I go to bed with you. I think making love with you would be on my mind constantly—" she paused "—if we were to do it."

"So it's best if we don't do it," he whispered.

She leaned closer as if to hear, and her leaning closer made him lean closer and their lips met again and pressed harder, and then his arms were around her pulling her to him and she moved into him easily and onto his lap.

His hands crept under her shirt and caressed her back

and she moaned against his mouth and sucked his tongue greedily.

A sound registered in Rick's brain at the same time the hot sucking sensation on his tongue ceased. Not a moan this time. A whistled tune in the distance. "Amazing Grace."

Summer straightened, pulling away from him slightly. "Kenny." The aggravation in her tone was almost palpable. Her bottom lip protruded in a pout as she slid backward out of Rick's lap and onto the couch cushion. Then the pout dissolved into laughter.

Rick laughed with her, feeling his upper brain clear with the additional oxygen. "I think I'd better go," he said, and she nodded.

They held hands as they inched toward the door. When they got there, she pulled him back and stood on tiptoes to slide her arms around his neck.

"We're adults, and we can do this," she said.

"Absolutely," he agreed. *Not a chance,* he thought.

"And there's no reason we shouldn't go ahead and have our time together at night when everyone else is asleep," she said.

I can think of several reasons, he thought. "No reason." He shook his head.

"We'll just have to keep ourselves under control and limit the contact to kissing," she said.

Big mistake, he thought. "Right. And we can do that." He kissed her softly. "Good night."

"Night," she said, and her voice caught in his ear and swirled around pleasantly.

He headed toward his cabin and the cold shower awaiting him. "This isn't Camp Sunny Daze," he muttered to the tree frogs he passed. "It's hell. Pure hell."

CHAPTER THIRTEEN

"HONESTLY, TARA, I THINK the urge is getting worse instead of better. I thought, after the first couple of days, it would lighten up. But it's been a week since we had *the talk,* and it's getting to the point that it's all I think about when I'm not busy."

A ripple of laughter from Tara echoed around her friend's bedroom as she continued folding her laundry. Ginny and Charlie were showing the kids a movie in the dining hall—a special treat to kick off the week. It was nice having a couple of free hours in the middle of the day.

"I'm not kidding." Summer huffed. "The corn dog at lunch nearly sent me over the edge."

Tara gave a hearty laugh and managed to land a towel over Summer's head. "So just do it, and get it over with."

"No, I can't. We made an agreement, and I don't want him to think I'm some kind of sex addict." Summer let out an anguished groan. "I mean, I love being with him for the hour or so we have at night. It's really romantic. We swim or go for walks in the woods. And we talk…about everything. I've learned a lot about him and his family and his career, so I'm not complaining. I just want more time with him. Lots more."

"You shouldn't be getting this serious so soon. You may have learned a lot about him, but you've barely scratched the surface. I mean, Louis and I have been together for eight years, and I'm still learning new things about him." Tara's voice trailed away on the thought.

"I think that's a good thing. You don't want a relationship to go stale." Summer folded the towel Tara had thrown at her and set it aside. "Have you noticed that look Rick gets in his eyes sometimes? Sort of a sad, faraway look?"

Tara pursed her lips as she thought. "No. Not really. He always seems pretty upbeat to me."

Summer shrugged. "Maybe it's just me. I think he worries more than he lets on. His best friend's dog tags tattooed over his heart? You've got to admit that's pretty heavy."

"But sweet." Tara wrinkled her nose and added, "Sweet in an over-the-top manly kind of way."

"Maybe I'll get a couple of tattoos." Summer kept her face serious as she traced a finger across the top of one breast. "Rick—" and then moved to the other "—Warren."

"Aye!" Tara shuddered, and Summer smiled that her comment had gotten the desired result. Aggravating her older sisters had been a favorite pastime when she was growing up. Being with Tara was kind of like being with them.

A grin tugged at Summer's lips. "It would be a way to show him I'm taking this seriously."

"You're losing it. You need to breathe." Tara took some exaggerated deep breaths. "C'mon. Take some deep, cleansing breaths."

Summer did as she was told and started to relax a bit. She lay back on the bed again as Tara's breathing continued. "Okay, c'mon! Now you're being creepy. And the heavy breathing is gonna sling me right back into thinking about sex with him. Talk to me about something else."

Tara obliged and started chatting about details of the pageant the counselors were planning for the last night of camp. "I have my costume ready, and Rick said his mom was mailing his. How about you?"

"I've got a fairy princess story I think the boys will enjoy as much as the girls."

"How are the parties going without you? Is Kate handling things to your satisfaction?"

Summer smiled at Tara's intuitiveness. Fairy Princess Parties was probably the only subject that could truly pry her thoughts away from Rick for a while. She shared some new activities Kate had added that she was planning on keeping in the rotation permanently.

"See?" Tara smiled. "You haven't lost your focus. It's still on the kids."

"Unless Rick's around." Summer sighed and then felt the smile break across her lips unbidden. "Mmm, I love thinking about him."

Tara cleared her throat. "Today's field trip should be fun *and* educational." She was obviously trying to direct the conversation away from Rick again.

"Yeah? I've never been to this place we're going to today." Summer didn't add that a replica of an 1850s farm sounded hideously boring or that the kids were going to hate it. She'd tried to steer Rick away from this particular idea, but he'd remained adamant.

And he *was* the assistant director.

His title didn't bother her nearly as much as it used to, though her parents' preference of him over her still tightened her gut when she thought about it.

She tried not to think about it. Her time would come.

Tara gave a wistful sigh. "I practically grew up in the Land Between the Lakes. All our school field trips were there. I know you think the kids are going to be bored." Tara had gotten to know her well. She hadn't made her negative comments about this field trip to anyone except Rick. "But I think they'll enjoy it. Learning what life was like back then. The chores and all. It's…entertaining."

"How do you think people had sex back in those days?" Summer wondered aloud about what Tara said previously about the pioneers. “Those log cabins were tiny, so the kids would’ve been just a few feet away. There wouldn’t have been any privacy, and you know the beds had to creak really bad.”

“I dunno. Maybe they went to the barn?”

“But what if you had hay fever?” Summer paused. “I’ve always thought sneezes and orgasms feel kind of the same. Not literally, but both of them have that buildup, like a bad itch that needs to be scratched, and then when it happens, it’s such a relief—”

“Aaiiee! Would you get a hold of yourself?” Tara drew in a loud breath. “Hey, wait! Maybe that’s not a bad idea. Maybe you should—”

“No!” Summer protested. “I’m saving myself for Rick.” That sent both of them into a fit of laughter. Summer rolled over and looked at the time. “The movie will be over soon, and I want to get my laundry folded, too.”

“I’m going to keep an eye on you when we get to the farm. Stay out of the barn,” Tara warned before Summer got out the door.

With a little time to spare, Summer showered and changed clothes. She’d never sweated through so many changes of clothes before. She folded and put away her laundry. Thank heavens Ginny was willing to wash the staff laundry; otherwise, they’d have to change it to clothing optional for the staff, which wouldn’t be such a bad thing if it involved Rick in the buff.... She mentally rebuked herself for letting her thoughts stray that direction again.

As she crossed the parking lot to move the bus to the loading area, Kenny drove in, pulling his new camper behind him. It was bigger and newer and shinier than the one destroyed in the storm.

Summer waved. “Wow! She’s a beauty, Kenny.”

“Thanks.” Kenny grinned from ear to ear. “The storm turned out to be a good thing, after all.”

Rick would be relieved, too. He would get his cabin to himself again. He hadn't felt free to go back to his cabin during the day with Kenny trying to sleep, so he'd roamed around a lot—making notes in the file folder he kept with him all the time.

Yesterday, she'd walked in on him measuring the dining hall, and she'd questioned him about it. He answered that her parents were thinking about repainting the floor, which irked her that they'd talked to him about it and not her.

She reminded herself that the folder only contained a bunch of notes, but Rick still seemed almost sheepish every time she found him writing in it. Maybe a little embarrassment over his borderline OCD, and she now wondered if it was OCD or just all the rigid upbringing from his dad. Whatever it was, she wished he'd let his guard down more often.

She'd learned a lot about Rick Warren over the past week, but there was still a whole lot of man to uncover.

That task she would enjoy every minute of.

FERN WOODROW THREW HER ARMS around Rick's neck and held on a little too long. "You haven't called me in way too long," she whispered.

Rick didn't have any sisters, but he gave Fern what he hoped was a sisterly pat on the back before he straightened up and broke her hold. He'd been hoping she'd left the job playing the role of the Browns' daughter at the Old Homeplace, but here she was. And the sweet smile on Summer's face as she watched the display of affection didn't match the coolness in her eyes.

"It's good to see you, Fern," Rick lied. "And Peggy." The older woman let M&M take over the churning for a moment while Rick gave her a hug of real affection. "Man, I've missed your Dutch oven blackberry cobblers."

He watched Summer wander out of the log cabin behind a group of girls.

"Well, you need to quit making yourself so scarce," Peggy chided. "Now, catch me up on what's going on with you."

Much as he wanted to follow Summer, Rick felt obligated to chat for a while with his old friends. He covered the past three years of his life—the time since he'd left the park ranger's job—as succinctly as possible, but by the time he'd finished, Summer had vanished. She could be in any of the sixteen log structures.

The farm was a place where the kids could roam free and spend as much time as they wanted learning about what interested them. So now that he'd spent some time visiting with his old friends and extricating himself from the clutches of Fern Woodrow, he and Summer could have two hours of free time together. Well, as free as they could be surrounded by thirty people.

But he'd take what he could get.

He tried to decide where she might've gone after the kitchen. Toolshed, maybe? She drove a bus, after all. The corn crop looked good, he observed as he walked the edge of the field toward the toolshed. Felix Pratt stopped his saw-sharpening demonstration long enough to shake hands with Rick and welcome him back. Rick felt the sting of another delay stealing precious minutes away from time he could have with Summer.

Some of the girls were going toward the cabin where they could make cornhusk dolls, so he headed that way in hopes of finding her. But just before he stepped through the doorway, he caught the flash of sunlight on her braid, going into the barn. He had to force his legs to a walk rather than the jog they were insisting on.

The doors at both ends of the barn were open, pulling

a breeze through that smelled of leather, straw and horse manure.

When his eyes adjusted from the bright sunlight to the shade, he found her, cooing and nuzzling the neck of one of the horses, looking so tiny and delicate standing next to the giant animal. He paused just to take in the sight.

"I'm not sure that's appropriate behavior with a horse you just met." He strolled up beside her.

She raised her chin and tilted her head to lean it against the animal's jaw as she continued scratching its neck. "Well, you certainly seem well acquainted with everyone."

The horse snorted and bobbed its head.

"You stay out of this," Rick scolded. "These were my stomping grounds for four years," he added by way of explanation to Summer's question.

Her eyes squinted in challenge. "I think you did more than stomp."

"Fern and I had three dates." Rick shrugged, hoping that ended it. "There was never anything between us. She just wanted a man."

"Bless her heart." Summer's fingernails found what must have been the perfect spot. The horse stretched out its head, and she scratched harder.

Rick couldn't hold back the grin. "I never pegged you for the jealous type."

Summer cast him a sidelong glance. "Because I've never been jealous."

"Never?"

"Nope. I have this philosophy. A guy you have to fight for isn't worth having."

Rick scratched his head. "That's pretty harsh."

"Not really." She gave a shrug. "If he wants somebody else, then he doesn't want me."

He reached out and caught her chin on two fingers, turning her face to him. "I want you."

A smile teased at the edges of her mouth, and he realized he was being played. He brushed his thumb across her lips, watching her eyes close in response. He couldn't have stopped himself from kissing her if the whole world had been watching.

But the world wasn't watching. They were alone. He kissed her forehead and both of her eyes and the tip of her nose.

"Somebody might come in." Her words had hardly any breath behind them.

"I don't care," he said, and kissed her on the mouth long enough to elicit a sigh from them both when they broke away.

"Mmm." She smiled as she opened her eyes slowly. "Tara told me to stay away from the barn."

"Why is that?" He smoothed back a strand of hair that had worked loose from her braid.

"She didn't want it to stir up my hay fever." She patted the horse's neck and laughed at the joke he'd somehow missed.

She seemed totally at ease with the horse, which intrigued him. "If you grew up in Paducah, how'd you get so comfortable around horses?"

"Kate's grandpa has a farm, and he had horses we used to ride. I loved it. I begged Mom and Dad for a horse, but they didn't think I was responsible enough to take care of one." She shrugged. "They were probably right."

"At least you realize that now."

"That...and a whole lot more."

The talk was taking a serious turn that Rick didn't want right then. They only had a few minutes. "Bet you're looking forward to the ride next week, then, aren't you?"

"I am, but it's been a while, so it'll probably make me really sore." He watched her demeanor change, saw the impish gleam come into her eyes as she tilted her head and looked up at him. "How about you? Has it been a while since you've… ridden?"

Rick wasn't sure she was still talking about horses. "Yeah, it's been a while." He tried to keep a straight face. "But I think I can remember how to do it pretty well."

She licked her lips, her eyes never straying from his. "I love sitting in the saddle, the feel of the horse beneath me, increasing its speed slowly from a walk to a trot and then a gallop."

Rick trailed a finger down her arm and felt her shiver. "My favorite way is bareback. Using the movement of my body to control the direction. Running my hands into the silky mane…"

She drew a long breath, closing her eyes in an invitation he gladly accepted. He kissed her again, feeling the fire from her tongue consuming him, throwing his world into a spin he had no desire to control.

He drew back and looked at her, not even trying to contain the awe he felt. "Is kissing you as wonderful as I think it is? Or is it just all the pent-up passion? I mean, do you think it will be this good…afterward?"

She shook her head. "I don't know, but I'm looking forward to finding out."

"Me, too." He brushed the backs of his fingers down her cheek, flushed with desire and from the heat in the barn. "Think we better leave before we catch this place on fire?"

She kissed the horse's neck and gave him a final pat. "Yeah, I feel my hay fever kicking in."

They started toward the barn door, but she stopped. When he turned toward her, her brows were drawn together in concern.

"What is it?"

"Something I've been wanting to ask you about, but I

wasn't sure I should...yet." She took a deep breath, and he could see this was difficult for her.

He met her eyes straight on. "You can ask me anything. What's bothering you?"

"Semper fi."

"O-kay." Confused and more than a little surprised, he drew the word out. "What about it?"

"You still take it seriously."

He rested his fists on his hips and nodded. "Very."

Her teeth chewed at her bottom lip before she spoke. "Will you always be a marine? At heart, I mean?"

"Always. Forever. That's what it means." He remembered the look of doubt in Summer's eyes when the girls asked him about the slogan.

"Do you ever take time off from duty. I mean, you know... time just for yourself?"

His gut tightened. "Not very often," he admitted. "But... maybe the right person could help with that."

"Yeah? What kind of person would it take?" A shadow darkened her eyes.

"Somebody very different from me, I think. Somebody uninhibited. Somebody with a vivacity for life. Somebody with a wild-child nature..."

Her smile was gentle, like she was talking to one of the kids. "I know somebody like that."

"Well." He gave her a wink. "Maybe you could fix me up with her."

She pursed her lips as she considered his suggestion. "I dunno, Warren. You may be beyond fixing."

She was kidding, but Rick flinched involuntarily at her words. How many times after a particularly grueling nightmare had he thought that very thing?

Her smile tightened, worry marks forming between her

brows. Rick hurried to lighten the moment. “Yeah, I might require the motherload of all fairy princess magic.”

That brought a smile to her lips.

They moved from the barn into the sunlight. The Old Homeplace looked like a beehive swarming with kids.

“I have to disagree with you about one thing, Summer.”

Sarcasm tinged her laugh. “One thing? You disagree with me about everything. What this time?”

He stopped and made sure he had her full attention before he spoke. “There are people worth fighting for.”

He heard her sigh, and he couldn’t tell if it was one of contentment or something else completely.

SUMMER TRIED TO LOSE HERSELF in the tranquil chirping of the crickets outside her bedroom window, hoping to find enough peace to allow sleep to come.

She stared at the clock. Thirty-four minutes had passed since Rick left her, and she was still dizzy with desire for him. The heat of his hands on her back as they’d wandered under her shirt during an extremely long, hot kiss blazed in her imagination as if she’d been branded by them. The nerves in her palms still tingled from smoothing over the muscles in his back, which tapered down to his waist.

They were playing with fire, but keeping their hands off each other was asking the impossible, and not something either of them wanted to do. And while it didn’t exactly give relief, it helped move things to a more adult level.

She concentrated on the ache in her core. It wasn’t an ache—it was a need…and it didn’t hurt. In fact, it was quite yummy and it made her feel alive and breathless with anticipation.

She laughed, realizing that she was, indeed, panting, just at the thought of the time when she and Rick would finally get to make love.

Tara had been right about getting to know each other first. She'd barely broken through that shell, and there was so much more she wanted to know about him. The outside was all steel and rock, but sometimes—and apparently she was the only one who saw it—she glimpsed vulnerability beneath. He kept it covered well, but it was there. It came out at certain times. Usually with the kids...or when he mentioned Dunk...or the way he looked at her in the moonlight.

It made her want to open him up and examine everything inside that made him who he was.

But right now, it made her hot...and thirsty. A cool glass of lemonade might offset enough of the heat to allow her to sleep.

She eased out of bed, not bothering to turn on any lights as her eyes were well adjusted to the darkness, and the sparse furnishings left the space uncluttered.

Coming out of the bedroom into the living room, her eyes caught the movement and her body froze, paralyzed by fear.

A second later, the adrenaline kicked in. A scream tore from her lungs.

CHAPTER FOURTEEN

OH, GOD! HE'D KNOW THAT VOICE anywhere. *That's Summer!*

The scream propelled Rick out of bed and onto the path with no thought of shirt or shoes. His only thought: *Get to Summer.*

He and Kenny reached her porch at the same time.

"What do you think's going on?"

"I don't know, but I'm going to find out." Rick used his size to jockey through the screen door first, noticing it was slightly ajar. Kenny followed close at his heels.

The door to Summer's bedroom was closed. "Summer?" Rick called as he crossed to it.

"Snake." Her voice sounded far away and an octave higher than usual. "In the front room. Big snake."

A faint scent of ammonia that hadn't been there a half hour before made the hairs on Rick's neck rise. His hand was on the doorknob when he caught sight of the movement in his peripheral vision.

A long, dark line undulated from beneath the couch.

He leaped and turned on the light in time to see the black snake making for refuge under the refrigerator.

He pointed toward it. "Snake."

"Shitfire!" Kenny pulled his gun.

"Damn it." Rick pushed the young man's outstretched hand toward the floor. "For God's sake, put that thing away. You can't shoot it in here. You'll put a hole in the floor… or in me."

Kenny made no movement to holster the pistol, but he kept it aimed at the floor and used his other shaking hand to wave toward the creature. “We’ve g-got to…to…g-get that thing…outta here.”

“Agreed. But it’s a black snake, Kenny. Not a cobra.”

Kenny retreated a few steps toward the door. “Th-they’re all co-cobras to m-me.”

“Well, trust me, this one’s on our side, and from the size of him, he’s a good mouser, so we want to keep him around.” Rick put his hands on his hips and deliberated. It wasn’t an idea he relished, but there was only one way to get the snake out of the cabin unharmed.

He turned to the security guard. “Put the gun away.” Kenny hesitated, but then did as he was told. “And stay out of my way.”

Kenny’s eyes went wider than Rick thought possible. “Wh-what are y-you gonna do with it?” The guard’s backside was already pushing the door open.

“Just stay out of my way,” Rick ordered.

The snake stopped with several inches of its body sticking out from under the refrigerator. Rick flexed his hands open and closed a few times, taking deep breaths, reminding himself that black snakes could be quick to bite, but weren’t poisonous. “Grab, tug, run, toss. Grab, tug, run, toss.” *And try your damnedest not to piss your pants.*

One last breath, and it was time. The snake started to move again and would soon be settled under the fridge… *and a mad son of a bitch to deal with.*

Rick grabbed the tail, tugged and ran as fast as his legs would take him, keeping the writhing creature at arm’s length and thanking the Lord the whole time for long arms.

A leap off the porch and a few long strides gave momentum to his slinging movement. The black snake sailed through the air, landing with a *thump* near the path into the woods.

Rick leaned forward, bracing his hands on his knees, taking deep gulps of air as he watched the shadowy mass slither into the shadows.

"If he comes crawlin' outta there during my watch, he's a dead son of a bitch, good guy or not," Kenny called from a safe distance away.

"You don't have a tranquilizer dart, do you?" Rick walked back toward Summer's cabin.

"No, why? You want to put him to sleep if he comes back?"

"I was thinking I may need it for Summer."

He heard the night watchman's nervous laugh…headed away from the direction of the woods.

"Summer, it's okay," Rick called. He crossed the small living room and opened her bedroom door. The room was empty, but light shone from under the bathroom door.

He went over to it and rapped lightly. "Summer?" Listening for an answer, he caught the sound of her soft cry. Slowly, he opened the door and peeked in.

She was huddled in the bathtub, eyes wide and wild. "It was a big sn-sn-snake. I nearly stepped on it."

Rick pushed the door wide-open. "It's okay. It's gone now."

"Oh, Rick!" She launched herself at him, and he caught her. Her arms clutched his neck, and her legs wrapped around his waist. "I was so scared."

He held Summer close as he walked to her bed and sat down with her, too keenly aware of her breasts pushed taut against him with only the thin material of her top separating them from his bare chest. "It's okay." He stroked her back and used what he hoped was a soothing voice. "I'm here. You don't have anything to be afraid of."

"Did I wake the kids?"

He snorted. "Those old A/C window units in the dorms are so loud, a helicopter could land and it wouldn't wake the kids."

"I shouldn't have screamed like that, though. It caught me totally off guard. How do you think it got in?" Her cheek rested on his shoulder while her warm breath came in jerks, bathing the side of his neck.

"The screen door doesn't shut well." He leaned back to look at her, brushing away the wet hair clinging to her face. "We'll get Charlie to fix it tomorrow. I should've already taken care of it."

"Tomorrow?" Terror returned to her eyes and she shuddered. "I can't stay here tonight. Can I stay with you? Please? I can sleep on your couch, and I'll be really quiet."

He pulled her to him, trying to ignore the erect nipples and remain logical as he thought it over. The logical answer would be to share his bed and make love all night, but that would go against the agreement they had. He was positive he couldn't share a bed with her and not make love to her, but he didn't want her sleeping on the couch, and the couch wouldn't be nearly big enough to accommodate him comfortably.

"Do you want to go home for the night? I could take you if you're too shaky to drive." He hoped she didn't jump on that option. She shook her head against him. "By the time we got there, it wouldn't be three hours until we'd have to get up and come back."

They could switch cabins for the night. Other than knowing he was sleeping in her bed and her scent filling his head all night and keeping him so hard he probably wouldn't be able to sleep, he couldn't think of a reason that wouldn't work. "You can sleep in my cabin. I'll come back here."

"No." She shook her head in protest. "I won't let you sleep in this snake-infested place."

Her drama made him laugh. "One snake, which probably came in through the open door, does not qualify a place as infested. And sleeping with a snake around doesn't scare me nearly as much as the thought of sleeping under the same roof as you."

She huffed and grabbed a tissue from the box on her nightstand to wipe her nose and eyes. "I promise I'll be good."

He hugged her. "That's what scares me."

SUMMER'S STOMACH DREW INTO a lead weight as they walked out onto her porch. Rick's strong hand clutching hers helped, but the snake was out there somewhere in the darkness, so when Rick stepped off the porch, her feet wouldn't follow. She froze in terror, jerking his arm back. "I can't do this."

"No problem." In one smooth move, he scooped her up. She clutched his neck, feeling the security of his steel body as he strode toward his cabin, loving the feel of his bare skin pressed to her side, against her arms, under her hands.

An unexpected flashlight beam illuminated Rick's face, causing her to gasp. Kenny.

"Summer's going to spend the night in my cabin," Rick explained.

"'Bout time." Kenny continued on his rounds.

With Summer's help, Rick maneuvered the door to his cabin open and kept going toward his bedroom without breaking stride.

"Just put me on the couch, Rick."

He ignored her and passed it by. When he laid her on his bed, she opened her mouth again, but his lips closed down on hers, smothering her protest, causing her breath to sputter in her chest.

Fear of the snake ebbed away into the recesses of her body while another emotion coiled and struck with a vengeance.

Rick brushed his knuckles down her face as he straightened. "Good night," he whispered.

She flung her arms around his neck. "Don't leave."

"You're safe here." With an arm to each side of her, he leaned down to touch her lips again with his. "You don't need to be afraid."

She moved her hands to his face. Their gazes tangled. "I'm not afraid. I want to be with you, make love to you. I don't want to wait any longer." She watched him swallow, and he straightened again. Her hands slid to his chest and on down to the chiseled planes of his abs. His breath caught beneath her touch.

"But we agreed that making love would only be a distraction."

She sat up, too, bringing her face within inches of his, brushing the backs of her fingers against his temple and into his hair. "*You're* the distraction. Not sex. I can't keep my mind off you whether we make love or not." She inched closer, speaking against his mouth. "I think *not* doing it is making it worse."

His relieved rush of air warmed her lips. "I thought it was just me."

Their lips came together in a kiss that burned with urgency. Their tongues collided, and she moaned into his mouth as the heat swept through her heart and outward to every part of her, burning away any doubt that this was the right thing to do. She wanted this…wanted him.

She raised her arms, and his hands slid under her tank top to sweep it up and off in a motion that interrupted the kiss for only a second, but when his fiery mouth reconnected, it wasn't to her mouth. He nibbled along her jaw to her earlobe and behind her ear. She gasped and sighed until her breathing became so erratic she grew dizzy.

Throwing her head back, Summer sucked in a quick breath at the sensation he created as he lowered her back into the pillow, his mouth caressing each inch along the path from her neck to the peak of her breast.

He sucked a nipple into his mouth, the tantalizing pull making her arch up against him. He took advantage of her raised hips by gliding his hand into her pajamas and caressing her bottom. "Take them off." She encouraged him and wriggled her hips until she felt the material around her knees. A few good kicks sent the last of her cover sailing. Being naked had never felt this fabulous.

Rick was everywhere around her. He'd become all hands and mouth and the weight of his hard body pressed the bed down next to her and she rolled to her side against him. She couldn't anticipate where his touch would land next. He had her gasping for air and she wanted to reciprocate, wanted to feel him and taste him, but he had her so wild with need, she could do little more than claw and pant. Thinking was out of the question.

IT'S LIKE MAKING LOVE TO A little wild cat, Rick thought as Summer's hands moved through his hair and then scratched along his sides and back while she made little mewling sounds of pleasure. He'd never been with a woman this uninhibited and this passionate…nor one this small. Summer's diminutive size worried him. Her amazing body was perfectly proportioned, and he had to assume that meant *every* part of her was tiny. He'd heard a woman could accommodate any size—and he was hardly porn star status—but the tiny body writhing so feisty under the ministrations of his hands and mouth didn't seem big enough to hold even a man of average size.

As he hesitated, Summer's thumbs caught the waistband of his athletic shorts, pushing them down until his erection sprang free, and she stroked her hand tightly along the length of him.

Her movements felt so good he shuddered and drew back

a little, trying to give her the space she needed to evaluate his size. The nymph made quick use of the distance to let go of him long enough with one hand to rid him of the shorts. Then her mouth was on him, sucking in a way that was going to make him lose his rational abilities quickly. He had to act fast.

RICK PRESSED HER INTO THE pillow with a kiss that stopped her breath, but not her determination. She let her hands replicate the action her mouth had been pulled away from and was rewarded when Rick's hand finally glided past her stomach to stroke between her legs. She opened easily for him, greedy to receive the finger he offered, but knowing it wasn't enough to extinguish the need for him burning at her core.

"Rick." She panted. "I want you in me."

She felt his hesitation. "Summer, you're so small...."

You gotta be kidding me! He was afraid to follow through. She fought to keep her voice calm and lucid. It wouldn't do to let him believe her words were fueled by frustration. "I'm woman enough. I promise."

She nibbled on the shoulder that loomed in front of her mouth as his weight shifted, and she continued to knead whatever part of his body her hands fell on as she recognized the sound of the bedside table drawer sliding open, followed by the sound of ripping cellophane. It ran through her mind to question why he'd brought condoms to the camp, but whatever the reason it didn't matter much right then.

After some of the most agonizing seconds she'd ever experienced, Rick settled between her legs, his weight on his elbows, his gaze capturing hers with its heated intensity. "Are you sure about this, Summer?"

She nodded. "Uh-huh."

"I mean, really sure?"

She ground her lower body against him, punctuating each word as she spoke. "I'm. Absolutely. Certain."

He released his breath and reached between them to guide himself, sliding into her with agonizing slowness, as if she were a piece of fragile porcelain he was afraid of breaking. Inch by inch, he filled her until she couldn't stand the delay any longer.

"Oh, for heaven's sake, Rick, do me before I combust." She ground the words out as she thrust against him hard enough to bury his full length deep inside her.

He let out a groan of pleasure. "You're so tight."

"Cut the praise." She wrapped her legs around his waist. "Just pump."

Summer felt his muscles relax as he fell into a rhythm, but they tightened again just as quickly as the thrusting started to heighten the effect for both of them.

The buildup intensified, and he followed her lead. She raised her hands above her head and pushed against the headboard, wanting...needing to meet and give back his pounding rhythm as he drove into her. She arched her back higher and higher, pressing against him harder, faster and faster until her body and her mind reached their peaks simultaneously and she cried out as relief from the delicious agony swept through her.

Had Rick been holding back? His movements intensified at her cry. A violent shudder shook his body as the breath-stealing spasms continued to course through her. He kissed her hard and rolled to the side, holding under her knee to slide her thigh atop his. This position kept him firmly planted deep within her. He held her tight against him until her quaking stopped.

"Did I hurt you?" The arm beneath her loosened its hold slightly, but still kept her close.

She snuggled her face to his chest. "Of course not. Was I too tight?"

"No such thing." His leg still lay between her thighs and

he shifted closer, his palm making lazy circles around her rear. "You're perfect…in every way."

He kissed the top of her head, and she tickled his chest with her tongue, and they lay together quietly, words seeming unimportant and useless to describe the delicious bliss she was drenched in.

Her sensitive breasts picked up the rumble of laughter as it started in his stomach, felt it pull him free from her at last. She poked him playfully. "What's so funny?"

"'Do me before I combust'? Is that fairy princess talk?"

She laughed, leaning her head back to look into his eyes, which were smiling and sweet, and it ran through her mind that she could look at him looking at her this way for the rest of her life. *First-time glow,* she told herself, though her heart was sending a different message to her brain. "Hey, even fairy princesses have needs. And if I'd known what kind of magic your wand was packing—" she brushed her fingers along the side of his penis and felt it jerk to life "—I'd have told the girls not to waste the other one." She tapped the granite star wedged between them.

He grinned and tucked his hand behind the back of her neck to guide her mouth up to his again. "Has anyone ever told you how amazing you are?"

"It took a real fairy prince to ascertain that, I think." His thumb caressed her cheek, and she turned her face to press a kiss into his palm. "But it wasn't just me." She breathed deeply, a relaxed breath that filled her lungs like she hadn't felt in months. "*We're* amazing," she answered.

The question that had risen vaguely in her mind earlier resurfaced, disturbing her tranquility. She sat up to point at the open drawer beside them. "Seriously, condoms? Were you that confident, or did you just come to camp prepared for anything?"

Rick took her hands, threading his fingers between hers. "Trust me when I say I was never prepared for anything like you." He kissed her fingers and her relaxation evaporated into a bubbly sensation like she'd taken a huge gulp of champagne. "Kenny left them. They were his thank-you for the use of the cabin."

Rick must have felt the bubbling, too, as she saw the stirring of another erection. She gave him a mischievous grin and crawled on top to straddle him. "Did he leave plenty?"

Rick shrugged. "That depends, I guess. At the rate of one a day, we could stretch them to last a month."

Summer gyrated her bottom against him unabashedly. "But this session only lasts for two more weeks."

"Was one of the degrees you pursued in math?" He gave a playful groan as her figure-eight movements had the desired effect.

"Economics." She pulled her hands loose and brushed his nipples with the backs of her fingers, causing him to suck in a quick breath.

"I guess if we run out, we've got other means we can make use of."

Summer reached back with one hand to feel his erection spring to its full length. She feigned surprise. "Uh-oh. I think we might have another snake in the house."

Rolling to one side, he flung her to the bed and pinned her with his leg. "Well, this time—" he grabbed her wrists and pulled them over her head, holding them easily with one hand "—we're going to torture the snake slowly." He used his free hand to make long, bold, leisurely strokes down her body. "None of that fast catch-and-release stuff like before."

Summer closed her eyes and smiled at the delectable vibrations already thrumming through her. "Be sure to thank Kenny for me," she purred.

"Rick!"

They were thirteen and flying down the hill on their bikes. Dunk stood on his bicycle pedals, one arm holding a basketball stretched over his head. "Hell-pee-roo!" he yelled.

Rick scrunched his nose. "What?"

"Hell-pee-roo! Hell-pee-roo!" Dunk chanted at the top of his lungs.

"What's that mean?"

"Don't mean nothing. Just made it up. Sounds cool, huh?" He sat down and extended his legs out straight. "Hell-pee-roo! Say it, Rick."

"Hell-pee-roo!" Rick yelled. It was fun. He repeated it a couple more times, then they screamed it together.

Dunk held the basketball up again. "Catch!" He bounced the ball on the middle line of the street, timing it to make its ascent as Rick passed. "Hell-pee-roo!" he shouted.

Rick scooped it up as it rose from the ground, amazed to find it in his clutch. "Hell-pee-roo!" he answered.

They laughed.

"Lemme try!" Dunk held his arm out in anticipation.

"Hell-pee-roo!" Rick dribbled the ball, not hard...just enough to get it across the line and back up.

It hit the asphalt and exploded upward, shrinking in size, becoming a bullet, heading straight for Dunk!

Rick tried to shout a warning, but his voice froze in his throat. He watched in horror as the bullet buried into Dunk's neck, the force of it pitching his friend from his bike.

Rick was rushing toward him, picking him up, running with him, aware all the while of bullets zinging around him. Sweat poured from his forehead into his eyes...his ears. He glanced down. Dunk's eyes were closed. He couldn't sleep now...had to stay awake. "Dunk!" he screamed.

"Rick!"

A voice broke into his consciousness. A light flashed on,

blinding him momentarily. He shaded his eyes with his hand, feeling the sweat from his face against his palm. He took deep breaths to slow his heart rate to something resembling normal.

"You were having a nightmare."

"Sorry."

"You don't have to apologize." Summer leaned over and he was treated to the view of her perfectly sculpted back just before she switched the lamp off. "Are you okay now?"

"Yeah." *Embarrassed as hell, but okay. Gotta get these damn things under control.*

Her yawn drifted through the darkness. "You sleep at attention. How come?"

"We were trained to sleep that way." He scratched his head. "I didn't realize I still did it."

She took advantage of his raised arm to snuggle her naked body against his side. She felt warm and delicious, and he rolled over on his side to wrap his other arm across her.

His mind drifted back to their lovemaking and, surprisingly, his body relaxed. After one of his nightmares, it usually took a while…if he could get back to sleep at all.

She kissed his neck. "We're gonna retrain the tight-ass right out of you, Mr. Warren."

"That's gonna take some strong magic, princess." He buried his nose in her hair. It smelled nice…like the tea his mom used to make in the afternoon…she'd serve it with honey cakes. He hadn't thought of honey cakes in a long time. "You're good for me, Summer."

Her breathing deepened, and she didn't answer.

He took several long breaths, matching them to hers. If he dreamed again tonight, the woman in his arms would take the starring role at center stage.

CHAPTER FIFTEEN

For the seventh morning straight, Rick woke up at five but couldn't coax his body out of bed to run. He would run during quiet time, even though it would be during the heat of the afternoon. An hour of drowning in sweat was a small price to pay to enjoy another half hour of Summer in his bed—and his arms. Hell, with the workouts she'd given him the past week, he probably could cut out running completely.

It struck him as odd that he didn't feel compelled to run, and the irony of that thought made him smile. He hadn't reached the age of thirty-four unmarried by falling in love too quickly. And even the serious relationships he'd been in made him feel as though he would have to give up a part of himself to make it last.

This morning, he had no compulsion to bolt mentally or physically. He just felt relaxed. Maybe starting out disliking each other had been a good thing. Coming through the bad before the good certainly gave him a much truer perception of the woman he held than all the flirting and courtship crap that went along with dating when everybody was on their best behavior.

What a woman she was, Ms. Summer Delaney. She took his breath in so many different ways, not the least of which was the way her ass wiggled against him as she woke up just now.

"You awake?" she whispered, and he pulled her closer and kissed the crown of her head in response. "Can we talk?"

He stiffened. “Uh-oh. The ‘can we talk’ thing, already?” What had gone wrong? The week had been wonderful, hadn’t it?

“Tell me about the nightmares,” she said.

He didn’t want to start the day thinking about them. “There’s nothing to tell.” He closed his eyes. Maybe he could doze back off for a few minutes.

“They’re every night, Rick.”

“But they don’t last long.”

Her sigh had a disgruntled edge. “They disturb your sleep…*our* sleep…every night. What’s going on?”

He’d never trusted a woman enough to talk about the story behind them. But Summer understood…or was beginning to understand. He cleared his throat. “I told you Dunk got shot.”

“Yeah.”

“He was covering me when it happened. I had an injured kid in my arms.” His stomach clenched at the words. God, he hated talking about it.

Summer pulled her arm from beneath his and laid it on top, guiding his hand to her breast. “Go on. Tell me the rest.”

“I couldn’t stop. The kid needed medics.” He closed his eyes and breathed through the pain. “I went back and got Dunk. But he didn’t make it.”

Summer rolled over to face him, sadness darkening her eyes. “I’m sorry.” She ran her fingertips across his temple. “Have you tried therapy? I mean, it might help to talk to somebody.”

“I can handle it. It’ll just take time.” He saw the crease form between her eyebrows. “And I don’t want to talk about it anymore.” That was the truth. It was better to leave it hidden in the darkness. He latched on to another subject. “Happy anniversary, by the way.”

“It’s been a week today, hasn’t it?” He could hear the smile in her voice, and he relaxed. She snuggled her forehead against his neck and kissed his collarbone. “Did I tell you how good you were last night?”

“Mmm-hmm. I think Kenny might’ve heard you telling me how good I was last night.”

She sighed. “We’ll need to turn the air conditioner on if you’re going to keep doing those yummy things that make me want to pant so loudly.”

“Or, if you want to continue sleeping with the windows open, we could stop doing those things,” he teased.

She looked at him under half-lidded eyes and gave him a lazy smile. “I’ll pant more quietly.”

“I thought so.” He kissed her eyelids, admiring the thick lashes that lay against her cheek. In the breaking light of dawn, they glistened like gold threads.

She opened her eyes slowly. “What are you looking at?”

“You.” His chest tightened as he used the tip of his finger to trace the side of her face, so delicate in its bone structure. It was difficult to think he’d ever found much wrong with her. “This is the only time of day I get to look at you. I mean, *really* look at you. During the daylight, I hardly have time to even glance at you, and that bulb—” he pointed to the bedside lamp “—doesn’t begin to do you justice at night.”

Her lips pursed. “The shadows it puts out make you look pretty hot.”

He raised on an elbow and tossed the sheet that covered them to the foot of the bed. “Stand up.”

“Why?” She propped herself on both elbows and tilted her face toward him. “Are you treating me to a stand-up quickie?”

Rick shook his head, then stopped to consider her willingness. She thought *she* was the one who was being treated? Her sexual appetite was like no other woman’s he’d ever known. But he felt satisfied right now, like the urge was there and it was good, but it would be even better if he waited. “It’s tempting, but I'm pretty mellow right now. I just want to look at you in the natural light…naked."

A tender smile crept to her lips, and she crawled over him to stand at his side of the bed. Her hands swept her hair behind her shoulders, baring her breasts and her nipples, which were standing at attention. Then she dropped her arms to let them hang loosely at her side.

"You're beautiful." His eyes roamed over her slowly, for once taking in her beauty at his leisure.

"Beauty's on the inside, Rick. This is all just cover."

"I was talking about the inside." He grinned. "But the cover sure makes me want to read this book."

Her eyebrow rose as a smile twitched the corner of her mouth. "Well, it might hold a couple of interesting passages."

He chuckled at her quick wit—another plus in the long list of things he found adorable about her.

A recent tan line that outlined the modest swimsuit she wore at camp gave way to lighter areas that denoted a bikini. But nowhere was there an area that didn't have at least *some* tan.

"You sunbathe in the nude?" His finger traced a lazy, meandering path from the base of her neck between her breasts and down to her navel.

She gave him one of her mischievous grins. "Every chance I get. Which used to be pretty often with Mom and Dad traveling so much. I visited my sister in Florida last month. She has a very private patio."

He brushed the back of his finger across her deeply tanned and toned thighs. Her weight shifted forward to press against him, and the temptation almost proved to be too much as he felt himself stiffen. He thumped her playfully on her stomach like he was testing a watermelon.

"Turn around, soldier," he growled. "This inspection's not finished yet."

Summer stuck her hip out in an exaggerated sway and undulated her body around in a belly-dancing move until she faced away from him.

She'd given out two more wands the night before, so her hair was still in fairy princess mode. Golden waves splayed down her back in a disheveled mass that gave her an intoxicatingly sensuous look. Rick couldn't resist combing his fingers through the enticing tangles, noticing the way the sunlight picked up the natural highlights, which separated into myriad colors.

The wild cascade ended just above the small of her back. He let his fingers trail out through the ends and follow the dip in her spine to the crease between the cheeks of the perkiest, most perfectly formed ass he'd ever had the pleasure of knowing. The brown luster of the mounds looked like a pair of buns toasted to delicious perfection and made his mouth water. He leaned forward and nipped the fleshiest part, which brought a surprised yelp.

Summer swung around and popped him on the head with her palm, then tried to scamper away, but he proved faster. Seizing her around the waist, he pulled her between his legs, and began planting loud raspberries across her belly, ignoring her squeals of protest.

Laughter shook her until she finally collapsed onto his lap. "I surrender."

Their smiling gazes locked, and Rick felt his desire for her make a slow burn through him. Not just the desire for sex, although that was part of it. It was a desire to take possession of this woman, body and soul. Her mouth lowered to his and he could swear he felt the surrender of it all in her kiss.

She straightened, pulling her face back a few inches. "Do you regret this, Rick? Making love was my idea. Do you have any regrets about it?" She searched his eyes for an answer.

He thought about it for a moment, wanting to be as honest as possible. “Yeah. There’s one.” Clouds gathered in her eyes at his words. “We met almost two months ago, and we didn’t make love until last week. I regret all that wasted time.”

He’d never been more truthful, and honesty had never felt so good…especially when Summer rewarded him by inviting him to join her in the shower.

SUMMER DECIDED NOT TO EVER distrust her instincts again. Making love with Rick had filed the edge off and smoothed her into a new woman. On one hand, she felt relaxed and laid-back. On the other, she had energy to burn and felt as though she could take on the world with her bare hands. The bubble she carried inside made her float through her days knowing she would end them in Rick’s arms.

Normally, the current midafternoon activity would have catapulted her into zombie mode, but not even the boring fossil hunt could sap her giddiness.

“Yep, another crinoid stem.” She nodded and repeated the words for the seventeenth time…but who was counting?

The recent storm had eroded a huge portion of the bank along the pebble beach surrounding the cove, so Rick came up with an idea to combine some geology and paleontology by having a fossil dig.

Neil ran with the idea and had arranged for a professor from nearby Murray State University to come and talk to the kids and demonstrate the proper procedures to follow during an archaeological excavation. He explained to them the different eras of Earth’s history and how fossils were formed.

Of course, Howie asked question after question about the dinosaurs that roamed this region, but the professor, Dr. Shelton, showed a great deal of understanding and patience for the kid’s high-octane energy. Howie just seemed to be one of those kids people responded to.

Summer was pleased with the improvement in his attitude toward females since they'd made the groups coed. She'd even heard a couple of the girls arguing about who he liked the best. She imagined how charming he would be in a few years. It would be difficult not to love him…the little twerp.

So she reminded herself it was his enthusiasm that had him heading toward her once again, lugging another big rock. A couple of groups down, she saw Rick smile and shake his head as he watched the kid carrying the huge rock in her direction. It ran through Summer's mind that putting Howie in her group for this activity had been by design rather than the random way it appeared.

"I think I found something cool, Ms. Summer. Look at this." Roughly the size and shape of a partially deflated football, it took both hands for Howie to hold the rock up for her inspection.

Summer glanced down, expecting more of the same-old-same-old, but what she saw made her do a double take. Ridges. One side of the rock was flat but cut by a series of ridges separated by shallow grooves. It was unlike anything she'd ever seen in nature, though it did look kind of like the sole of a running shoe. She ran her fingers across the pattern, her quickening pulse convincing her Howie had found a treasure.

"Howie, I think you're right." Her voice shook with excitement. "You need to show this to Dr. Shelton." She scanned the bank until she found the professor swishing one of the large screen sieves in the water.

"Dr. Shelton," she yelled, and he looked up at the sound of his name. She pointed to the rock, which Howie now held proudly over his head. "I think we have something here."

Even from a distance, she could see the spark of recognition on the professor's face as he tossed the sieve onto the gravel and broke into a meaningful jog.

The beach came alive with the scurry of children and adults alike, running from all directions toward Howie and his treasure.

"A MAMMOTH MOLAR. Who would've thought?" Rick repeated the words on everybody's lips since Howie's find that afternoon.

"How much do you think something like that's worth?" Tara leaned on her hand, looking sleepy, which Summer couldn't imagine with all the excitement surrounding them right then.

Neil shrugged and took his glasses off to clean them with the hem of his shirt. "Dr. Shelton says not as much as you might think." He expelled a breath on the lenses and rubbed. "You can find them for sale online anytime for a couple hundred dollars. But he says this is a really fine specimen that a collector might pay more for." He put the glasses back on and used a finger to ram them into place.

"But it could mean a lot more than that to this place." Summer was too excited to hold back the news.

Rick gave her a quizzical look. "What do you mean?"

"I talked with Dr. Shelton privately for a little while, and he says there's a possibility a whole mammoth could be buried in the bank down there. He says it's not that uncommon for a river like the Ohio or the Tennessee to give up a mammoth tooth, but the banks should be checked to see if any ribs have been exposed by erosion. He wants to bring in a team during the week between sessions to do some digging. I'm going to stay here that week, and they're going to rent out one of the dorms. He said there'd be a team of probably six."

"Did your parents talk to you about their plans for that week?" Rick's mouth drew down at the corners.

"No. What plans?" What was he talking about?

"Um..." He hesitated a moment. "I suggested to them

that we use the week to spruce things up around here. Paint the buildings. Put in some flower beds. Your dad called this morning and said he was all for it."

A flash of annoyance ran through her. Her dad had called Rick about it—not her. "That's the first I've heard about any of that."

"I'm sorry. I was going to talk to you about it tonight. But I assumed your parents or Charlie had already said something...."

"Nobody told me anything." The admission clogged her throat. Her parents still saw Rick as the one to turn to.

"Dr. Shelton's team can still come." Rick's placating tone was meant to sooth her fractured ego, but it only made things worse because it was like he was giving his permission. "Neither of the projects should hinder the other," he said. "I don't see any problem—"

"The *problem* is nobody told me anything."

"Well, it was my idea, so naturally they called me...."

"Naturally. And I'm not important enough to be brought into the loop, naturally. So Charlie knows, too?"

"Yeah. He told me at lunch that he and Ginny were going to stay through that week, too, to help."

A frustrated sigh exploded from Summer's chest.

"Don't get all huffy about this, Summer. Charlie's the director, and I'm—"

"The assistant director." Her frustration was quickly giving way to indignation and anger. "How could I have forgotten they picked you over me? I'm just their daughter, so it's not like I have any investment in the place." Looking around, she noticed that Tara and Neil were on their way back to the dorms. She gathered her things and headed toward her cabin, Rick following quickly on her heels.

"Summer, don't be like this."

Aggravation tinged his voice, and she wheeled around

on him, letting her own aggravation fly. "Like what, Rick? Say it."

"Don't pout. You're acting like a child."

She ground her teeth at his words. "I'm not acting like a child. I'm acting like a woman who's insulted that she's considered to be no more important in the administration of this camp than any of the kids who are attending."

Rick reached out to take her hand, but she jerked it from his grasp and hurried on toward her cabin.

"Furthermore, as a grown woman, I'm perfectly capable of being by myself." Her insides churned hot, and she needed time to cool down. "And that's precisely what I intend to do tonight. Good night, Rick."

"Oh, for heaven's sake, Summer."

She stepped onto her porch without a backward glance. "I'll see you tomorrow."

His disgruntled huff followed her into the cabin and stayed with her long into the night as she thought about her situation.

People had to start taking her seriously. She had to prove to her parents—and yes, to Rick—that she was capable of making good decisions.

Charlie was retiring soon and Rick wouldn't be available past this summer. Her chance to take over the camp was coming soon. She had to show everyone she was capable of running this place—that taking it over wouldn't be biting off more than she could chew.

Hell, she had a mammoth molar to help with the task!

CHAPTER SIXTEEN

RICK WOKE AT HIS USUAL FIVE o'clock, and because he had no reason not to, he went for a run and hoped the morning air would clear the fog in his head. The Summer Delaney–induced fog.

Last night during the staff meeting, he'd forgotten all about telling the group about today's special event. That had never happened before.

He'd always considered himself levelheaded and rational. Hell, in Afghanistan he was the one who volunteered for dangerous missions because not many things fazed him enough to muddle his thoughts. When Dunk got hit, and while enemy bullets whizzed over his head, that head stayed clear and focused.

Then along came a slip of a woman dressed like a fairy princess, who, in three weeks' time, had him forgetting important things, questioning things he knew and regretting actions he'd taken. Even when his head told him he was right, his heart wasn't so sure.

The Delaneys hired *him* as assistant director. They had put their faith and trust in him that he would make the best decisions. Next year, maybe Summer would get her chance. He hoped she would, and he would recommend her without hesitation. But this year, they were counting on him. It was his reputation on the line, and he wouldn't disappoint.

Honor. Courage. Commitment...Semper fi.

Surely, Summer understood that. They'd gotten to know

each other well enough for her to understand he would give this place his all.

He ran faster, trying to rid his body of the restlessness he'd put up with all night. Restlessness because Summer hadn't been beside him. The small granite star thumped against his chest as he ran. He'd never really noticed its presence before, yet today it felt heavy.

Maybe during the second camp session, they could share assistant director duties.

It wasn't much, but it was the best he could come up with until his brain cleared from the Summer fog.

He broke out of the woods at full speed and detoured from his usual route to beat a path around her cabin, hoping he'd find her stirring, and they could talk.

He slowed. *No sign of life yet, damn it.* He veered toward the lake to finish up with some laps and his homage to morning and Dunk, hoping the plunge into the cool water would shock his system and clear his head.

PROPPED AGAINST the pillows, Summer watched Rick run by her window. She'd missed him last night.

But the loss of sleep had been worth the amazing idea she'd come up with—a way to become an active part of the administration of the group, even if she didn't hold the assistant director's title. Around two o'clock in the morning, she'd shot off an email to the *Paducah Sun* newspaper, relating the news of a mammoth molar being found by one of the campers. The story would surely be picked up, which would translate into free advertising. Not even her parents could poo-poo that.

Her clock read five-thirty...the time she usually left Rick's cabin. She went ahead and got up, hoping that tomorrow her schedule would return to the normal she'd grown accustomed to the past week.

Thirty minutes later, she was about to leave her cabin when her computer pinged that she had a message.

Received your email about the molar tooth. Leaving tomorrow for two weeks off, but would like to run a story in tomorrow's paper. Am available at 2:00 today. Can we make that work? Cal Perry.

That would be during quiet time. She'd be free. The kids would be free.

"Oo-rah!" She pumped the air with her fist before she typed her answer.

Two o'clock will be perfect. See you then! Summer Delaney.

She hit Send and gave herself a congratulatory hug.

"BUT SID'S COMING IN and opening the planetarium just for us. He was nice enough to work us into his busy schedule, and I'm not going to call him at this late hour and change it."

Summer's chin came up in that stubborn gesture Rick had learned to recognize. "And this is our only chance to get this story while the kids are still here. He's going to be gone for two weeks, Rick. We're talking about free advertising here." She slapped the backs of her fingers against the other palm to emphasize her point.

Rick reminded himself to be supportive. "It's a great idea." Neil and Tara had the kids lined up by the dining hall for breakfast. He waved at them to go ahead. "It's just coming at a bad time."

"If I'd known you had the field trip planned, I would've tried to schedule it for this morning. But as it is..."

"As it is..." Rick wiped his hand down his face. "The kids

won't have any time after the star show to explore the exhibits, and that's a shame because they're very interesting."

Summer snorted. "I'm sure the kids will be more than ready to leave by the time we have to go."

Her sarcasm about his educational activities unleashed Rick's irritation. "You should've checked with me or Charlie first," he snapped. "You're not in charge here. We are."

Summer's face blazed red. "And you won't ever let me forget that, will you?" She stomped away toward the dining hall.

Rick headed back to his cabin to get his measuring tape. Charlie had told him he could measure the square footage of his and Ginny's apartment today. Might as well do that now since his appetite was nowhere to be found.

AS HER PARENTS' OFFICIAL representative of the camp—her dad wasn't feeling well, which bothered her more than a little—Summer forced herself to smile throughout the interview and photo session with the young reporter from the newspaper. Cal Perry seemed as interested in flirting with her as he was in gathering facts about Howie's story. In fact, after finishing up with the mammoth molar, he'd announced he'd like to stick around and do a story on the camp itself, spending the better part of the afternoon.

This was the opportunity Summer had dreamed of, literally, and she made the most of it. Ginny had spent the morning calling parents and getting permission for their children's photos to appear in the newspaper. Mary Margaret's mother had been a hard sell, but had finally acquiesced.

Summer divided the kids into small groups and sent each group out with an adult. Cal had the opportunity to photograph them practicing archery, canoeing, swimming, geocaching, hiking and cooking. Then they all ended together with a hike to the Byassee place.

During the entire afternoon, Rick kept his distance, and

Summer missed his presence by her side. Despite their differences in opinion, she wanted to straighten things out with him as soon as possible. She hated the anger hanging between them.

"The kids have been telling me about this fairy princess philosophy of yours." Cal was standing beside her again with his pad open. "I think it would make a great angle for the story."

His statement sent a surge of satisfaction through her. More free publicity was a good thing. Her mom and dad would be impressed!

WHILE THE YOUNG MAN FAWNED over Summer, Rick stayed out of the way, watching from a distance, taking his own photos for his Delaney file. The besotted reporter was sure to give Summer some great coverage in the article. Rick just hoped the camp got some mention, as well.

When the guy first arrived and attached himself to her, jealousy pricked at Rick. But he'd recalled Summer's words that a person who made you fight for him—or in this case her—wasn't worth having. The adage made sense. And though the twangs continued throughout the afternoon as he watched her smile and converse, he realized they weren't so much twangs of jealousy as they were twangs of remorse.

He didn't mind her smiling at the reporter—he just wanted her to smile at him, too. Her smile warmed his heart, and he missed that feeling.

Cal Perry put his gear into his backpack, finally. Rick waited until he was pulling away in his car before he approached Summer.

She heard him and turned his way, but the smile he was hoping for wasn't present. She raised an eyebrow. "See? I told you it was a great idea."

"I never said it wasn't a good idea."

His friend Sid at the planetarium had been none too pleased that he'd given up time in the middle of his day off when he found out they would have to rush through everything.

Once the kids had loaded back onto the bus, Sid had chewed Rick's ass thoroughly for his poor planning, making Rick wonder if he'd hurt his chances for the park ranger job he was hoping for this fall. He'd counted on Sid's support, but now he wasn't sure that was a given. It ate at him, and he shrugged noncommittally, still feeling the sting. "It was just bad timing."

"The timing was perfect, actually. Maybe Mom and Daddy will finally see that I'm capable of making good decisions for this place." Her face broke into a smile of smug delight.

"Is that what all this was about?" Irritation flickered in his gut again.

"Proving myself?" She gave a curt nod. "Damn right."

Proving herself to Mommy and Daddy? Grabbing some glory for herself with no thought of the consequences to others? The flicker flared higher. She was acting like a spoiled brat, and it was time somebody called her on it. "That's pretty selfish, don't you think?"

"Selfish?" Her smugness shifted to indignation.

"You heard me. You're thinking about Summer Delaney, not Camp Sunny Daze…not the kids."

"How can you say that?" she sputtered.

"How can I *not* say that? Don't you realize there's a ripple effect in life? Things are related? You're willing to waste educational time…time that could spark a lifelong interest… maybe even determine a life's calling—" he included the entire camp with a sweep of his arms "—in order to prove you could make one good decision?"

Her chin snapped higher at his use of the word *one*. "I would never preempt a *true* learning experience for the kids.

I'm all for their learning early about life and finding their place in it." She mimicked his arm sweep. "If you think anything different from that, you don't know me very well."

"I thought I did. But you're right. I *don't* know you very well, apparently."

They stood in silence, eyes locked defiantly.

Summer was about to say something—wanting to get in the last word, no doubt—when her gaze shifted beyond him and her face pinched in worry. Footfalls came up fast behind him.

He swung around to meet Tara, breathless and pale. She gripped her cell phone so tightly her knuckles were white. "Summer, I need to go home." Her voice quavered.

"What's wrong?" Summer's hands gripped her friend's shoulders. "What's happened?"

Tara held up the phone and shook her head. "I don't know. My mom just called. She said not to worry…everybody's okay and nobody's hurt or anything, but I need to come home. They need to talk to me about something."

"That's odd, isn't it?" Summer voiced Rick's exact thoughts. "What could it be?"

"I don't know." Tara's eyes filled with tears. "Unless they're getting a divorce or something, but I can't imagine that. I mean, with my dad being a preacher… They seem so happy and have never had any problem that I know of…." Her voice trailed off.

"Go," Summer insisted. "I'll find Ginny and Charlie and tell them right now."

Rick stepped in. "I'll find Ginny and Charlie. Y'all go take care of whatever you need to do."

Summer gave him one last glaring look before they took off in opposite directions.

CHAPTER SEVENTEEN

RICK SENSED HER FOUL MOOD. The tense lines between Summer's brows remained fixed the rest of the evening and all the next day. Her eyes and mouth were tight even when she smiled—and she'd smiled often, though never at him. She'd totally avoided eye contact with him since their argument.

Charlie had gotten up early, gone into town and had a souvenir copy of the *Paducah Sun* waiting for everyone at breakfast.

While a small photo of Summer included a caption about Fairy Princess Parties, the newspaper did a remarkable job of making Camp Sunny Daze look like a piece of kid-heaven on Earth. All of the kids were included in at least one photo, but Howie and his mammoth molar scored top billing, firmly establishing the little boy's celebrity status among his peers.

Rick noted that even the kids who'd rolled their eyes at the youngster's tall tales vied for a seat near him during morning snack, lunch, supper and bedtime snack. And with the wisdom of one who recognized the fickle nature of fame, Howie took it upon himself to group the kids into bunches of five and sat in the middle of one group each time.

Rick smiled as Neil led the boys toward the bunkhouse for the night. Howie was in the middle of the band of brothers, a line of ten comrades, arms around one another's shoulders as they marched along singing the Sunny Daze camp song.

Although the girls were just as giddy, the party attitude didn't extend to Summer. The *attempt* was there, but her raised, rigid shoulders spoke volumes. The one point of genuine pleasure he'd seen in her was when she presented Howie with his star. The boy's grin split his face as he held it up and proudly proclaimed himself "just like Mr. Rick."

A shudder passed through Rick at the words. He hoped like hell the boy's nights weren't haunted by nightmares like his were.

They allowed the kids to stay up later in celebration, so Rick canceled the staff meeting. It was for the best. His call to Sid to apologize had stirred up the cantankerous old man's ire again and rekindled his own frustration with Summer's antics. He could tell she was exhausted, having only Ginny's limited help with the girls, so it was just as well they both had time to cool off.

He watched her walk toward the girls' bunkhouse, where she would spend another night in Tara's room.

With all the talking they'd done, how in the hell could he have missed her self-centeredness?

The term *how in the hell* mocked him when he entered the stifling hot cabin. A threat of rain that morning had convinced him to close the windows, and he hadn't been back, spending the hour of quiet time getting a few photos of the archery field and the Byassee homestead.

He made quick work of opening all the windows, but it was going to take a while to cool the place down. Maybe a swim would cool his frustration, as well.

"Another hot summer night, eh?" Kenny appeared out of nowhere when Rick stepped out onto the porch, making him wonder if the security guard had been waiting for him.

Kenny loved to talk, so the long hours of the night shift probably passed slowly for him. Rick didn't normally mind company, but he wasn't up for small talk tonight. "Yeah." He kept his answer monosyllabic so as not to give encouragement.

"Speaking of hot Summer..." Kenny grinned and shrugged his eyebrows suggestively, which irritated the hell out of Rick.

"Off-limits," he growled, and stalked off toward the beach.

Kenny hurried after him. "Hey! Sorry, man. I didn't mean anything by it." He caught up, falling into step beside Rick. "Summer's a great girl. Y'all need to work things out."

Hell-pee-roo. "It's that obvious, huh?"

Kenny shrugged. "Just to me. It's my job to watch what goes on around here."

If the comment was meant to make Rick feel better, it didn't. He didn't say anything and hoped Kenny would take the hint and leave him alone.

But the security guard seemed bent on providing consolation whether Rick wanted it or not as he followed him down the path. "My girlfriend and I broke up for a couple of months 'bout two years ago. This girl I'd gone out with in high school showed up in town, and I—"

"Shhh." Rick grabbed Kenny's arm and motioned with his head toward the cove and the sound he'd heard in the distance—a vehicle of some sort...from the grinding, most likely a pickup truck. A sound familiar in these parts, for sure, but he hadn't heard one anywhere around since the camp opened.

He and Kenny raced down the path to the beach.

Headlights shone through the trees that bordered the beach on the far side of the cove. In the darkness, it was impossible to make out more than the vague outline of a pickup.

"Fisherman?" Rick asked.

"Nah." Kenny shook his head. "Parkers, most likely."

The sound of a door slamming drifted across the water toward them.

Kenny pulled his flashlight from his belt and tried to scan

the far bank, but the light wasn't quite strong enough to reach that distance.

The door slammed again and headlights flashed back on. They soon disappeared, backing away from the trees.

"Too much beer. Taking care of nature's call. Been there myself lots of times."

Rick's gut told him that wasn't the case. "He wouldn't have come so far off the main road."

"Well, whatever was taking place, it was off camp property and not really our concern." Kenny dropped the flashlight down through the leather loop on his belt and headed back up the path.

Rick followed him. "It was close, though, so keep an eye out and an ear to the ground tonight."

"I've told you before, it's my job to keep watch over this place." Kenny chuckled. "I'm real good at what I do."

SUMMER WOKE IN A COLD SWEAT. Shivering, she drew the blanket closer under her chin, trying to remember the dream that could cause such a reaction.

Or maybe it wasn't the dream. Maybe it was waking up for the second night to the strange surroundings of Tara's bedroom, wondering what had happened that shattered her friend's world. Ginny had heard from her, at least. She said Tara would be back in the morning, but Ginny had added that she was crying when she phoned.

While Summer was definitely concerned about her friend, more likely it was Rick Warren who was haunting her dreams. Waking up without him for the third morning and facing the fact that waking up *with* him might not be a possibility ever again made her shiver just thinking about it.

Selfish.

The word he'd used to describe her squeezed her heart and then moved down to squeeze her stomach just for good measure. She got up before she puked in Tara's bed and went to the bathroom to apply a cold washcloth to her face. It kept her from throwing up, but didn't stop the pain.

She eyed her reflection in the mirror. There were plenty of men in the world, so how did she come to fall in love with one who didn't understand what she was most passionate about?

She peered deeper, shocked by the question. *In love? Oh, for heaven's sake...when had that happened?* She'd been in love before, hadn't she? But breaking up had never felt like this—like she was shriveling up inside…like something was squeezing all the important stuff out of her and leaving an empty shell in its place.

Selfish. She'd been called that so many times in the past the word shouldn't have any effect…and maybe it had been deserved then. But she wasn't like that now. Why couldn't anybody see that? Rick, of all people, surely should be able to see it…*would* be able to see it, if he loved her back.

But he hadn't seen it, and she had to face what that meant.

She jerked away from the mirror and turned the shower on full force.

An hour later, she and the girls approached the boys, who were waiting at the trailhead for the morning hike. Rick's eyes locked with hers, the grim set of his mouth confirming he hadn't changed his mind…about her…about anything.

"Kenny and I saw a pickup in the woods across the cove last night." He kept his voice low as they followed the group being led by Neil. "Might have been parkers, and we apparently scared them off. But…"

He hesitated, and his reluctance to finish the sentence stopped Summer in her tracks. "But maybe it was someone planning to go digging for mammoth bones."

Ricked shrugged. "That idea did enter my mind."

A fierce, protective anger shot through her. "No one can do that!" She turned and paced the opposite direction to gain more distance from the kids. "The mammoth molar was found on *my property!*" she spewed. "My parents' property. Whoever it was has no right!"

"Thieves generally aren't great respecters of other people's rights." Rick had followed her.

His hand slipped around her bicep to slow her down, but she jerked out of the grip, pulling the cell phone from her pocket. "I'm calling Sheriff Blaine right now—"

Rick snatched the phone from her hand and stopped the call. "I've already spoken with him."

"And?"

"And he said he doesn't have enough deputies to patrol areas accessible only by water with any consistency. He'll do what he can, but that's not going to be much. Marshall County has miles and miles of shoreline, and the areas that don't have residents near are always going to be a problem."

Summer's mind whirred. She turned again to follow the campers. She walked fast out of frustration and to catch up. "We're only talking three more nights until this session is over. Then Dr. Shelton's group will be here. I'll sleep down on the beach if I have to."

"No, you won't."

Her jaws clenched at Rick's commanding tone.

"Why don't we move the group after-dark activities to the beach?" he suggested. "Then Kenny can keep watch down there the rest of the night. That's really all we can do."

His words conjured memories of the after-dark activities the two of them had enjoyed on the beach, and she swallowed hard. How long would it take until those thoughts stopped popping unbidden into her head?

Stop it. She mentally slapped herself. More pressing matters were at hand. She didn't have time to moon over a man who thought the worst of her.

"After lights-out, I'll stay on the beach until I'm ready to go to bed," Rick said. "And then Kenny will include the area in his rounds every half hour or so."

"*I'll* stay on the beach," she corrected. "It isn't right for you to give up your own time for this."

Rick seemed unaffected by her insistence. "I don't want you down there alone. We'll stay on the beach together."

Hours alone on the beach with Rick? That would be torture her heart couldn't bear. It threatened to gallop away now merely at the thought. She could hear the blood pulsing in her ears. "No. This isn't your problem. It's my problem, and I'll handle it." She cast a sidelong glance at him. The muscle in his jaw twitched, but he said nothing.

Neil turned onto the path that led to the Byassee homestead, and Summer's breathing finally caught up with her stride. This was where she needed to be. The place and its guardian angels would calm her.

The past two mornings, they'd been treated to the view of a skulk of red foxes that had made a den in the old house. A vixen and six kits—Rick made sure everyone called them by the correct names—identical in their furry red coats and white-tipped tails. Mama would scurry out each morning as she heard the group approach and make for the woods, leading her babies to safety.

This morning, the vixen didn't appear, leaving the kids disappointed, but an apprehensive twinge ran between Summer's shoulder blades.

"She probably moved 'em," Carlos suggested. "My cat moved her kittens. My mom said we bothered 'em too much."

"I'll bet you're right, Carlos." Rick smiled his approval at the boy's observation, but Summer couldn't shake her odd feeling. The area was too quiet.

"But look who's here." Neil pointed to a log that had four box turtles nestled beside it.

While the campers got a short lesson on the species from

Rick, Summer ambled toward the back of the house. A couple of minutes by herself in the peaceful sanctuary should slow the world down some.

The bit of fur, fluffed by the morning breeze, drew her eye and then sucked her breath completely out of her lungs.

One of the kits. Dead. Run over. Tracks in the grass showed a vehicle had turned in from the old roadbed.

Summer's head swam, and she leaned against the wall that had once held the back door, letting the anger and frustration rush through her. Someone had been here yesterday. Last night. A low hum nearby called her attention to a spot of golden brown liquid that stained the wall, and was now covered with flies. A broken whiskey bottle lay in the weeds below.

Was it the same person who'd been across the cove? Had the news story brought him here? Anguish nipped at her heart. This was her fault.

Looking at the dead kit brought the bitter taste of bile into her throat. All those years, this place had been isolated and quiet. That someone had been here the night the story was in the paper seemed too big a coincidence. In her haste to garner attention, she hadn't considered any bad consequences. Her selfishness *had* caused this. All of it. Her knees grew weak at the thought.

Willing her legs not to buckle under her, she half staggered back around to the front of the cabin. Rick glanced up over the heads of the kids. When his eyes locked with hers, he seemed to read her mind.

He clapped his hands together. "You know, if we travel very quickly and quietly on down to the lake this morning, we might be lucky enough to catch that eagle again."

"You heard the man." Neil spoke in a stage whisper, jerking his head toward the path. "Let's go, gang."

Rick leaned down and whispered something in Neil's ear.

The young man's eyes shot to Summer, and he nodded. He hustled the kids out of the clearing as Rick approached.

"What's wrong?" His fingers skimmed down her arm and caught her hand. The touch was warm and soothing, and she knew she should pull loose, but it was what she needed right then. She let it stay.

Swallowing didn't rid her throat of the tight lump lodged there. "One of the kits is dead. Run over." Her voice quivered on the last phrase. She cleared her throat. "Somebody's been here."

Rick's face darkened. He dropped her hand and stalked toward the back of the house. She had to jog to catch up.

Stooped beside the lifeless form of the small creature, he smoothed its fur gently with the back of his fingers. She watched his eyes fill with grief as they took in the tracks left in the grass.

"Do you think it was the same person who was in the cove?" She motioned toward the wall and the whiskey bottle.

Rick's eyes flashed from sorrow to anger, and he shook his head. "I don't know."

Summer swiped at the tears on her cheeks. "This is my fault. We've never had trouble before. It can't be coincidental this happened right after the story was published."

"Don't jump to conclusions, Summer." The sympathy in his voice battered at the wall holding back her emotions. Her body shook with the effort of keeping them in check.

When he stood and pulled her to him, her resolve crumbled amid the bombardment of anger and frustration. She clung to him like a child and cried against his chest as his hands smoothed over her hair and back.

"It's okay. Quit crying now." He sounded like he was soothing one of the kids.

No way was she going to let him think of her that way. Pulling herself together, she pushed out of his hold.

His hands settled on his hips as he blew his breath out in a discontented sigh. "Go back to the camp and get a shovel. Bring it here, and leave it. We'll meet you on the way back. You can accompany the kids with Neil, and I'll stay and bury the kit."

They walked silently to the main trail, but he gave her shoulder a pat before he broke into a run in the direction of Neil and the campers.

Summer's legs felt like weights were attached to them as she jogged back to camp. Or maybe her heart had sunk so low it was now in the vicinity of her ankles.

The shovel Charlie kept near the campfire leaned against a tree. She got it and headed back toward the wooded path just as Tara turned in the drive.

Burying the kit was important, but welcoming Tara back took top priority. Summer went to meet her as her friend parked the car.

Tara's face was unreadable as she got out, but when she turned to Summer, she took off her sunglasses, and Summer felt an involuntary gasp slip between her lips.

The skin around Tara's eyes was swollen, and the blotchy red areas stood out against her fair complexion. She'd been crying, obviously hard, probably for a while. Two days, maybe?

Summer stood quietly, waiting for her to speak first. Tara's eyes darted away, then back, and a heavy sigh settled in her chest.

"Louis came home from Honduras the day before yesterday," she said finally. "A month early."

While the news sounded like it should bring Tara joy, that obviously wasn't the case. Summer took her hand to lend moral support, then braced herself for what would come next.

"He brought…" Tara stopped and took a deep breath. "He brought his wife back with him."

His wife. The words seemed to hold their shape in the void between them.

"His wife?" Had Louis been married all this time? "His wife for how long?" Anger stirred Summer's already-churning stomach.

"They met shortly after he got there, and a month ago they decided they were in love." Tara drew a ragged breath, but there were no tears. Probably none left, if her face was any evidence.

"He wanted to tell me in person. Not over the phone or in an email. When he told Mom and Dad, they thought it would be best if I came home right away instead of hearing it from someone who might call me here."

"Oh, Tara, I'm so sorry." Summer hugged her, and Tara's answering embrace was strong. Her friend was holding herself together well, but that didn't stop the anger from vibrating through Summer. "The no-good bastard."

Tara pushed away, shaking her head. "No. Louis isn't a bastard. He's a great guy, and I want him to be happy."

How could she be so calm? Summer wanted to shred his hide with her fingernails, and she'd never even met him. "But he hurt you," she said, like she needed to draw her friend's attention to that fact?

Tara's snort held a bitter edge. "Yes, he did. But not as much as he would've hurt me if he'd married the wrong woman."

Summer's head swirled with vicarious resentment. "All those years of saving yourself?"

A half smile raised one corner of Tara's mouth. "I've got a lot of years to make up for. And I need to think about something else now and get on with the rest of my life." She gave a dismissive wave. Her eyes darted around, searching for something to attract her focus. They settled on the shovel.

"I saw the article. Is Howie laying it on so thick now you need to shovel it out?"

Summer held up the shovel, but thought better of telling Tara just yet about all that had transpired during the night. "One of the kits is dead. I'll explain later. Right now, I need to go meet the kids."

Tara nodded. "I'll put one of Ginny's ice packs on my face for a few minutes. Maybe it'll help with the redness. Then I'll meet y'all at breakfast?"

"My stuff's still in your room, so stay in my cabin tonight." Summer didn't give her a chance to disagree. "Another night away from the girls might be good for you...." *In case you decide to cry your eyes out again.* She kept that to herself as she trotted away, shovel in hand.

Arriving back at the Byassee place ahead of the group, she leaned the shovel against the house, noticing her hand trembled under the movement. The heavy stress of the past couple of days was beginning to show.

She breathed in, trying to recapture the peace and tranquility she'd always felt here, but the panicked beating of her heart was anything but tranquil as it drummed a frightening message into her brain. The disturbance bored deeper into her psyche, deeper than a dead kit or a corrupted mammoth dig, deeper than the possibility of her parents' lost retirement...deeper even than the breakup with Rick.

The serenity of her favorite place had been violated, the angels chased away by some evil that still lurked. She could feel it despite the heat of the morning—an icy edge to the breeze warned her to leave and not come back.

She ran back to the main trail to meet the group, channeling the instincts of the vixen.

She couldn't give a good reason why, but for the rest of the camp session, the Byassee homestead was off-limits.

CHAPTER EIGHTEEN

DANIEL'S SMILE SAID IT ALL as he rose from the water a couple of seconds ahead of Carlos. Not only was he a fast learner, he was also a fast swimmer, beating all the other boys in every race during the past week.

Summer released the sigh that pressed in her lungs as she watched M&M. The girl was still only dog-paddling in waist-deep water while wearing a life jacket...another screwup on her side of the scoreboard.

Her phone conversation with Dr. Shelton had at least made her feel a little better about the publicity the newspaper had given the camp. He didn't think it likely that anyone would try to dig for a mammoth. According to him, only a scientist would know what to look for, and a scientist wouldn't run the risk of working in the dark. And, as he'd pointed out, what would a layperson do with something he found? Any find would be suspicious, thanks to the publicity the site had received.

So while she was breathing easier about that situation, she still couldn't shake the uneasiness about the Byassee place. No one was searching for fossils there. She squeezed her eyes shut, trying to rid them of the image of the dead kit and the smashed whiskey bottle.

"Why's everybody so sad?" M&M stopped in front of Summer and peered into her eyes.

Summer forced a laugh. "Everybody's not sad."

M&M nodded sagely and glanced around the swimming area. "A lot of people are. You. Ms. Tara. Mr. Rick."

"Maybe we just hate it that the camp is coming to an end. We'll miss you all."

A mischievous twinkle lit the child's eyes. "I know something that will make y'all happy."

"Oh, yeah?"

M&M nodded and unbuckled her life jacket, flinging it onto the beach. "Watch."

Her form wasn't perfect. She slapped the water hard and shifted her face from side to side with every breath, but the child swam across the area from rope to rope.

The entire camp population came to a halt, silently watching the feat.

When she popped up on the other end, a roar of applause greeted her, and she acknowledged the ovation by raising both hands and waving like an Olympian.

"You little imp!" Summer called. "When did you figure out you could do that?"

"Last night," the child shouted. "I dreamed it. I think it was my pretty heart speaking to me. It told me I could swim and make people happy."

That announcement was met by more cheers, and M&M beamed.

Neil hoisted her onto his shoulders for a triumphant ride through the crowd, being met with high fives all around.

RICK JOINED IN THE CHEERS as Neil picked the child up. From somewhere in the distance, a noise floated around his ear—a boat motor backfired with a *pop.*

The beach...the kids...Summer...Neil—everything in his vision zoomed away as if he were watching through a camera lens and needed a wide-angle shot.

He watched Dunk lift the child with tender care, stag-

gering under the additional weight that should have been an easy carry.

"Can you make it?"

Dunk nodded, his face etched in determination as he turned and fled.

Another lap around the burned-out shell of a building turned up no survivors, and with every step, a sickening realization coiled his muscles tighter. The child had been left behind to die. A decoy, most likely.

Rage fueled his movement as he sprinted to catch up.

He could hear Dunk's labored breathing.

"Let me have her, Dunk."

"The name's Neil, remember? And I've got her." Neil glared at him, the indignation in his eyes magnified by the thickness of his glasses. "I may not be a marine, but I'm capable of carrying a child."

"No, I, uh..." Rick ran a hand down his heated face, trying to gain his equilibrium. He glanced around the group of still-cheering kids, thankful no one else had heard. Thankful Summer hadn't heard. She would've known immediately what had happened. "I didn't mean to imply you weren't strong enough to carry her. I just thought since it's time to go, maybe I would carry her on up the hill."

Right on cue, Tara blew a whistle. "Time to get washed up for dinner."

The swimmers started slogging to the shore, gathering up their towels and shoes.

Neil looked at the hill, obviously sizing it up and making a quick calculation about the slope and the additional weight he carried on his shoulders.

Rick made use of the time by dropping under the water to rid himself of the cold sweat oozing from his pores.

"Okay, man." Neil grinned, the indiscretion forgiven. "She's all yours."

M&M gave a delighted squeal as they exchanged her from one set of shoulders to the other.

On the way up the hill, Summer fell in step beside them. Rick's heart thumped a double beat that had nothing to do with the extra weight of the child, which he hardly noticed, and everything to do with the fact that Summer was going to speak to him again.

"You know, M&M," she said, "I think listening to your pretty heart has earned you a wand."

The child let out another excited squeal, beating her hands on top of Rick's head.

They reached the summit, and M&M held her arms out to Summer, who lifted her down with Rick's help. They both were engulfed by the other members of the female group, chattering noisily about the turn of events in the past few minutes.

Rick watched them, thinking about the same thing, but with none of the enthusiasm. Oh, he was happy for M&M. But after the incident this morning at the Byassee place, Summer had returned to her cool distance, while the concern and fear in her eyes had put a choke hold on him he couldn't break loose from.

Plus, he'd had to admit to himself that his own recent frustration had been fueled in part by self-serving motives. He'd wanted Sid to know what a good job he was doing…wanted his approval…wanted his nod for the pending job.

Were he and Summer really so different?

He touched the star beneath his shirt.

M&M had earned her wand, and at the same time the magic in his was sifting away.

While that should lighten his load, the heaviness in his heart told him he was losing something precious.

And he sure as hell didn't want that to happen again.

"LOVE SHOULDN'T BE this difficult." Summer dug her feet into the soft sand and patted it to cover her ankles. "I was watching the kids' tug-of-war this afternoon and thinking how much that game is like love. You pull and tug, first one way, then the next. It goes back and forth, and then somebody weakens and ends up losing."

"Tell me about it." Tara's voice lacked its usual spark.

It was such a relief to have her friend back to talk with again, even if the subject made Summer's heart feel like it was being grilled on a spit over an open fire. Neither of them was in the mood for lemonade and chocolate in the cabin tonight. Instead, they'd chosen to hang out on the beach, despite the drop in the temperature—which Tara insisted on blaming Summer and Rick for.

"Selfish. He actually called me that to my face." Summer bit her lip to stop it from trembling.

"He doesn't really believe that, and you know it. We all see how much you love this place." Tara tossed a pebble absently into the water, and they watched the ripples fan out.

Summer pointed to them. "The ripple effect. Another term he used. Every action leads to another one, and before you know it, it's gotten out of hand and can't be controlled. The hell of it is he's right." She formed a circle with her hands and let it grow larger as she spoke. "I get this great marketing idea for the camp, but Rick gets pissed because the kids miss part of the space lesson he's sure might direct one of them to astronaut training. The article gives us some amazing coverage, but maybe too much because somebody finds the Byassee place, and a kit gets killed. I try to do something that I think will benefit my parents, but Rick sees my motives as selfish. I fall for him in a big way, and he thinks I'm a spoiled brat." She folded her arms across her chest, warming her fingers under her arms. "My dad's right. I'm a total screwup."

Tara's eyebrows drew together in concern. "Does your dad say that?"

"He doesn't have to say it. I see it in his eyes. Hear it in his voice. But he trusts Rick. Trusts him implicitly." A hard lump formed in her throat, and she took a deep breath. "I wish there was some way to get them out from under this debt. I'm terrified this worry will be the end of my dad." A tear crept from the corner of her eye. "I mean, Charlie's going to retire soon. Rick's not going to be around next summer. The whole point was to prove I could run this place, thinking that might take the pressure off."

Tara held out a tissue. "Have some faith in yourself, Summer."

"Why? Nobody else does."

"You've got good intentions."

"Yeah…right. You know what they say about the road to hell…" Summer wiped her eyes with the tissue.

Tara snorted. "That's one I'm definitely familiar with." She pulled another tissue from her pocket and wiped her own eyes. "But I want to believe good intentions are rewarded sometimes, too."

They sighed in unison.

A fish jumped out of the water, making a light splash. They watched in silence as the ripples widened in the cove until the tiny laps crawled onto the beach.

"The ripple effect," Summer murmured. "Once they've started, you can't pull them back in."

RICK WAITED UNTIL HE SAW the shadowy figure making her way back to the girls' dorm.

He'd watched Summer and Tara go down to the beach after the quick but tense staff meeting. No doubt Tara had needed some time to discuss whatever it was that had happened at home. She was obviously still upset. Ginny and

Summer had clucked around her all day like mother hens, while the men in the camp had been kept in the dark about the entire situation.

A welcome cool front had come through on the heels of the blistering heat. Rick kept an eye on Summer's cabin as he grabbed a jacket. The cabin stayed dark, so she must still be on the beach.

He could discern the small figure, huddled with her knees under her chin and her hood up.

She didn't move as he approached, not even when he called to her from the edge of the trees.

"Not speaking to me, eh? Then I'll have to do the talking." He plopped down on the towel beside her.

A startled Tara threw her iPod with an "Eeep!"

"I thought you were Summer, Tara. I'm so sorry." Tara wiped her eyes. *Damn.* She'd been crying.

"Summer's staying with the girls tonight." The young woman retrieved her iPod and sat back down beside him with a sniff.

"That bad, huh?" Not a great opening, but one she could either take or back away from.

"Yeah, but getting better." She still didn't offer to tell him what was wrong, so he didn't ask.

"Help me understand men, Rick."

The sadness in her voice clutched at his heart. "We're very basic creatures actually," he answered. "Feed our egos and our stomachs, and our hearts are in your hands."

"Well, I'm not a very good cook, so maybe that's where I went wrong."

He wasn't sure what happened, but he reasoned it had to do with another woman. He'd noticed that men, as a rule, wouldn't leave one without another to go to. "Not that this is an excuse or anything, but sometimes guys leave their favorite dish just to try something new. Later, they figure out they still crave that favorite dish."

"And sometimes the new dish suits their palate perfectly."

"Then it was meant to be," he answered softly.

She nodded and her breath stuttered.

"Want to talk about it?"

She shook her head with a sigh. "I've thought about it to death. Time to let it go."

They sat mutely for a few minutes, avoiding eye contact.

Rick broke the silence. "Any words of wisdom for me? Any deep insights into the feminine psyche?"

"Summer's an interesting person." She didn't hesitate on the name, so she knew whose psyche interested him. "She comes across as a free spirit, but she's really a worrier about some things, especially her dad."

Rick thought about the few times he'd been around Herschel Delaney. "He seems to be doing okay. I mean, he needs to lose some weight and get more exercise, but for a man his age, he's not that bad."

"Did you know Summer blames herself for his heart problems? She thinks she worried him too much in the past, so she's determined to keep him worry free now. That's why this place has such a hold on her. I didn't realize how deep it was until a few minutes ago. She's obsessed with getting her parents out from under the debt."

Put that way, her recent actions didn't seem so selfish… didn't seem selfish at all. The conclusions he'd jumped to and the things he'd said to her gnawed at his insides even harder than before. Big chunks of regret landed with a *thud* in his stomach.

"She loves her parents…and she loves you," Tara said.

The statement jolted Rick. The few looks he'd received from Summer the past couple of days had been anything but looks of love. "Your woman's intuition may be a little outta whack right now."

Tara turned to look at him squarely. "You're not that clueless, are you?"

"Well." He rubbed a hand down his face. "I never thought so until now. Does she say she loves me?" His breathing held as he waited for her reply.

"Yeah, and it's tearing her up that you accused her of being selfish. She wants to prove she can run the place so her mom and dad will quit worrying. She really was doing what she thought was in their best interest."

He picked up a pebble and hurled it as far as his arm could throw. "What an ass I've been. I need to apologize. But that's not going to take care of her parents' debt problem."

"Sorry. I can't help you there. Financial planning's not my forte. Maybe that magic wand you earned can go *poof* and fix everything." Tara gave a heavy sigh and stood to leave, brushing the sand from her feet and legs. "I'm getting chilly. Think I'll call it a night."

"Try to get some sleep." Rick watched her go up the hill until she disappeared from sight. *Poor kid.* It was obvious she was hurting.

And, much as he hated to admit it, so was he—because he'd hurt Summer. *Damn it all!* He had to fix this. He wanted her in his arms…in his bed. Not just for the night. Forever. She brought a special magic to his life.

He pulled the chain hanging around his neck out of his T-shirt and fingered the star. His eyes fell on his dog tags, reminding him of the flashback that afternoon. That had never happened before…during the day. Were they getting worse? He shivered in the cool night air. He'd have to find a way to stop them.

He stood and stretched, dreading sleep and what it might

bring, wishing he had Summer's soothing warmth to share the night.

Seeing the camp and her parents' retirement lost…needing to prove herself to them…fearing the decline in her dad's health—those were Summer's nightmares. What could he do to stop them?

His phone beeped when he walked into the cabin. He picked it up from the table, wishing for a text from Summer.

It was his mom. He'd missed her call, but she'd still be up. He pressed the button.

"Hi, sweetheart." She answered after the first ring.

"Hey, Mom. Did you need me?"

"I wanted to see if you ever tried the costume on and if it fit okay?"

Rick chuckled. "It fits fine. Neil said I need to get a wide, flashy belt and tell my story in an Elvis Presley voice. Thank you. Thank you very much." He tried an Elvis impersonation.

"Or maybe not." His mom laughed. "But I'm sure you'll look very handsome. Summer will love it." She picked up on his pause immediately. "Everything okay with you and Summer?"

"I wouldn't exactly say everything's okay." He blew out his breath. "What would be the opposite of everything's okay?"

"Oh, Rick." In his mind's eye, he could see her leaning back, getting comfortable in her desk chair. "Things were going so well between you two. What happened?"

Rick gave her a brief rundown, leaving out the more intimate details, but focusing on his biggest mistake. "So I can apologize, but I want to do more than that."

"Well, we know that selling the camp is a possibility. That would get rid of the debt, and ease Summer's worries as well as theirs."

Rick shook his head, then realized his mom couldn't see him. "If there's any chance of the property becoming a subdivision, she'll completely freak out. I mean, she'd let it happen if it meant getting her parents out of debt, but it would break her heart."

"And I agree with her. That would be a shame. But the place has just received some terrific coverage as a camp. If you could find that quick buyer who would offer a good profit and tie it to Summer's promotional campaign, she could feel good about what she's done and rest easy about her parents' retirement." Mom was on a roll now. Rick listened to her ideas with a growing interest. "Surely there's a buyer out there who'd want to keep it as a camp. You've got contacts in the state government. Don't you know somebody?"

Rick's heart lurched. He *did* know somebody! "Riley Gibson," he answered. "The state director of Parks and Recreation. He's a friend. State money's tight, but this place would be a great investment, and there would be no worry of subdivision development. Mom, you're a genius!"

"Look how smart you are. It took your dad forty years to figure that out."

"I'll call Herschel first thing tomorrow and run the idea by him."

"And you'll apologize to Summer. That's an order."

"Yes, ma'am," Rick answered.

"And you'll quit worrying about Sid. The department has your personnel records from when you were a ranger, and those are going to mean more than that silly old coot's grumbling."

How come talking to Mom always made things better? "Yes, ma'am," he said again, noticing how the weight had lifted from his chest.

"Good boy. Now get some sleep."

"Love you, Mom."

"Love you, too, bedbug." She hung up.

Rick shook his head at the endearment. He and Dunk had

brought bedbugs home from basketball camp one summer—their moms hadn't found the real critters quite so endearing. He brushed his fingers over the tattoo and gave it a pat.

Then, grabbing the granite star, he pumped it in his hand. There might be a little magic left in the thing, after all.

SUMMER'S HEART NEARLY JUMPED out of her chest. Had the answer really been that easy all the time?

"From the mouths of babes," she whispered to herself.

Returning to the bunkhouse after the talk with Tara, she'd met M&M coming out of the bathroom, apparently too keyed up over the events of the day to go to sleep.

The child, still clutching her wand, had given Summer yet another hug. "I wish I could live here with you."

Maybe it was the wand or the magic behind it, but that phrase had started the wheels spinning.

For the past hour, Summer had been exploring the possibilities of leasing the camp from her parents...with an option to buy.

If she moved into Ginny and Charlie's apartment and lived there full-time, her mom and dad would have rent income coming in every month. Insurance might even go down if the camp were occupied.

That thought spurred her ideas in a different direction.

What if she moved Fairy Princess Parties here? She would have the facilities for full-day parties...sleepovers? She could drive the bus. For an additional charge, picking the kids up and taking them home could be arranged.

And what about renting the facilities out for seasonal retreats? Her parents had never wanted to be tied down by the camp, but leasing it and living here opened up a world of possibilities. Churches? Businesses? Writers? Paducah had a huge population of artists in the Lowertown district! And

Sunny Daze was central enough to pull from other surrounding towns rather than just Paducah.

Her breathing came so fast hyperventilation seemed likely. She stretched out in the bed to concentrate on calming down, but being there turned her thoughts to Rick.

She'd been looking forward to the end of this camp session when they'd have a week of downtime together, but now it was going to be a grueling week of awkwardness and longing. She'd never in her whole life felt so miserable.

She fended off the suffocating sadness by grabbing the pad off the bedside table and making notes of her ideas for the camp—anything to keep her mind from being idle. Her mom and dad would be here Saturday to say goodbye to the kids. When they arrived, she wanted a plan laid out to show them how serious she was about this endeavor.

The pen flew across the page as ideas poured from her pretty heart, keeping thoughts of Rick, and the part of her heart that ached for him, at bay.

CHAPTER NINETEEN

RICK CAUGHT SUMMER IN A POSE that had been all too rare the past couple of days. She was smiling. A *real* smile rather than one of those fake things she'd been producing, and he wondered if perhaps she'd spoken with her parents. On closer study, though, he recognized the wary edge around her eyes, the tightness around her lips, which told him she probably didn't know yet about his calls that morning.

His first inclination was to ask Charlie for a few minutes alone with her so he could apologize and make his big announcement in private. In his imagination, he was already picturing her reaction to the news that Riley Gibson was indeed interested in purchasing the camp as a future state facility. He was so interested, in fact, he was driving down from Frankfort today to meet Herschel and Agnes for a tour in approximately—Rick checked his watch—forty-nine minutes.

It wasn't a done deal by any means. The meeting had come together without a hitch, however, so he couldn't help believing that was a good omen.

But it wasn't his place to tell her. The news should come from her parents. When she heard it, Summer would understand he'd used what power he had to make her dream of saving the camp and her parents' retirement come true, and that realization along with his genuine apology would coax her back into his arms...where she should've been all along. Or, at least, that was the plan. He flexed his fingers, his arms already reacting to the mental stimulus.

When her stance shifted and her smile landed on him, he hoped it wasn't accidental. But his heart, which had been riding high in his chest all day, sank a bit as he watched her cheerful expression waver and fade when he moved in her direction.

An itch to be near her propelled him forward nonetheless. Whether she knew it or not, reconciliation was only a few hours away. Probably some of his longest hours since Afghanistan. But being near her would help the time go faster.

"You seem in a better mood today. Not anxious to get rid of the kids, are you?"

Her answering smile encouraged him. "Never entered my mind." She chose a plate of ants-on-a-log over the apple wedge and cheddar cheese combo snack. "Did you and Neil finish your project?"

"Yep." His arm brushed against her as he reached for a plate of apples. She made a quick sidestep away. Yesterday, the movement would've caused an expletive to rise in his throat. Today, he put his hope in Tara's theory. If Summer loved him, touching before they'd made up would cause the fire to burn too hot. It certainly fueled an instant heat in him. "We need to keep the kids away from the fire pit area until after dark, though. If they see the monofilament line, it'll spoil the whole effect."

While Summer studied the raisins on her celery as if they were the most interesting things on earth, he studied her. She couldn't touch him…couldn't be near him…couldn't even make eye contact with him without being miserable? Hell-pee-roo. Tara *was* right!

Summer loved him.

Joy rolled out of him in a louder-than-warranted chuckle, which did draw a questioning glance. "Um, I was just thinking about how surprised the kids are going to be when the fireball comes swooshing out of the sky." *And how surprised you're going to be when your parents arrive with the news.*

She chewed her lip for a couple of seconds. "If Neil doesn't catch the tree on fire in the process."

The pleasant breeze had enticed everyone to snack outside under the trees, so Rick took advantage of the private dining hall, keeping his voice low. "All this talk of combustion reminds me of the first time we made love."

"Don't, Rick." She stopped at the door and looked at him then. The longing in her voice and her eyes confirmed his suspicions and stretched his patience to the limit, but he reached above her head to push the door open, allowing her hurried escape. Agnes and Herschel couldn't get here too soon.

As Rick and Summer joined the group, the mail truck arrived. Charlie shuffled across the parking lot to meet it, returning with a stack of letters, a plastic Walmart bag and a grin that spread from ear to ear.

He continued grinning as he called out the recipients' names on the letters, passing them out one by one until he was left with only the bag, which he held up for everyone to see. "And this," he announced, "is fan mail for Howard Gerard, Jr."

The boy's eyes widened in delight. "Wow!" Howie grabbed the bag and rummaged through his mail as the other kids swarmed around him. He proudly showed off several small packages, then dove in again, surfacing with a clutch of letters in his hand.

"Open thomething!" Willard's request was seconded all around.

Howie made quick work of tearing into one of the packages. As he tilted it to one end, a letter and a carefully folded and taped mass of tissue paper fell out into his hand. He ripped it open, exposing two arrowheads fashioned from pieces of flint.

He unfolded the letter and read aloud. "'Dear Howie, my parents read me the article about your mammoth molar. I like looking for old stuff, too. These are two arrowheads I found in one of the fields on our farm. If you would like to come visit me sometime, we could go look for stuff together. It would be fun. Write me back. Love, Brandy Sherwood.'"

Reggie's nose crinkled in a sneer. "Ew, a girl?" He glanced around the group, drumming up support. "Howie's got a girlfriend. Howie's got a girlfriend."

"Shut up!" Howie, his face blazing with humiliation, shoved the letter, arrowheads and all, back into the sack, pulling it tight against his chest.

A couple of others picked up Reggie's chant, and Rick thought he best put an end to the ribbing before things got out of hand. He spoke loud enough to be heard over the ruckus. "Howie's got a *fan,* not a girlfriend. Big difference."

"So, Ms. Summer." Carlos's mischievous grin passed from Summer to Rick and back. "Are you a fan of Mr. Rick or a girlfriend?"

Summer choked on her bite of celery, her face soon matching Howie's in hue.

"Well, we've got more exciting things than girlfriends and boyfriends to think about," Charlie said as he stood and held up his hands, drawing everyone's attention. "Finish up those snacks and get on back to the bunkhouses to get ready for our last big adventure. We leave for the zip lines in less than an hour."

A shout of excitement went up as the kids scurried to throw away their paper plates.

Rick watched the girls pull Summer and Tara into a jog, and he couldn't keep from thinking how wrong Charlie was.

Having Summer as a girlfriend was more exciting than zip lines any day.

He imagined her back in his bed tonight…the things they would do to each other.

Much more exciting…and he wouldn't let them zip along too fast, either.

SUMMER WAS TOO…SOMETHING…to stay still. She meandered in and out among the buildings, waiting for everyone else. Or anyone else.

She dialed Kate's number. No answer, so she let it go to voice mail. "Just wanted to see how yesterday's party went. We're going zip-lining, so I'll talk to you tomorrow." She slid the phone back in her pocket and picked up her nervous pace.

She couldn't name her emotion exactly. It was a conglomeration of too many things, pulling her from different angles, stretching her too thin and exposing raw nerves.

That it was the last day with these kids stung like a hornet. She would miss them and their cute ways…even Carlos and his mouth.

The possibility her parents might not be enthusiastic about her plan pricked at her, but she couldn't come up with a good reason for them not to be. Her fiercest foe who might screw things up was herself, or rather her former self. The flighty ne'er-do-well who'd never before taken much of anything seriously. Well, this time she had the beginning stages of a five-year plan to show them that she'd changed.

But if all that wasn't enough to fray her composure, Rick was flirting again, and the longing for him had come back with a vengeance. Her heart and her body had thrown up their hands in surrender—only her brain held out. He still hadn't apologized for believing the worst about her, but was he coming around? She could hope. Maybe the week between sessions would give them time to work things out. Maybe they could even go out to dinner or on a real date.

She rounded the corner of the girls' bunkhouse as a car turned in the gate. Her parents? What were they doing here? Had some fairy princess magic pulled them to the camp today? Her heart galloped away at the thought. If she gave the outline to them now, they'd have tonight to look it over, and the three of them could sit down and talk it over in-depth tomorrow afternoon after the kids were gone.

She ran to her cabin and snatched up the pad she'd been working on and then ran out to greet them. Her hurried walk slowed when she saw Rick already shaking hands with her dad, handing him the file folder he always made notes in. She wanted to talk to her parents about her plan alone. Perhaps she could get Rick to load the kids on the bus for her, which would grab her a few minutes with her mom and dad.

Her dad held out his arms when he saw her coming their way. "How's my Nubbin?"

"I'm fantastic!" She hugged them both with enough enthusiasm to bring a question to their expressions.

"Well, camp life certainly seems to have agreed with you." Her mom smiled, her glance shifting from Summer to Rick and back.

She hurried with an answer before her mom got too carried away. "I love it here. I think I've found my calling."

That brought a laugh from her dad. "For…let's see…the nineteenth time?"

"Now, Herschel…" her mom scolded. She turned back to Summer. "Well, if you're serious, Rick might be able to help you get a job if things work out today the way we hope they will."

Summer's glance shifted to Rick. His huge grin startled her. "What's going on?" Her gaze darted back to her mom and then her dad. "Why are y'all here, anyway?"

Her dad clapped Rick on the back. "Rick's arranged for someone from the state to come look at the property. They might be interested in buying the camp."

The words delivered a hurricane-strength punch straight to Summer's gut. "The state might buy the camp?" *No!*

"It's just a possibility." Rick's eyes were set on her as her breathing became stuttered. His smile started to waver. "I thought of it last night, so I made the call to Riley Gibson this morning."

"We hadn't considered selling it this quickly, but if the offer's right, it could be our chance to get out on top." Her mom gave Rick an adoring look.

"Summer should get the credit." Rick flashed a smile again in her direction. "Having the news article to flaunt during the visit should make them sit up and take notice."

Summer's stomach lurched.

"Rick's been drawing maps and diagrams and taking notes to help us out the whole time he's been here. He's got a whole file here with photos, measurements.... Everything's laid out and ready."

One glance at the folder and Summer's stomach turned over completely. She turned an accusing eye toward Rick. "You've known this the whole time? That they were interested in selling?"

"I, uh, yes." His face reddened.

"We swore Rick to secrecy." Her dad chuckled and gave her shoulders a squeeze. "Didn't want you getting upset if we decided to sell it to a developer for a subdivision. But we think Rick's taken care of that."

No, no, no! This could ruin everything...all her plans. She closed her eyes and breathed, groping for a light to lead her out of this dark spot. *Think...quick!* If they were considering selling, anyway, maybe this was her chance.

A group of boys came out of the dorm and moved in the

direction of the bus. Rick waved at their calls to him. "Sorry I won't be here to introduce you." He addressed her parents but kept throwing questioning glances Summer's way. "But you'll like Riley. He's very laid-back. Easy to talk to."

"I'm sure we'll get along fine," her mom assured Rick as he turned to leave.

Her dad spoke up. "Actually, today was perfect. With the kids gone, we'll be able to give him a thorough look at everything."

Now the girls were making their way to the bus, also, and Rick shot her a look over his shoulder. "You coming, Summer?"

"I'll be there in a minute." This was her only chance. She squared her shoulders and took a nervous breath as he walked away. "I've been doing a lot of thinking and…and figuring, trying to come up with a way that I could buy the camp myself. Or, at least, lease it to buy." She held up the notepad so that it faced them. "I've even been working on a five-year plan of things that I could do to make it pay for itself."

Her parents moved in unison. They stared at her, turned to stare at each other, some unspoken communication passing between them, and then moved their placating looks back to her.

She recognized the look. It was the same one they'd given her when she told them she'd decided to go to culinary school…and take up massage therapy classes…and…

Her dad ended the silence with his laugh. "With the imagination you've got, Nubbin, you need to be writing fantasy stories." He gave her a hug and nodded toward the bus. "Go on now. We've got business to tend to." He took her mom's hand, pulling her in the direction of the dining hall.

Summer followed, determined to make them listen. "No, you need to hear me out." She walked with them, holding out the tablet again. "I have some great ideas, like moving

Fairy Princess Parties here, and renting the facilities out for retreats for various groups—"

Her mom took the tablet out of her hand and glanced down it. "She does have a lot of ideas here."

"I don't care how many ideas she has, it's not going to happen." Her dad's face turned a deep red as he snatched the tablet from her mom's grip and thrust it back toward Summer. The three of them came to a stop in the shade of the picnic shelter. "You don't have money for a down payment, we can't afford to finance it for you—"

"I'm not asking you to finance it for me, Daddy—"

"—and you don't have any collateral, so no bank is going to finance it *for* you." His forehead broke out with sweat even though there was a cool breeze where they stood. He mopped his face on his sleeve. "If we sell to the state, we'll have the money in hand, free and clear."

His breathing labored, and the sound ran shudders up Summer's spine. She had no right to ask them to give up a sure thing and gamble on her dream. They'd gambled on too many of her dreams in the past.

Don't be selfish.

She took the tablet without further protest.

"See you tomorrow, dumpling," her mom called as they headed away from her once more.

"Yeah. See ya." Summer stared down at the tablet, watching the words blur. She wiped a hand down her face, still stunned that things had happened so quickly. The hurt was too deep to even cry about yet.

Slowly, she made her way to the bus, following the last of the girls onto it, and plopped into the driver's seat with a heavy sigh.

A trash can sat under the lever that closed the door. She let the notepad drop into the receptacle, feeling its *thud* at the bottom of her heart.

RICK SAT IN THE SEAT BEHIND the driver's—the one that had become his usual spot for all the road trips. Summer moved like she'd been trampled by buffalo as she got on the bus.

He watched her, scrutinizing every movement to try and figure out what in the hell had gone wrong.

The woman was impossible to please. He'd just given her exactly what she'd wanted—and now she wouldn't look at him except to give an evil glare when their eyes happened to meet in the rearview mirror.

She'd thrown away a large notepad when she got on the bus. His gut told him *that* had to be significant, though he couldn't for the life of him decipher what a notepad would have to do with Riley Gibson's visit—a visit she didn't even know was going to occur until a few minutes ago.

When they arrived at the zip lines, the crew divided them into four groups with a camp counselor in each group, effectively squelching any hope Rick had of a private word with Summer.

But a bit of luck was with him. His group finished first. While they waited for the others to return, his kids played hacky-sack in the parking lot, and he went back to the bus and retrieved the tablet from the trash. One glance at it had made him wish he hadn't.

Shitfire and damn it all to hell! She'd written out a plan. *To own the camp herself!* His stomach drew tighter with every flip of the page. Ideas for moving the Fairy Princess Parties to Camp Sunny Daze. Ideas to rent the facility out to groups for private parties, church groups, businesses, weekend retreats.... She had some wonderfully imaginative ideas that sounded like they could work.

Too late the realization came to him that he should have talked with her before he'd made the call to Riley. He'd tried to anticipate what she wanted, what she needed. Why hadn't he just asked and listened to her answer?

Because first he'd been too busy judging her, then he'd been trying to impress her, trying to win her adoration, trying to fix everything.

Oh, he'd fixed everything, all right.

He'd led the enemy directly into her camp.

Literally.

Hell-pee-roo.

CHAPTER TWENTY

RICK STEPPED ONTO SUMMER'S front porch. Catching a glimpse of her through the window, he paused. She was sitting on her couch. Not doing anything. Just sitting. He'd never seen her so still except when she was sleeping.

The memory of her body pressed against him, her leg slung over his in the abandon of sleep, motivated him forward in a last-ditch effort to make things right between them again.

He knocked and she opened the door, looking at him dully. "What do you want, Rick?"

"Can I come in? I need to talk to you. It won't take long."

They didn't have long. Dinner would be served in about twenty minutes.

She didn't answer, just turned and moved back to sit on the couch, leaving the door open. He noticed then that she held her cell phone.

"Have you heard from your parents?" He took a couple of steps into the cabin. She didn't offer him a seat, didn't look in his direction.

"Just now. The guy you put on to them seems very interested. He told them he'd get back to them soon. Probably early next week."

"Summer, I'm sorry. I didn't know you wanted to buy the camp yourself."

That got her attention. Her eyes shot to him and narrowed. "You read my plan."

"Your reaction to the news was the opposite of what I expected it to be. I thought you'd be happy, but you weren't. I was trying to figure out why."

"It was my plan, and it was none of your business."

"It was in the trash."

"Where it belonged. You should've left it there."

"Maybe you're right, but—"

"But you can't leave things alone, can you? You always have to get involved because you know how to fix it, and you know better than anyone else."

"That's not fair."

Anger brought her to her feet. "I'm not fair? That's the pot calling the kettle black, don't you think? Does it ever occur to you that someone else might know more about something than you do? I went to camp here for six years. My parents have owned it for five. That's eleven years my family has invested here. You've been around for eight weeks, but in that time you've managed to come in and take over and jerk away something precious in my life. What's fair about that?"

"You're right. I should've talked to you, but I thought—"

"No, you didn't. You didn't think. You just reacted. You rushed in to save the day, playing the part of the hero like you always do."

"If I was playing the part of the hero, it was only for you. I was trying to be *your* hero."

"Don't feed me that line. You're still trying to be Dunk's hero. You set out every day, trying to save Dunk, but every night, he's still dead, so the nightmares torment you. The next day, you get up and start it all over again."

Rick's gut twisted. "This has nothing to do with Dunk. Leave him out of it."

"You're the one who needs to leave him out of it, but you can't. You save your friends from the cave, save Kenny in the storm, save me from the snake, save the camp.... No matter how hard you try, how many people or things you save, you're never going to save him. Dunk's gone, Rick. Let him go."

Her words drove into his brain like a fist, grasping something from its secret depths and jerking it unbidden to the surface.

"Dunk's gone, Rick. Let him go."

The sunlight around him fractured and the camera in his head zoomed Summer out. Her mouth moved, but her words were lost.

Dunk was in his arms.

Heat. Fire. Bullets zinging all around, the repetitive whine of ricochets off the stones. No plan, no strategy. Just run like hell. Get Dunk to someone who can get the bullet out of his neck.

Damn! He's losing so much blood! Slick...hard to hold on to.

His muscles protested the double exertion, shook violently. Sweat poured into his eyes.

Can't see...can't see. Keep running.

Hands trying to pry Dunk free.

"Dunk's gone, Rick. Let him go." Asa's voice.

No! Won't let go! Letting go means... Oh, God! Not Dunk... please, not Dunk.

The film rolling in his head stopped and rewound. Back… further back.

The child was in Dunk's arms.

"Give her to me. You can't carry her."

Dunk handed her over. They were running.

Zing! The bullet...one bullet...only one shot when they had the child. One shot...aimed at whoever wasn't carrying the little girl.

And he'd taken her from Dunk's grasp seconds before.

Rick's eyes cleared to reveal Summer's upraised chin, right in front of him. She advanced a couple of steps and stood close enough to touch him, but she didn't. She couldn't feel the icy tremors rolling down his spine, reverberating out to his fingers and toes.

He took a step backward toward the door. Retreating. "I'm sorry I called you selfish." He barely recognized his own voice through the thin ringing in his ears. Oh, God! Was he going to pass out?

Summer reached around him and opened the screen door. "It doesn't matter now."

Rick backed through the door and off the porch, an eerie numbness settling deep in his chest. It seemed to originate from the granite star hanging on the chain and bored its way through the tattoo over his heart.

He stumbled to his cabin and into the bathroom where he heaved up the contents of his stomach. Filling the sink with cold water, he rinsed his face repeatedly until the nausea passed…but the truth remained.

Summer was right. He always had to be the hero.

And it had cost him the life of his best friend.

THE EXCITEMENT FROM THE afternoon of zip-lining had run its course, replaced by a mellowness that settled over the group like a cozy wrap…for everyone except Summer.

A chunk of ice hung in her chest, occupying the area that had once held her heart.

Everyone sat in a semicircle on the beach, where the gentle waves lapping behind them should've been mesmerizing and calming in their regularity. But Summer's insides were a matted, twisted conglomeration of emotions.

"I know all of you have seen a crow." Rick's mellow voice captured her attention. "But did you know that the crow wasn't always black? Back in the earliest times, when the world was first created, the crow was the most beautiful bird of all. He had feathers the colors of the rainbow, and his song was the sweetest sound ever heard."

Tara's idea for each of the counselors to tell a story while dressed in costume had been a stroke of genius. The kids had remained entranced throughout Summer's story of the ill-equipped fairy princess who tamed a dragon using only a bubble wand. Neil's ninja tale, purposely chosen so he could be dressed in black for the next part he was to play in tonight's drama, was a huge hit also.

Tara's true story, told in full Irish brogue, of her great-grandmother's coming to America during the potato famine had moved some of the girls to tears, giving Summer the perfect opportunity to wipe away the occasional tear of her own.

Now Rick, dressed in a Native American garb of buckskin, had the kids captivated by his tale. "Rainbow Crow couldn't stand to see the animals freezing beneath the heavy snow and ice, so he told them, 'I'll go to the Creator and ask him to stop the cold.' The journey was a long one. Rainbow Crow flew for three days and nights."

So Rainbow Crow chose to be the hero. No wonder he chose that particular story. Summer forced her mouth into a smirk.

In contrast, her stomach churned of its own accord as she remembered the way she'd lashed out at him, saying what she had about Dunk. It needed to be said. He needed to hear it. But that kind of thing shouldn't have been spewed in retaliation.

The look on his face was like nothing she'd ever seen. Anguish personified. She'd been angry…lashed out to hurt him…wanted him to feel some of the pain she carried.

Well, she'd been successful there.

But instead of vindication, her guts were twisted by shame.

She brushed away another tear.

"I was trying to be your *hero."*

No one had ever tried to be her hero—except her dad.

"The Creator jabbed the end of the stick into the sun, allowing it to catch fire, then he handed it to Rainbow Crow. 'Take this back to Earth,' he said. 'It is fire and it holds the warmth you seek to save your world.'"

Rick's eyes met Summer's for only a split second, but long enough for her to be reminded of the fire she'd seen in them when they made love. The chunk of ice in her chest melted a little. She could feel the trickle worming its way through her, leaving a warm trail where it meandered.

"Rainbow Crow flew and flew as fast as he could, afraid the fire would go out before he reached Earth."

Summer filled her eyes with the striking image Rick posed. An exterior chiseled out of granite, yet a touch tender enough to calm a scared child…or melt a woman's heart. Hers.

"Too close to the sun and his beautiful rainbow tail feathers were scorched black…"

Even now, she wanted to undo the leather laces holding his shirt closed and press against the taut ripples of his stomach. Wanted to pull a feather from his headdress and stroke it along his length, drawing grunts of pleasure.

"Too close to the moon, which scorched the lovely feathers on his wings and body to a dull black, also…"

She wanted to look him straight in the eye and tell him she was crazy for being so crazy about him…but looking at him turned her brain matter to goo.

"The smoke burned his throat until his beautiful voice was choked out…"

Pulling her eyes away from Rick, she picked up a stick and scratched in the dirt at her feet. Next week, when there wouldn't be any kids, and she'd had time to get over the shock of losing the camp and her life's dream, they'd be able to talk…without all the drama.

"Because of his unselfish acts, the Creator coated the crow's charred, black feathers with a beautiful gloss that would still show the rainbow colors when the sun hit them. And the Creator made the crow's meat taste bad like smoke so that man wouldn't be tempted to hunt him."

Summer's upper teeth gnawed a piece of skin from her bottom lip. She hadn't told Rick her dream of owning the camp. He'd acted based on what he thought she wanted.

Another drip trickled inside.

"Each time you see a crow, remember the sacrifice he made, and how he put the other animals' needs before his own."

*Just like you, Rick...like you always do. Forever faithful...*Semper fi.

She sighed, not wanting to wait until tomorrow when the kids were gone to talk. She couldn't. She wanted to talk to him...make things right between them...tonight.

A long breath expanded her lungs, filling the space in her chest and warming it, making it feel not nearly so cold or hollow.

"We stand and unite our hearts by the joining of our hands," Rick said, motioning everyone to their feet, and she was relieved for some action to shake her out of her lethargy.

They stood, each one clasping the hands of the person next to him or her.

A vibration of excitement thrummed through the group as Rick turned to face the trees, raising his arms and his voice. "The sign of fire from the unselfish act of Rainbow Crow to forever remind us of the unity of our hearts even as we walk the separate pathways of our lives."

The echo of his voice sent an uncomfortable shiver up Summer's spine. She didn't want a separate pathway from Rick. Every part of her wanted unity—especially her pretty heart.

And then, even though she'd been in on all the planning, astonishment filled her, and she gasped right along with the kids as a flaming fireball shot out of the sky. The fire pit at the edge of the beach burst forth in flames.

Carlos's and M&M's grips tightened on each side of her, their eyes wide with wonder. After the initial shock, they regained their wits, and their hands, still clasped, shot into the air along with cheers. The campers' awe soon gave way to a deluge of questions centered around "How'd he do that?" while Summer and Tara shrugged in response.

The kids didn't need to know that the fireball was actually a roll of toilet tissue Neil had soaked in kerosene and lighted before sliding it down the monofilament line to the fire pit.

Let them believe in the magic.

Neil appeared out of the woods along with Ginny and Charlie, carrying a tray of Hershey bars, marshmallows and graham crackers for s'mores.

The kids toasted marshmallows on sticks that Charlie had whittled into points as Summer and Rick guarded the fire pit area to make sure no one got stabbed, stuck, burned or pushed. The others helped with assembly of the treats.

Summer was sweltering, standing so near the fire in the fairy princess costume. But the sight of Rick dressed in buckskin, rugged and sexy with his tanned skin burnished by the glow of the firelight, drew her unwittingly like a moth.

He seemed distracted…didn't look her way—not once. Damn him and the way he made her feel. Totally confused, she didn't know what her future held. And yet, more sure than she'd ever been, she wanted Rick to be in it.

"Great story, Rick," she called over the fire, hating being ignored by him.

"Thanks. Yours, too."

Silence.

She tried again. "Where'd you get the costume?"

"Mom drove to Oklahoma."

A bead of sweat trickled between her breasts and onto her stomach as the last child marched away from the fire.

Her breath caught as Rick moved her way, but the smile froze on her lips when he brushed past her as if she wasn't there and went to join the rest of the group.

Sheesh! He was driving her insane!

"Can we play hide-and-seek, Mr. Rick?" Howie's tongue snaked out to lick a smear of chocolate from the corner of his mouth. "P-please? One last t-time?"

The emotion in the boy's voice and eyes made a bite of Hershey bar stick in Summer's throat. This had been a special time for him—a time to bask in some glory. Be the star. Earn his star. A time of learning, acceptance…safety. Tomorrow he would go back home…to what? Had his mom decided to give Howie, Sr., another chance? So often, abused women did.

Summer shuddered, wishing the camp could go on forever for Howie.

"Tell you what." Rick tousled the boy's hair with such a fatherly gesture, Summer's eyes stung. "How 'bout the counselors be 'it' this time, and all the kids can hide."

"Yeah!"

"When we find you, go sit in the pavilion until everybody's in," Neil instructed as the kids scurried away.

Ginny and Charlie gathered what was left of the snacks onto the trays and headed to the kitchen.

Rick drew his comrades into a small circle as he began counting, and Summer felt childish, wishing she could stand by him.

Tara laughed. "We look like a prayer group."

"Oh, Lord, we want to thank you for these children," Neil intoned below Rick's counting. "And thank you that our time with them is drawing to an end. Mmm-hmm. It's been a fine time we've had here, Lord, with these fine children, who've blessed us with their antics. Blessed us so that the stars in our crowns have been given a greater chance to multiply with each and every passing day."

Summer and Tara ruptured with laughter at Neil's last statement as Rick called out, "Thirty!"

"Let's make this quick, y'all," he said, and Summer noticed that his eyes slid over her, but landed briefly on Neil and Tara. She hurried away in response. The sooner they found everybody, the sooner they could get them in bed and the sooner she could talk to Rick alone.

Would he talk to her? Her mouth went dry. Maybe not. But he'd have to listen. He couldn't ignore her forever.

Without even having to discuss it, the counselors fanned out in different directions as they headed away from the beach into the trees surrounding the camp.

Most of the kids hid behind the large trees and, although they tried sneaking around the sides, were easily spotted by one of the adults. A few braved the relative darkness to hide in the shadows of the buildings. They seemed the most relieved when they got found.

It didn't take long until everybody was in except for Lucy and, as usual, Howie.

Tara and Neil stayed at the pavilion with the large group as Rick went around the dining hall toward the storm shelter. Summer searched the opposite direction.

At the edge of the woods, a hand caught her arm. "Aaiiee!" Summer let out a startled yelp. "Lucy, you scared me."

"Ms. Summer, I know we're not supposed to tattle…" The child bit her bottom lip.

"What is it, Lucy?" She didn't have time for one of Lucy's whiny accusations of being left out. The sooner they found Howie…

"Howie went in the woods." Lucy's chin buckled in aggravation.

Summer didn't relish the idea of traipsing through the woods in her fairy princess dress. "Are you sure?" She squinted and tilted her head to let the child know this was no time for games.

"I promise, Ms. Summer." Lucy traced a quick cross over her heart. "He went in there."

Summer's eyes followed the child's pointing finger—to the path that went by the Byassee place. A cold dread filled her as she remembered her frightening premonition. Something bad could be out there again tonight. Howie had a good head start…might already be walking into danger. She pulled a small flashlight from the pocket of her dress and kept her voice calm, trying not to scare the child. "I'm going toward the Byassee place, Lucy. You tell Mr. Rick, okay?"

Whether or not Rick followed, she knew this path well enough to walk it blindfolded if she had to.

Not waiting for Lucy's answer, she hiked up her costume and ran.

CHAPTER TWENTY-ONE

"Howie! C'mon in, bud. You've won again." Rick listened but there was no answer. No feet scuffing in the dirt. No branches cracking. "Howie, did you hear me?" he tried again. The voices of the other children calling Howie drifted around the buildings.

It wasn't like the boy to stay hidden this long. Usually, by the time they confirmed him as the winner, he was anxious to take his victory lap.

He *had* been quiet all afternoon…not showing his usual enthusiasm during the zip-lining, hanging back in line rather than pushing to the front like he normally did. At the time, Rick had wondered if perhaps he was afraid of the zip lines. But looking back on the rest of the evening, the boy had been silent throughout dinner and the stories. In fact, Rick couldn't recall that he'd said anything since mail call. He'd been embarrassed by Reggie's teasing but that hardly seemed the type of thing that would upset him for very long. He generally shrugged anger off pretty quickly.

Something else was going on. Dreading going home? Afraid his mom and dad might have gotten back together while he was gone? Rick's insides coiled. If Howie were worried about his dad coming back to live with him, would he hide out to try to prolong going home? Worse yet, would he run away?

Rick beat a hasty retreat back to the pavilion, trying not to jump to conclusions. They were dealing with a nine-year-old. The thickly wooded area around the camp would let in only a minimal amount of starlight…a pretty scary place for a kid to tackle alone.

"Still no Howie, huh?" Rick's quick headcount answered his question.

Tara shook her head, worry tightening her eyes. "Neil's gone down to the beach." She kept her voice low. "He thought maybe Howie stayed behind down there while we were counting."

Rick understood leaving no stone unturned, but Howie had never broken the rules about where they could hide, and the beach—or anywhere near the water—had always been strictly off-limits.

Rick scanned the area, deciding how to divide up the space for a search. "Where's Summer?"

Tara pointed in the general direction behind the cabins. "The last time I saw her, she was looking for him over there."

"I know where she is."

The small voice beside them caused Rick and Tara both to look down in surprise. Lucy looked at them wide-eyed and shrugged. "I didn't want to be a cheater, but I thought if I followed Howie, maybe I could win this time." She sighed dramatically. "But he went into the woods, so I told Ms. Summer. She's gone after him."

"Which way did she go?" Rick's fingers gouged into the skin on his hips as his grip tightened involuntarily.

Lucy pointed to the dark path beyond Rick's cabin. "I'm supposed to tell you she's going toward the busy place."

"The busy place?" Rick looked to Tara for a translation. "What does that mean?"

"The busy place." A whine entered Lucy's voice. "The old house where the foxes live."

"The Byassee place!" A coldness gripped Rick's insides

as he remembered the dead fox kit and the broken whiskey bottle.

"That's what I said." Lucy pointed toward the path that snaked through the dark woods.

Rick walked casually in the direction Lucy pointed.

But once within the trees and under the cover of darkness, he ran. His legs pumped furiously, working to keep up with the frantic beating of his heart.

SUMMER DIDN'T HESITATE WHEN she reached the turnoff to the Byassee place, but she did slow to a walk purely out of necessity. Trying to move fast in her costume was like swimming against the tide. A stitch in her side caught on every intake of ragged breath.

"How-wie?" she called, trying to coax the child out of hiding, and trying to warn anyone hanging out at the Byassee place she was on the way in, giving them a chance to grab their whiskey and make a quick exit.

Any other time, the sounds from the frogs and cicadas would be welcoming. Tonight, she wished they'd shut up. The small beam of light helped, but vision was still limited. It would be her hearing that would alert her to Howie's presence—she cleared her throat of the dry lump—or anyone else's.

She reached the clearing and stopped. The ramshackle old cottage stood before her, swathed in shadow. A barely crescent moon gave little illumination…and yet, too much. She'd never considered how the two empty windows on each side of the doorway might take on the appearance of staring eyes and a mouth gaping in horror.

Fear tightened the muscles at the back of her throat, and swallowing didn't help much. Would Howie come this far? They'd been here often, so he was familiar with this area, but it seemed over the top, even for the little attention-seeker.

A movement behind the house brought her to a stop. Just a fleeting shadow, but enough to drag a cold finger up her spine. Maybe an animal. Maybe her imagination. Or maybe the child…hurt…scared?

"Howie? Is that you?" She inched around the front corner of the house. "You can come out now. The game's over." A rustle in the woods brought her to attention and she flashed the beam that direction. She strained, but her eyes couldn't discern anything beyond the edge of light. Keeping her palm pressed against the wall, she began to move again, hesitantly, toward the back of the house.

The glint of moonlight on metal stopped her shy of the back corner. A truck. Parked in the driveway. Painted in camouflage.

She smelled him before she felt him, a sickening mixture of body odor and whiskey with undertones of pot. Her mind screamed at her to run, but her feet froze to the spot. She gasped as a hand gripped her upper arm, jerking her around and shoving her back against the stone wall, making her drop the flashlight. The wire frame of one of her wings snapped. Its sharp point stabbed below her shoulder blade.

"You got tha' right, bitch. Game's over, sure as hell."

His hot, rank breath bathed her face, along with a spray of spit. Her stomach convulsed, and she swallowed hard.

"Where's my boy? Why you callin' him?"

My boy? "Y-you're Howie's dad."

"Tha's right." He nodded and the movement caused him to sway. His fingers tightened around her arm as he stumbled against her. "Is 'e lost? Wha've you done with 'im?"

She fought the urge to wince, her gut telling her that this guy preyed on weakness, used pain to intimidate.

He wasn't a big man. Medium height and thin—skinny, actually. Wobbly on his feet. A hard shove might knock him down and give her a chance to run. But the grip on her arm might take her down with him. If he got her on the ground… She shuddered.

His head tilted, and his mouth curled into a sneer. "Where's 'e? Th' li'l bastard bet'r not've tol' you 'bout our plan."

He lowered his eyes until they were level with hers, and she could read the range of his emotions. Rage…fear…desperation. Of the three, the last was the most frightening. A desperate man was capable of anything. She had no chance against him, but Rick would. Rick could take him out with one swipe. Where was he? Had they found Howie yet? Surely Rick would come looking for her… If she could just stall.

Despite the stench, she took a deep breath, trying to control her trembling knees that kept threatening to buckle. "I don't know anything about a plan. We were playing hide-and-seek."

Howard Gerard's voice settled into a menacing growl. "Don't lie t' me!" He jerked her away from the wall and threw her in the direction of the truck. She didn't have time to pull her skirt up. Her feet caught in the hem, pitching her forward onto her knees. She struggled to get up, once again aware of a tight grip around her bicep, hauling her onto her feet. "Tell me where he's at."

"Don't hurt her, Dad." A timid voice drifted out of the darkness. "I'm here." The vise around her arm dropped away as Howie crept slowly from the shadow of the opposite side of the house.

"Why'd you come early, boy?" The threat of a beating lay in the tone.

Howie's shoulders absorbed his scrawny neck as he cowered, looking like a whipped puppy. "I wasn't sure…wasn't sure I could get past…past Mr. Kenny. I thought this'd be better. I knew you'd be here already." His eyes darted toward Summer.

Was the lie as obvious to Howard Gerard as it was to

her? Howie had been there all along…led them to his dad… waited, hoping…

"Git 'n the truck."

The child moved quickly to obey.

Adrenaline shot through Summer's veins. "He isn't going anywhere with you!" She lunged at the man, catching his side with her shoulder like she'd seen football players tackle the opponent. His reaction time was stymied, giving her the advantage. She watched the ground coming up to meet them, felt the air forced from her lungs as they landed in a twisted heap.

Howard Gerard threw her off him with a roar, and she hit the ground a second time. She scrambled to rise, but the costume tangled around her legs, slowing her down. By the time she got squared on her feet, so had he.

He advanced on her, a bull seeing red, but she stood her ground. If she ran, Howie didn't stand a chance.

"Nobody's gonna keep m' boy away from me, bitch." His fingers dug into her arms, just below the shoulders, and he shook her so hard, her head bobbled as if her neck were a spring. He shouted, venting his frustration at the world. "You hear me? Nobody! Not m' wife…not th' law…not you!"

He held her upper arms tight against her sides, allowing no reach to her blind slaps, but she threw as many kicks as she dared, fighting to stay upright. And she screamed…over and over. "Run, Howie! Get help!"

One hand left her. Seizing the opportunity, she drew her free arm back, mustering all her strength into the intended punch. Before she could follow through, the back of his hand connected with her jaw. Her head snapped sideways and back with such force her body had no choice but to follow.

The ringing in her ears grew to a roar. The moon whirled above her in a sickening dance as she fell.

RICK BUSTED HIS ASS, TRYING TO catch up with Summer before she reached the Byassee place. This whole ordeal smacked of something that churned his insides. It felt too coincidental…too contrived.

As he neared the place where the path veered right, an off sound registered in his hearing. One that didn't belong to the night. Faint, but definitely human voices. He kicked harder, and the sounds grew into shouts…angry tones. One he recognized.

Summer.

As he tore into the clearing, the sounds stopped abruptly. He slowed his movement to a guarded walk.

He listened. The house's dark facade stood sentry, no hint of turmoil on its watch. Then a noise came from the back of the house. A slamming door.

Rick rushed toward the sound. As he rounded the corner of the house, the sight of Summer's body sprawled on the ground ripped a combined cry of anger and anguish from his lungs. "Summer!"

She struggled to sit up as he bounded toward her. Shaking her head in protest, she pointed to the truck in the driveway. "Howie!"

Rick's mind instantly processed the situation. A camouflaged truck. Howie's dad. The engine started as Rick jerked open the door on the passenger's side, and Howie flipped the latch to unhook his seat belt.

Rick hauled the child from the cab, scanning him quickly. He appeared unhurt. "Run, Howie." Rick gave him a push. "Go back to camp."

The child's eyes widened with fear and hesitation. He stood frozen to the spot.

"Now!" Rick used his most menacing marine voice.

A cloud of dust rose in the boy's wake.

Rick heard the truck's gears shift into Park. He threw a

glance toward Summer, who'd made it to her feet, albeit wobbly. That she could stand was a good sign.

He started around the back of the truck, but Summer took a step in the direction of the driver's door. He moved in fast, blocking her. "Don't." He used the same tone he'd used with Howie, but not as loud.

Her chin snapped up in defiance.

In the meager light he saw it—a lump the size of an egg on her jaw, and his insides wound into a tight coil. Blinded by rage, he sprang toward the driver's door, loaded for action, intent on tearing Howard Gerard apart with his bare hands.

The door swung open, and he gathered the son of a bitch's shirt into his fists and hauled him past the steering column with one jerk.

Something wasn't right about the man's sneer, and Rick's senses went on alert, but his body had the momentum of his weight behind it.

Too late he saw the flash…heard the *pop.*

A vacuum sucked his body in upon itself, bringing with it a pain like nothing he'd ever experienced before. He gasped and the very act of breathing caused him to lose his grip. He staggered backward, toppling, with no control of his movements, welcoming the feel of crashing onto solid ground.

Fireworks went off in his head, blinding his sight, but his sense of touch registered a hot, sticky wetness covering his hands.

He became aware of two distinct sounds piercing his brain. On one side, the roar of a truck engine being gunned.

On the other, screams of terror. *Summer's.*

He cursed his idiocy. A marine didn't make this kind of mistake.

Or maybe it wasn't a mistake.

Maybe the bullet was meant for him all along…it just took seven years to find him.

CHAPTER TWENTY-TWO

"Do you want to lie down? There's a couch in that empty waiting room over there." Tara pointed to the room across the hall. "I'll come get you if the doctor comes out."

Summer shook her head, glad it was just the two of them for a little while. Guilt for not joining everyone else in the chapel where Tara's dad was holding a prayer vigil for Rick pinged at her, but she couldn't leave the waiting room. The nurse who'd come out most recently said the hospital had contacted his family, and they were on the way. It would be several hours.

That was several hours ago.

What if…

"What if he dies, Tara? It's all my fault. I shouldn't have gone into the woods by myself." Summer's jaw ached when she spoke, bruised and swollen from Howard Gerard's backhand, tense and stiff from clenching in fear.

"You did what anyone would do. A child was in danger. When minutes count, we don't stop and think about consequences. We just *do*. You did the right thing."

Tara's words should've soothed, but they didn't. Summer kept hearing the argument with Rick from the afternoon repeating in her head…kept seeing the anguish on his face when she said what she did about Dunk. It was like an acid eating away at her insides.

"I was so hateful with him this afternoon, and all he did was try to give me what he thought I wanted. He said he wanted to be my hero, and I threw that back in his face like it wasn't worth anything."

"You were angry and upset. He knows that. We say things we don't mean…do things we shouldn't do. We're human."

"Rick's not. He's an angel. The most perfect man I've ever known."

Tara knelt in front of her, covering Summer's hands with her own. "He's not perfect. A month ago, you had a whole list of his faults you bombarded me with every day." She tilted her head lower to catch Summer's gaze. "You remember what was at the top of your list? His stubborn streak. And that stubborn streak is going to keep him alive. He's not one to give up."

"He lost so much blood." Summer's eyes blurred as she looked down at her blood-soaked costume, evidence of her futile efforts. She'd wadded fistfuls of the fabric, trying to staunch the flow of blood from Rick's chest until Ginny showed up and took over. "Thank God Howie got back to camp safely and alerted y'all. He tried so hard, bless his heart. But didn't it seem like it took the ambulance forever?"

Tara stood and squeezed in beside Summer in the large chair. Her arm fell across Summer's shoulders, pulling her close. "They got there faster than I thought possible, considering the remote location."

Fast…but maybe not fast enough. The swell of emotion broke again as it had time and again for the past six hours. Summer could only hold it for so long, and then it was like tears filled every available space in her body, and she had to let them out.

Had she cried when it happened? She couldn't remember. She remembered screaming. And trying to stop the blood. But no matter how hard she pushed, it wouldn't stop. It kept coming and coming.

She told him repeatedly to hang on. Held his hand…felt it grow colder as the blood ebbed away from his extremities.

"Don't let go, Summer," he'd said, and she'd answered, "I won't."

But what if *he* let go?

She closed her eyes and took a deep breath, the antiseptic scent filling her nostrils, burning her raw throat. None of this was make-believe, and Rick wasn't Superman. This was real life and real bullets.

And the real-life hero was in there fighting for his real life.

Why? Why did he always have to be the hero? Anger pounded in her temples, throbbed in her jaw.

Yet, when she was facing the desperation of Howard Gerard's rage, who had she wanted to come to her rescue?

Rick Warren, the hero. The kind of man she and everyone else in this country depended on when the job had to get done.

He hadn't asked for the role—it had been thrust upon him. But he accepted it and gave it his all.

She loved them both—Rick Warren the hero, and Rick Warren the man.

Tara stiffened beside her, and Summer's eyes flew open, expecting to see a doctor. Instead, she focused on three people standing just inside the doorway. A man, a woman and a younger man who looked enough like Rick to make her stomach do a somersault.

His family.

Summer stood and moved toward them on wooden legs, evaluating the degree of grief on their faces as she approached, trying to determine if they knew something she didn't.

"I'm Summer Delaney." Her hand shook violently as she held it out. "I'm one of the camp counselors. You're Rick's family?"

"Oh, Summer. Rick speaks fondly of you." The woman took Summer's hand and covered it with her other one in a kind gesture.

The kindness would evaporate once they heard the whole story…how this was her fault. A few seconds more and Gerard would have driven away. But…she remembered the look in Rick's eyes when he saw her face. He'd gone after Gerard because of *her.* He'd gotten shot because of *her*...might die because of *her.*

The ripple effect she'd caused expanded wider and wider as emotion stopped her breath.

"I'm Nolan Warren, Rick's dad." The older man's voice was deep and smooth. Controlled. "My wife, Babbs. Our youngest son, Luke."

Not yet trusting her voice, Summer nodded. She turned to make the introductions to Tara, and found her friend standing at her elbow.

"I'm Tara O'Malley, the girls' assistant counselor. I'm sorry we didn't meet under better circumstances."

Babbs loosened her hold on Summer to shake hands with Tara, and Summer breathed a little easier, finding her voice again. "Have you spoken with the doctor?"

"We have." It was Luke who spoke this time, and Summer said a silent thanks that his voice didn't sound like Rick's. "He made it through the surgery." Summer sent up a second round of thanks.

"Let's sit down." Rick's dad raised his arm to indicate the chairs, and for the first time Summer noticed the bag in his hand. A glimpse of its contents made her head swim. The blood-soaked buckskin.

Nolan and Luke waited for the women to be seated. Summer saw the horrified look on Babbs's face as her eyes took in the stains on the fairy costume.

Summer clasped her hands in her lap, getting a grip on

her emotions as Nolan cleared his throat. "Rick's condition is critical, but stable for the time being." He looked her squarely in the eye. This was a man who would be brutally honest—like Rick. That was a huge comfort.

"The bullet lodged in the upper abdomen, and they were able to remove it successfully, but he lost part of a lung. He, ah." He paused to clear his throat again. "He's already lost a vast amount of blood, so hemorrhaging is possible…and could be fatal." He seemed to lose his train of thought as his eyes took in Summer's gown. "And, of course, there's the threat of an air leak…infection…pneumonia." His Adam's apple bobbed as he swallowed hard.

A long stretch of silence followed before Babbs asked the question Summer had been dreading. "Can you tell us what happened? The sheriff said they caught the person who did this. One of the kids' fathers? Why?"

"I'll tell you what I can." Summer blinked several times, clearing away the protective fog that obscured the memories.

Worry tugged at the corners of Tara's mouth. "Are you sure about this?"

Summer nodded and licked her lips. They needed to hear it…from her. "We had this little boy whose father was abusive." She forced the words around the knot in her throat. It was an abbreviated version of Howie's story that she told, but she tried to include the little kindnesses Rick had shown to the child that might be important and comforting to them. They surprised her with what they already knew about the camp…and her. Rick mentioned his family often, but she hadn't been aware he called home on a regular basis.

When she got to this night's events, her speech became labored, but she pushed through it. Tara had filled her in on the details once all the kids had been picked up and the adults had gotten to the hospital.

"One of the packages that came in the mail to Howie

had contained a prepaid cell phone and a note from his dad. When Howie called him, like he was instructed, Howard, Sr., laid out the plan."

Tara handed her a bottle of water. Summer sipped it, the cold bringing a dull ache to the back of her head. "Howie was supposed to sneak away after lights-out, but he did it during hide-and-seek instead, thinking Mr. Rick would be the one to come after him and save him from having to go with his dad. He didn't expect me."

Summer paused, guilt stinging like a scorpion in her brain.

"If the child was afraid of his dad, why meet him at all?" Frustration clouded Babbs's eyes. "Why didn't he just tell somebody beforehand, and let the sheriff take care of it?"

"His dad threatened to hurt his mom if Howie didn't show up," Tara filled in, and Summer shot her a grateful glance. "In his childish mind, he felt like he was holding up his part of the bargain. So if something happened and his dad got away, Howie thought he was at least still protecting his mom."

Summer's eyes locked with Babbs's, and she braced herself for the hatred that would replace the frustration when she told them what happened next. "Rick got shot because he was protecting me. Howard hit me and knocked me down." She touched her swollen jaw. *If only I'd hidden it from Rick a few seconds more...just a few seconds...* Her chin quivered at the thought. "Rick got Howie out of the truck, sent him back to camp. He was safe. But then I'm sure Rick saw the handprint Howard, Sr., left on my face, and he went after him. Jerked him out from behind the steering wheel. That's when..." She couldn't say the words. She squeezed her eyes shut and wiped her palm down her wet face. Tara's hand rubbed back and forth across her back.

The Warrens were silent for a moment, and then Nolan let out a long breath. "Rick knows better than that. He's a trained marine, for God's sake! He should've assessed the situation better. In a combat situation, you don't walk blindly up to a vehicle—"

"Rick's reckless. He's been reckless ever since..." Luke hesitated. "Ever since Afghanistan." His jaw muscle twitched.

"Just say it. Ever since he lost Dunk." Babbs's voice was low, and she pinched the bridge of her nose. "He's always on a mission, driven by the guilt. He suffers so—" Her voice broke on a sob. She shook her head and waved the rest of the thought away with the back of her hand.

"He has nightmares every night." Summer's eyes went wide when she heard her own voice. *Did I really say that aloud? Now his family knows I've slept with him. Often.*

Nolan's face showed no change. He appeared deep in thought, and Summer wasn't even sure he'd heard her. But Babbs's eyes softened.

Luke's mouth rose slightly at one corner, and he nodded. "I've been with him when he's had one. Not a pretty sight."

"Damn PTSD." Nolan huffed farther back in his chair.

"Post-traumatic stress disorder," Luke explained, and Summer noticed he was speaking to Tara.

Nolan punched the air with his finger. "There's therapy available that can cure things like this. I talked to him about it a couple of weeks ago."

"EMDR." Luke's eyes were still on Tara. "Eye movement desensitization and reprocessing. There's a therapist here in Paducah who specializes in it."

"I've never heard of that," Tara said. "Would you write it down?" She leaned her head softly against Summer's and whispered, "You might want to consider it, too, after what you've been through."

Summer shrugged. Dunk died *in spite* of Rick, not because of him. No therapy in the world would take away her responsibility for what happened tonight.

"Well, this whole Dunk thing has gone on too damn long.

We've all lost friends in combat, but life goes on." Nolan's rigid tone raked down Summer's spine. "He's getting therapy this time. I won't take no for an answer."

I'll bet you never take no for an answer. Suddenly Rick's stubborn streak made much more sense.

Babbs laid her hand on her husband's arm. "Now's not the time to talk about that. Our son's fighting for his life in there." Her eyes fixed on the ceiling above her. "First, he's got to make it through the night."

The words squeezed the air out of Summer's lungs. "Amen," she whispered.

The walls of the room started closing in around her. She would suffocate if she stayed here another minute. Drawing a long breath, she pushed out of her chair to a standing position. "If y'all will excuse me, I've got to get some air, and then I'm going to the chapel for a while."

Tara stood up with her, and then Luke. "I could use a bit of fresh air myself," he said.

Tara pointed to the fairy costume. "I'm going to beg, borrow or steal a clean pair of scrubs for you to wear until someone can get to your house."

Summer followed them out, wondering if her heart would ever again beat a regular rhythm.

"I'M OKAY, DAD. HONEST." Summer walked with him out of the waiting room into the hallway. "Kate's waiting downstairs. Go on home."

Her parents had been here all night and the better part of the day. Her dad looked exhausted, and to be honest, she didn't need to have to worry about him. She had enough to worry about with Rick. Kate had agreed to take them home so Summer didn't have to be concerned about them driving in their sleepy state.

"You've been so strong through all of this." Her dad's

heavy arms gathered her to him, and she relaxed her head against his chest.

Swish...swish. What a glorious sound, the blood pumping through his heart. He'd been at death's door, too, yet here he was, strong and warm and alive. It gave her hope for Rick... but hope couldn't trump the guilt that lay like a lead weight in her stomach.

"I'm proud of you, Summer."

It sounded odd, her name coming from his lips instead of Nubbin. "Thanks, Dad." She'd waited so long to hear those words, yet somehow they didn't have the impact on her she'd expected. They sounded hollow. It didn't matter much anymore what anyone else thought about her. She'd finally seen herself as everyone else saw her. A screwup. She'd caused this. All of it. She was like a computer virus. Everything she touched went haywire.

Rick was the strong one, the one still fighting. The only thing that mattered was for him to be okay.

"We'll see you later." Her dad kissed the top of her head, then was gone.

Swinging doors separated her from ICU, but she could see through the windows to the nurses' station and beyond to Rick's room. It was comforting to stand there and watch, knowing he was close. Was he in pain? Aware of his surroundings? Could he hear her sincere apologies each time she was allowed to go in?

She watched for a long time. Anything was better than sitting in the waiting room, flipping through magazine pages that couldn't hold her attention.

"Thought you might like some coffee."

Luke held out a paper cup containing a caramel-colored liquid.

"Thanks." Summer took it, cupping both hands around

it for warmth. “They’re getting their money’s worth out of the air conditioner.”

“You want a jacket? I have one in the car.”

It was exactly what Rick would’ve said. Summer’s throat tightened and she took a sip. The heat burned her bottom lip, which she’d chewed raw. She could feel the hot, sweet liquid moving down through her chest. “I think this might do the trick, but thanks for the offer.”

“I wasn’t sure how you liked your coffee.” Luke gave her a lopsided grin. “But I figured you could use a pick-me-up, so I added a little of everything on the bar. Sugar, cream, a squirt of chocolate syrup and a dash of cinnamon.”

“I usually drink it black.” Summer smiled when he winced. “But this is delicious. And you’re right about me needing a pick-me-up.” The clock on the wall indicated visitation was in twenty-five minutes. Nineteen hours she’d been here. It felt like nineteen days. “Shouldn’t he have regained consciousness by now? I’d give anything to see his eyes open when we go back in there.”

“Sleep’s good for him. It lets his body do its healing work. Keeps him still.” Luke’s chin buckled as he pressed his lips together. “I hope he’s having good dreams this time.”

“Me, too.”

“It’d be a bitch to have nightmares while you were in a coma.”

Summer shivered, remembering Rick’s nightmares. She took a quick sip of coffee, seeking its warmth to offset the chill running through her.

One of the nurses walked over to Rick’s door, took the file out of the holder and scribbled something on it.

“He and Dunk had been best friends since the seventh grade. That’s when Dad retired and we moved to Little Rock.”

“I didn’t realize they went that far back.” Summer’s lip stung, and she flicked her tongue over it. “Rick wouldn’t talk about him too much. He explained to me about the tattoo over his heart. And he told me about Dunk dying in his arms…and trying to save him. That's about all."

Luke leaned against the wall, angling himself so he could see his brother's door. "They were inseparable. Dunk wasn't very big, so Rick always protected him from the bullies. It was Rick who talked him into joining the marines…they did it together. Rick thought he'd be able to protect him like he'd always done. That's why he took his death so hard."

"I see." Another shudder ran up Summer's spine.

"Luke."

Summer jumped at Babbs Warren's voice so close behind her. Some of the coffee sloshed onto her hand. She wiped the drops on the jeans Kate had brought her this morning.

"Why don't you go get Summer a jacket out of the car?"

"Oh, that's okay," Summer protested, but Luke nodded and started toward the elevator.

"I'll be right back."

"Men don't wait well." Babbs's smile turned a little sad. "It's always the women who are left waiting."

Summer looked her in the eye. "How do you stand it? The waiting, I mean. When your husband was gone…when Rick was in Afghanistan? With Jack in Lebanon and Luke headed to Syria in a couple of months? How do you stay so strong?"

"It's not easy, I can tell you that. And don't ever let anyone tell you any different." Babbs took Summer's hand. Her grip was strong and warm…more comforting than the sweet coffee.

"But I'm a military wife and mom, and I know in my heart they're fighting for a cause they believe in. I constantly remind myself what an honor it is to be a part of their lives… an honor I work hard to try to deserve."

A sudden movement drew Summer's attention. The nurse had rushed into Rick's room. A light blinked above his door, and some kind of call went out over the intercom. The doctor hurried from one of the other rooms.

"What's happening?" Summer set the cup of coffee on the floor and gripped Babbs's hand with both of hers.

"I don't know." Fear punctuated the words.

Summer held back the sob trying to force its way free as she watched a machine from the central desk being pushed through his door. She tightened her grip on Babbs, the woman's words echoing in her head. *"What an honor it is to be a part of their lives...an honor I work hard to try to deserve."*

"Fight, Rick," Summer whispered. "Please fight."

"He'll fight." Babbs Warren's voice was strong and sure. "Regardless of the outcome, he'll fight."

Her arm came around Summer's shoulders. Strong. Warm. Unsure how things would turn out, but capable of handling it with the dignity this man deserved. Without a doubt, Babbs Warren had earned the honor bestowed on her.

But the same acknowledgment pointed a condemning finger in Summer's direction.

She'd earned no such honor. She was a screwup...completely undeserving of a hero like Rick Warren in her life.

RICK RAN, PUSHING HIS BODY as fast as it would go, but he made no progress across the wide green meadow. No, he wasn't running. He was trying to run, but his body wouldn't cooperate. His legs were too heavy...wouldn't move. He gasped with effort, but no air entered his lungs. His heart pumped wildly in panic. He clawed at his chest. An odd growth protruded from the area over his heart. A stone. The tattoo of Dunk's dog tags had taken on dimension. Fossilized. As he watched in horror, its depth increased, taking up air space in his lungs, piercing his heart. The weight increased until he could no longer hold his torso upright.

And then, he was falling, but the ground didn't get any

closer. He was floating. The stone in his chest grew larger... heavier...would split him wide-open soon. The pressure was growing unbearable.

Thunder crashed through the trees, like a gunshot, reverberating through him, making his body quake.

"Losing him!" He heard the cry...knew it referred to him...but the voice was unfamiliar.

The pain in his chest intensified with every beat of his heart. He could feel it rupturing out through his fingernails.

A fleeting image of Dunk scampered across his consciousness. Smiling...running...whole again and happy. No pain. No suffering. Rick tried to call to him, but his friend was gone before he could form the words.

A surge of electrical shock ripped through his nervous system like a flash flood through a dry gulch. The fossilized mass of tattooed stone broke free of his body, pulling with it the fibers that held his being together for so long, shredding his essence.

He was vaguely aware of voices around him.

"...in rhythm but weak."

"...have to wait and see."

"Rick, can you hear me?"

Someone kept messing with the volume of the speakers. Voices lowered to whispers, then faded away. Some were familiar. Some weren't. Concentration was impossible...and unimportant.

Cold hands touched him. "...seeing improvement."

"...damage from the bullet..."

Oh, yeah. There'd been a bullet. A truck. Someone on the ground.

No, he was on the ground. A shadowy figure hovered above him. Screaming. Then someone turned down the volume. Quiet talk. Whispers.

"Don't die, Rick. Please don't die."

He recognized that voice…liked its soothing quality. It faded. Why wouldn't they leave the volume up? It was too hard…straining to make out the words exhausted him.

"…hear me?…new IV…" He didn't know that voice. It was loud. He'd heard it several times, but he couldn't place it. Thinking was too hard. His thoughts raced around his brain like the remote control cars he and Dunk used to play with.

He put his finger on the joy stick and backed the thought up to the voice he recognized.

A name formed on his lips and he breathed it out, laboring under the effort.

"SUMMER?"

The voice wormed its way into her consciousness a nanosecond before she felt the touch on her shoulder become a wakening shake.

She jerked to a sitting position. The world tilted and then righted itself. Her eyes strained to focus through the bright sunlight as her brain regrouped and placed her in the too-long-familiar confines of the hospital waiting room. The hands on the clock indicated it was 2:34…Sunday afternoon.

Babbs's hand clutched her chest while the other lay heavy on Summer's shoulder. She shook Summer again. "Rick's conscious. He's asking for you."

Summer jumped to her feet, swaying. Babbs stilled her with a brusque hug. She pointed to a nurse standing in the doorway, who nodded to Summer and motioned for her to follow.

"Thank you." Summer prayed, her heart brimming over at the news. She followed the nurse down the frigid hallway, keenly aware of the profound sadness lurking simultaneously just below the surface of her joy.

For almost two days, she'd had nothing to do except think, and those thoughts had replayed the ripple effect of her selfish actions over and over in her head. She'd brought nothing but heartache to too many people.

Her parents' retirement investment was surely gone. They'd had to cancel the second session of camp as parents pulled their kids left and right from the list of attendees on the heels of the news.

Rick had lost part of a lung…had almost lost his life. His parents had nearly lost a son. Luke, a brother.

Her parents didn't deserve a failure like her for a daughter, but they were stuck with her.

Rick, on the other hand, was not.

She hoped he hated the sight of her now. That would make it easier.

Coward. If he's asking for me, that's not how this mission is going down.

But she wouldn't play on his sympathy with the "poor little screwup me" thing, either. That would only encourage him to stick around to save her from herself.

No, she would be cheerful and strong. She would hang around a few more days to make sure he was going to make a full recovery, then she would get busy with parties…or whatever. Too busy for visits or calls, totally self-absorbed and totally in line with her selfish nature.

Rick could wash his hands of her with a sigh of good riddance.

Summer squared her shoulders and walked into his room with a smile of hello on her lips, every fiber of her keenly aware that this moment started her countdown to goodbye.

CHAPTER TWENTY-THREE

"HELLO?" SUMMER DIDN'T HAVE to look at the caller ID to know who was on the line.

"Did you know Rick's going home today?"

Tears stung at the backs of Summer's eyes. Again she sighed in resignation. "Yes, Mom. I know. Tara called earlier with the news."

She'd cried with relief and happiness when she'd gotten the call from Tara. After she hung up, the tears had been of anguish because she wasn't ever going to see Rick again. According to Tara, he was considering a job offer in Arkansas. That was a good thing, but it still hurt.

Maybe these tears would be cathartic. The ones that would wash away everything else and leave her feeling resolved. Healed.

"Are you going to visit him?" Her mom's tone took on that testy edge that came right before a lecture.

Summer considered lying, but that would just be putting off the inevitable. "No. I'm not going to visit him. I've made my break from Rick. It was the right thing to do...probably the most right thing I've ever done."

"This isn't like you, Summer." The voice on the other end rose at least an octave. "You've been flighty and selfish, but I've never known you to be cruel before."

Ouch. "I'm not being cruel, Mom." *No matter what you and the rest of the world think.* "It wasn't meant to be. He needs someone…different from me." *Someone worthy of a hero.* She wiped off the tear scalding a path down her cheek.

"He asks about you every day."

And I think about him all the time. "He'll get over it."

"Well, I can see talking to you about it isn't going to do any good. You've made up your mind, I can tell. And when you get your mind made up, you're just like your fath—"

"I've got a party to get to, Mom." That was a lie, but her battered heart couldn't withstand any more blows. "Was there anything else you needed?"

"Actually, I called with other news."

The words held a note of apology, so the news had to be about Sunny Daze. Summer gripped the phone tighter.

"We sold the camp this morning."

"You took the state's offer." Irritation burned Summer's throat. Sunny Daze was worth so much more than the paltry sum Riley Gibson had offered the day after the shooting.

No doubt, he was convinced the bad publicity of the incident would ruin the camp—which it might—and that her parents would jump at any chance to have the property taken off their hands. He wasn't far off the truth. They *did* want to be rid of the camp and the memory, but they still had their retirement to think about.

"We didn't have to. Another offer came in. A respectable one."

For a second, Summer's world came to a halt. Her knees wobbled, forcing her to sit. "Who from?"

"Chance Brennan."

"Rick's friend?" The news sent Summer's heart in two directions. One half leaped for joy. Chance and Kyndal Brennan were good people…heroes in their own way, deserving of the property.

The other half splattered at her feet. A subdivision was probably in the property's future.

"He came to see Rick a couple of days ago while we were there," her mom continued. "Rick introduced us and told him about the property. He called the next day and said he was interested and had some investors."

So Rick was directly responsible. Was he still trying to save the camp, or was this his way of getting the last word?

It didn't matter. This was the news she'd been waiting for.

The end of the story.

"I'm so happy for you, Mom." Tears were coming fast now. "I really am." She marveled at the words. She *really* meant them.

"Are you crying?"

"Happy tears." *Cry enough of them and maybe they'll fill up the hole that bullet left in my heart.* "I do need to go now, though." It wasn't a lie this time. Too much emotion clogged her throat to allow her to talk any longer.

"Okay, Nubbin." Her mom's tone modulated back to its normal sweetness. "I'll talk to you later."

Summer laid the phone down, grabbed a fistful of napkins from the basket on the table and sobbed loud and long until she had no tears left.

Eventually, the weight in her heart would lighten… wouldn't it?

Doing the same thing she'd done for the past week and a half to combat the grueling wait for nothing in particular, she pushed up from the table and moved. Keeping her body moving kept her mind at least partially occupied, and that kept the despair from consuming her. Her apartment had never been so clean, and she fell into bed every night, too exhausted to think…or dream.

She set to ironing the new fairy princess costume, a replacement for the one she had to throw away. It had arrived a couple of days ago, but she hadn't had the courage to put it on yet.

Go with the symbolism. Off with the old, on with the new.

Taking a deep breath of resolve, she slipped out of her shorts and top and into the dress. The zipper went up easily…too easily. She glanced at the mirror, grimacing at the woman reflected back. Dark circles shaded red, swollen eyes. Toothpick arms dangled from the sleeves. The dress hung slack on her, barely touching anywhere but the shoulders. The neckline gaped. The waistline needed cinching. She looked more like a zombie than a fairy princess. No child was going to believe this creature held the secret to a pretty heart.

A knock at the door jerked her attention away from the frightening image. Kate was early. Summer gathered up the dress and hurried to let her in.

She swung the door open. "Rick." She should've checked the peephole first.

"Hello, Summer."

His voice palpitated her heart, making it come alive for the first time since…

"I haven't seen you in over a week."

Since over a week. She sidestepped his comment. "You look good." He was obviously trying to stand in his normal, marine posture, but the slump of his shoulders hinted at the deep scar hidden beneath the blue dress shirt. He'd lost weight—his clothes fit baggy like her dress—and his hair was longer than she'd ever seen it, almost touching his ears on the side, the front combed off his forehead from a part that had never appeared before.

He was the most beautiful sight her eyes had beheld since…since the last time she saw him.

"Can I come in?"

No! her mind screamed. She wasn't ready to talk with him yet. Her emotions were still too close to the surface. But her mouth opened and "Sure" dropped out. She stepped back to let him in, motioning to the wingback where she thought he would be most comfortable.

He carried a box of candy, which he placed on the table by the chair, and waited for her to sit. She chose the couch, as far away from him as the small room allowed. As he eased into the seat, he looked around, the blue shirt bringing out the turquoise hue of his eyes. "Nice place."

"Thanks." Her eyes roamed over him. The way he sat so carefully. "Does it hurt much?"

"Only when I sneeze."

"That's good." She scratched an imaginary itch on her nose.

His steady gaze waited for more, and when it didn't come, he settled deeper into the chair. The subtle movement said, *I can wait.*

Okay, she could fake her way through this. She started with a fake smile. "How's the therapy going?"

"No nightmares so far." He rapped his knuckles a couple of times on the table. "Ironic, isn't it? I finally let go of Dunk, then you step in to haunt my dreams."

She tried to think of a snappy comeback, but her brain kept misfiring. She shifted uncomfortably and smoothed at a wrinkle she'd missed.

"Is that the way you generally dress at home?" He handed her an escape.

"No, I have a party." She clenched her teeth to stop her mouth from adding "in a couple of hours."

"Then I'll get to the point." He leaned forward like he was going to put his elbows on his knees, and then straightened and leaned back again. "You quit coming to see me, and you won't answer any of my calls. Obviously, you're finished with me. But I need to hear you say it…and I'd like to leave knowing why." The hurt emanating from those blue-green eyes spoke of more than just physical injury. They pierced her heart.

Her brain scrambled for a lie or even a half-truth that would satisfy his curiosity and squelch his desire to know more. Something, anything that would allow him to walk out of there and never look back. But also something that wouldn't make him hate her. No matter what she'd thought earlier, she couldn't bear him hating her.

"I…I…" she stammered, but the ocean of his eyes caught her thoughts in an eddy, swirling them around to the same point again and again, getting her nowhere. She was drowning in those eyes. Taking a deep breath, she changed her mind and plunged into the truth. "I think it's best if we don't get back into a relationship. I…I don't deserve you."

"What?" His eyes and words alike echoed disbelief.

"Your mom's a good woman. She deserves men in her life like you, your brothers…your dad. I don't. I'm not like her."

Even with several feet separating them, Summer could see the tightening of Rick's jaw in his thin face. "That's the craziest thing I've ever heard."

"It's not crazy." Summer raised her chin. It quivered, and she lowered it again. "The day after you got shot, Mom and Dad went home for a while. While they were home, the guy called with the offer from the state, which was terrible by the way. It got me to thinking again about how much I wanted the camp, and if I could find a way to counter that offer. But more than that, it got me to thinking how much I wanted to be there again with you. I was being selfish, just like you said. I wasn't thinking of Mom and Dad after all they've done for me. Just thinking of me, me, me and my happiness." A heaviness centered in her chest at the admission.

Hope softened the edges around Rick's eyes—a hope she couldn't let grow. It would be cruel, and despite what her mother said, that was one thing she wasn't. She continued her story. "Your mom and I were standing in the hallway, watching your room. We saw the commotion. Everybody running toward it. That's when your heart had st-stopped." Her voice was shaking now, and the tears fell freely, but she pressed on. "Your mom had been talking about deserving a place in your life. It hit me then—the ripple effect you talked about. The one I caused. My marketing idea, like you said, had a purely selfish motive. I just wanted the publicity of that newspaper article. The same article that Howie's dad saw, which gave him the idea to get Howie, which then got you shot." She'd been forming circles with her hands. She let them fall into her lap with a shrug. "Selfish acts hurt people, and I'd graduated from fairy princess to queen of selfish. My actions are undeserving of a hero like you."

Rick leaned forward again, resting his elbows on his knees, studying the ground intently. "So what kind of woman deserves a man like me?" He raised his eyes to lock with hers. "Describe her to me."

"She'd put other people first."

He nodded.

"She'd be strong in the face of danger. Courageous."

"With a pretty heart?" His mouth quirked at one end.

She gave him a real smile to show she was going to be okay as long as he was. "Yes, with a pretty heart, the kind that reaches out to protect the people she loves."

"Would she risk her own safety for a child in danger? Would she face a drunken father and fight him physically to try and keep him from driving off with the child?"

Summer saw where this was going. She shook her head in denial. "That wasn't being heroic. That was a reaction born of panic."

Rick's eyes widened, then he blinked slowly. He stood, picked up the box of candy and came to sit on the couch beside her. His nearness caused her skin to tingle. "This is for you." He held out the box.

"Thanks." She took the gift and placed it on the coffee table.

Rick picked it up and placed it back in her lap. "Open it."

She wasn't in the mood for chocolates—or anything—but his tone didn't allow for a refusal. She worked the lid off the box, which didn't contain chocolates, after all, but held a thick set of papers.

She unfolded them and scanned the legal document. Her hands began to shake so hard she couldn't keep it in focus. "What is this, Rick?"

He smiled. "The deed to the Camp Sunny Daze property. It's yours."

It couldn't be! Her pulse swished through her ears. "Chance bought it. Investors. How…?"

"My parents and I were the investors. We only let Chance put in a dollar so he could tell your parents he was buying it." One side of his mouth rose again. "We didn't want them to sell it to us out of sympathy at too much of a bargain price."

Summer shook her head, too dazed to think coherently.

The backs of his fingers brushed her cheek. "We want you to have it as a thank-you. You deserve it."

"For what?" The question exploded from her lips. "For… for almost getting you killed? No. No!" She thrust the papers back at him and tried to stand, but Rick's arm slid across her waist and held her in place.

"For saving my life." His voice was husky with emotion. He let go and fished in his pants pocket, pulling out a chain. His dog tags dangled from it, slightly bent, but still intact. He pressed the chain into her hand, holding on with both of his. "The doctor said the angle of the bullet should've hit my heart, but it ricocheted off something…something very hard. They found shards of green granite in the wound, Summer."

He cleared his throat, his gaze never wavering from hers. "If you want to talk the ripple effect, you need to find the true action that started the ripple. You started Fairy Princess Parties to empower girls. You taught them about their pretty hearts and how to earn their wands. I was given one of your wands, and it blocked a bullet from hitting my heart. It saved my life. *You* saved my life."

With a trembling finger, Summer caught the single tear as it left the corner of Rick's eye. "Oh, Rick..."

He took her hand and pressed it to his lips. "If you believe that everything happens for a reason, you're the reason I'm sitting here today. I think it's a sign we're meant to be together."

Summer's heart swelled with joy until she thought it would rupture. "I love you so much." The words came out as a whisper, although she felt like shouting.

"I love you, too." His hand caressed her cheek, then moved into her hair, pulling her face close to his until their mouths touched. He kissed her long and deep, and she responded with the fervor his lips were deserving of.

She leaned her head back to look him in the eye. "I get you and the camp, too? You're not moving back to Arkansas?"

Rick chuckled. "I'm planning on sticking around here. Forever."

Summer raised her chin and gave him an impish grin. "We've never even been on a date, and we're talking about forever."

"Would you have dinner with me tonight?" He leaned over and nibbled on her ear, sending a shiver from her head to her toes.

"I'd love to." She sighed, delirious with joy and thankfulness.

"Then I think our forever just began."

CHAPTER TWENTY-FOUR

Ten months later

RICK CLOSED THE DOOR of the dishwasher and hit the start button for the—he counted—*fifth* time that day. The next time they held a public event, he would insist they use the big kitchen…and maybe an outside caterer. If he was going to be this fatigued, it should be from something more gratifying than cleanup duty.

The open house had been a huge success. The calendar for their rustic resort, which they'd officially christened the Summer Place today, was filling up faster than either of them had ever dreamed it would.

Rick smiled to himself. Although Summer had been afraid the new name would sound too self-indulgent, everyone else gave it a thumbs-up.

The camp had definitely needed a new beginning.

He pulled out a chair and sank into it just as Summer came in the kitchen carrying their wedding picture. A frown pinched her mouth.

"What's wrong, babe? Not having regrets, are you?"

The corners of her mouth curved slowly upward as her eyes settled on him. She cocked her head. "What is there to have regrets about?"

He patted his leg, and she snuggled onto his lap. "Oh, I dunno. Marrying me?"

She shook her head. "Nope."

"Eloping to Vegas?"

"Nadda."

"Having a cheesy theme wedding?" He pointed to the picture. "You look beautiful as a fairy princess but your groom looks like a sweaty dork in his suit of armor."

She giggled as she examined the picture. "You don't look like a dork. You look dashing…like every woman's fantasy."

"That damn metal suit was like standing in an oven."

"Mmm." She nibbled his earlobe, sending a jolt of electricity straight to his groin. "Five months later and you're still hot, baby." Her mouth seared a line of kisses up his neck, and he decided he wasn't nearly as tired as he'd thought he was a few minutes ago.

"Know what Charlie said when he saw it?" she asked.

Rick cleared his throat to let loose his best Charlie impression. "Damn wild child."

"You got it." Summer laughed—a sound he would never grow tired of. She ran a fingertip down the slope of his nose and then pointed at the picture. Her mouth drooped again. "But look at all these smudges on the glass. I've used almost a whole bottle of glass cleaner today trying to keep it clean." She laid the photo on the table.

"Hide it next time."

She clasped her arms around his neck and hugged him. "No way. But I am going to find a prominent place on the wall so people won't pick it up."

Leaning back, she brushed her fingertips through one side of his hair and smiled. "Are you too tired to go for a walk?"

"To the bedroom?"

"We'll come back to the bedroom. Or the couch. Or…" She gave the table a pat and wagged her eyebrows suggestively. He watched the edges of her eyes soften. "But first, I'd like to go back to the Byassee place."

Until that morning, Summer hadn't gone near the Byassee place since the shooting. Rick thought once they'd moved into the apartment on the premises back in December, she'd get over the pain and stop avoiding the area, but she hadn't.

When Tara's dad showed up this morning to bless the camp, it occurred to Rick that blessing the Byassee homestead might give Summer back her favorite place.

Apparently, his idea worked.

She slid off his lap and held her hand out to him. "I've got something I want to show you there."

The early May evenings were still cool enough to require a light jacket. Grabbing the ones hanging by the door, they sauntered out into a world of wild dogwood blooms capped by a pink-and-purple sunset and scented heavily from honey locust.

They exchanged tidbits of information each had learned throughout the day from the plethora of visitors.

"Tara's ready for school to be out. She said she'd help me with those flower beds."

"M&M had grown so much I almost didn't recognize her."

"Buck Blaine said Nila Gerard's engaged, and the guy's a winner. Treats Howie like his own son."

Summer's hand gripped Rick's tighter at the last comment, and she quickened her steps.

"What's the hurry?" Rick was back to working out every day. His body still wasn't in marine shape, but it was getting there. Even with his long stride, he had to hurry to keep up with her tonight.

"We need to get there before it gets dark."

Maybe the blessing hadn't quelled all of her fears, after all.

Rick picked up his pace. *Everything in good time.*

They turned from the main path onto the less worn one and walked the rest of the way to the clearing in silence. A doe munching on sweet clover didn't hear them approach.

Startled when they broke from the tree line into the open, she bolted away.

They stood quietly, holding hands, listening to the sounds of the birds beginning to roost in the tops of the surrounding trees. An opossum beat a hasty retreat out of the broken-down house, glaring sullenly at them on his way to the woods.

"It's so quiet here right now." Rick swiveled his head to catch the sounds. "It's hard to believe a month from now, it'll be crawling with kids again."

Summer took his other hand and turned to face him. "Actually, a few months from now, this place may never be quiet again." Her mysterious smile didn't mesh with the tears shining in her eyes.

"Why is that?"

She let go of his hand and reached into her pocket, bringing out some kind of stick. She held it out to him.

"What's this?"

She laughed softly. "My new magic wand."

Rick squinted in the fading light. "Positive," he read aloud.

Summer nodded. "Positive by about two weeks, I think. So in about eight and a half months…"

Eight and a half months? It took several seconds for the math to catch up with him, but then his heart started to beat at a quick rhythm. "You're pregnant?"

Summer nodded, her face breaking into a radiant smile.

He couldn't, didn't want to, contain his happiness. "Ooh-rah!" He let out a whoop sure to be heard all the way to the lake.

In one leap, Summer was in his arms, her legs locked around his waist, and he was twirling around and around, in a dance of the most ecstatic joy he'd ever known.

They laughed and kissed and shouted, then laughed and kissed some more, until Summer finally begged to be put down.

"I don't want to get sick," she insisted, and he reluctantly set her on her own feet.

He looked around at the Byassee place. The ramshackle old house seemed an odd choice for such an announcement. Catching Summer's chin with his finger, he raised her face. "So the angels have returned?"

"The angels never left." She took his hands and kissed them tenderly. "They were here watching over us the whole time."

He pulled her close and lowered his mouth to hers. "I can't argue with that," he whispered. "Right now, I'm holding two of them in my arms."

* * * * *

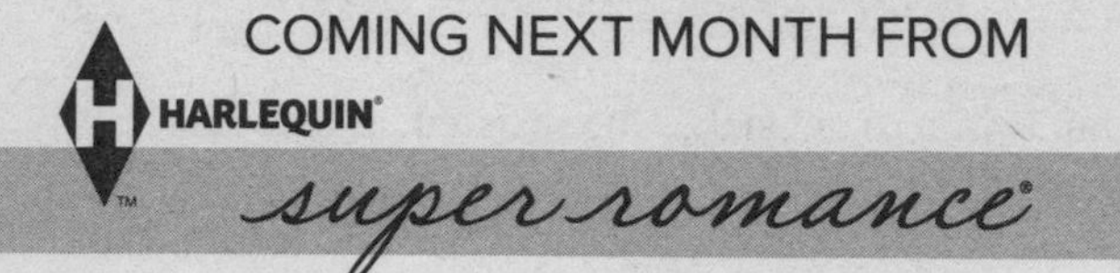

Available May 7, 2013

#1848 WHERE IT MAY LEAD by Janice Kay Johnson

Instant attraction? Madison Laclaire never believed in it—until she met John "Troy" Troyer. She's eager for the alumni reunion to end so they can kick this relationship up a notch. But when the college time capsule is opened, secrets spill out that could stop them before they begin.

#1849 A PRIOR ENGAGEMENT by Karina Bliss

Presumed dead, war vet Lee Davis returns home to discover that Jules Browne, who'd rejected his wedding proposal before deployment, has been playing his grieving fiancée. Well, she's not the only one who can act. And he intends to find out how far she'll take this so-called relationship....

#1850 JANE'S GIFT by Abby Gaines

Jane Slater would rather be anywhere other than back in Pinyon Ridge, but she's determined to help her best friend's little girl move on after her mother's death. Thing is, Kyle Everson doesn't want a Slater, especially Jane, anywhere near his daughter. Until Jane reveals a secret that changes everything.

#1851 A FAMILY REUNITED by Dorie Graham

The last thing Alexandra Peterson wants is to return home to Atlanta after her family has been torn apart. But when her brother is diagnosed with cancer, she has no choice. She'll move back—but only until Robert is well. Can Chase Carrolton, her high school sweetheart, convince her to stay?

#1852 APRIL SHOWERS • *A Valley Ridge Wedding*
by Holly Jacobs

Lily Paul is only trying to help pay back the kindness she's found in Valley Ridge. Seb Bennington, former bad boy, insists she's interfering with his family. Both agree the last thing either of them wants is to admit their attraction for each other, and yet...they may have no say in the matter!

#1853 IT'S NEVER TOO LATE • *Shelter Valley Stories*
by Tara Taylor Quinn

Two people come to Shelter Valley, Arizona, and end up as next-door neighbors. One, a rugged small-town man named Mark Heber, is there to accept a scholarship as a mature student. The other, Adrianna Keller, is not who she pretends to be. But Mark doesn't learn that until long after they've fallen in love....

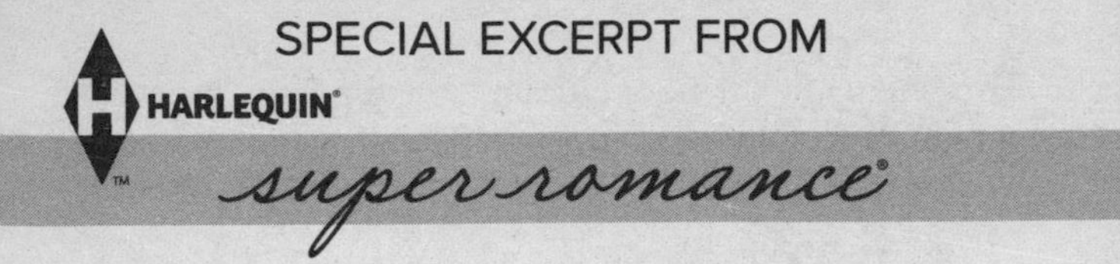

Where It May Lead

By Janice Kay Johnson

Being the police liaison for the local college's alumni event should be straightforward for Detective John "Troy" Troyer. That is, until he meets Madison Laclaire! Read on for an exciting excerpt from the upcoming book *WHERE IT MAY LEAD* by Janice Kay Johnson.

"I doubt we'll have any problems this weekend," Troy said, glancing through the schedule. "I think my role is going to be an exciting one. I'll hang around. Maybe even play golf."

Madison tilted her head in interest—and he liked being the object of her interest. "Do you play golf?"

"Poorly," he admitted. "I've got a hell of a slice. But from a security standpoint, having me lurking in the rough probably isn't a bad plan."

Her laugh was contagious…and unintentionally erotic. "I'll look for you there."

"You'll be playing?"

HSREXP0413R

"No. Actually, I'll be frantically arranging the luncheon." She rose gracefully to her feet. "Thank you for coming, Detective Troyer."

"Troy." He stood, too.

A smart man would bide his time, not make any move until after the weekend. He didn't want her to be uncomfortable with him when they had to work together. Troy had always thought of himself as a pretty smart guy.

Turned out he wasn't as smart as he'd thought.

"So. I was wondering." *Slick. Really slick.* "Any chance I could talk you into having dinner with me?"

Madison blinked. "Tonight?"

Tonight, tomorrow night, every night. Startled by the thought, he cleared his throat. "Tonight would be good. Or tomorrow." He hesitated. "Unless you're too busy."

Her expression melted into a sunbeam of a smile. "I would love to have dinner with you tonight, Troy."

Down, boy, he cautioned himself when his enthusiastic response threatened to overflow.

They agreed on a restaurant, then he left before he did something stupid. Like kiss her.

He grinned as he exited her office. She'd said yes. He *felt* young. Half-aroused, too.

He would definitely be kissing her tonight.

HSREXP0413R